THE BLOOD ZONE

MICHAEL ANGEL

The Blood Zone

ISBN-13: 9781712303047

Paperback Edition of The Reaper's Scythe printed in the U.S. and published by Banty Hen Publishing, November 2019

For more about Michael Angel, please visit MichaelAngelWriter.com.
For more about Banty Hen Publishing, please visit our website at: BantyHenPublishing.com.
Cover art by DerangedDoctorDesign.com.
Editing/Proofing by Leiah Cooper, SoIReadThisBookToday.com.

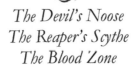

DEDICATION

To Dorothy Papin:
Your love and support
are all I need.
You are my muse.

To Leiah Cooper:
Without you, all of my
characters and stories
wouldn't gleam as bright.

To Alan:
Once again, this book exists
only because of your
willingness to pass on
your hard-won wisdom.

CHAPTER ONE

Tyrrhenian Sea, 250km south of Naples
Sirenica Dive Monitoring Center
Depth: 100 Meters

They'd lost contact with the dive team over a half-hour ago.

Reece Jordan looked up from her monitors and through the foot-thick tempered glass window. The one hundred meters of water above muted the sun's radiance. At best, it illuminated the depths like moonlight through a cathedral's windows.

Her chair squealed as she shifted back to the screens. She did her best to ignore the sound. *Everything* creaked, squeaked, or shed rust flakes in an underwater habitat like Sirenica. On a bad day, her monitoring center sounded like a fleet of cars with worn-out brakes.

A *rap-rap-rap* came from the open hatchway. Jordan didn't look up. She knew her boss' tics better than anyone.

"Anything?" Dylan Sawyer asked. The woman's short blonde hair clung to her scalp as if she wore a skullcap. Another perk of living in a high-moisture environment.

Jordan shook her head. "Not a peep. I've got both ROVs on a search pattern."

The remotely operated underwater vehicles were the size of large dogs. They sported a pair of grasping claws on either side of a cyclopean camera lens. Each could operate long distances without a tether.

But the ocean was a big place.

"Shouldn't have sent them down there in suits," Sawyer muttered under her breath. "I told them we needed that fourth minisub up and running."

"Peterson would've told you if he felt uncomfortable." That was an understatement. Peterson, Richter, and Lang had a combined fifty years of experience working under deep dive conditions.

"Even three people can get the *nark*. At the same time, too."

Jordan nodded. Nitrogen narcosis could hit hard and fast at this depth. A too-quick depth change could fog the brain as effectively as chugging a bottle of Tennessee whiskey.

She wiped a finger across her lips before catching herself. Jordan fiercely pressed her palm flat against the arm of her chair.

Don't you dare go down that path again, she thought to herself. *But as God is my witness, what I wouldn't give for a shot of Jack.*

Her monitor emitted a *ping*.

"I've got something."

In an instant, Sawyer was up and looking over her shoulder. "Show me."

Jordan tapped a few keys. The monitor switched over to one of her ROV's cameras. Her breath whistled out through her lips as the fuzzy image of two divers appeared on the screen.

Peterson swam with a crab-like motion. His right arm curled around one of his fellow divers, dragging him forward through the water. The other man moved feebly, if at all. Dark streamers of some strange material rippled from the edges of the two men's suits.

"The hell is that?" Sawyer peered at the screen. "And what's that black cloud trailing them?"

Jordan swallowed. "It's blood."

The picture finally snapped into focus. Both men's dive suits looked as if they'd been stuffed into a shredder while still being worn. The torn edges rippled like streamers in the current, leaking bright red blood that looked as black as squid ink in the dim light.

Peterson's suit had been ripped open along one side. His left leg hung uselessly, as if broken. His dive fin had a wedge-shaped chunk missing.

The other diver was in worse shape. The man moved only spasmodically, trying to assist his friend's efforts. Deep slashes crisscrossed his body from scalp to thigh.

"That's Richter," Sawyer finally said. "No sign of Lang?"

"I'm not seeing anything."

"Dammit. How far are they from us?"

A pause. "About two hundred meters."

"They'll bleed out before they make it that distance. Can you bring them in?"

Jordan took down a miniature control module from a nearby shelf. "I'll get them home."

"That's what I want to hear." Sawyer stood and reached over to tap the intercom. Her voice took on a metallic reverberation as it boomed through Sirenica's metallic interior. "All hands, we have a medical emergency! Clear the way to the sickbay. I need Dive Master Hanick and Doctor Lici down at the moon pool room in five minutes."

"I can be there in four shakes," Jordan added. "If you need another hand."

"The shape those divers are in? I could use you."

Sawyer left at a run. Her footsteps made a tinny echo as they receded. Jordan grasped the controller and plugged it into the network. Manipulating the nub of a joystick with finesse, she brought the ROV within grabbing distance of the two divers.

One of the ROV's manipulator arms appeared onscreen. She maneuvered the claw hand to clamp down on one of Richter's tattered dive fins. Peterson gave her a weary thumbs-up as he let go of his friend and grabbed onto the ROV's other arm.

Jordan kicked the vehicle into gear, the speed set as high as she dared. She rotated the ROV's camera to see Peterson clinging desperately to the metal arm. Richter lolled in the propeller's wake like a rag doll.

Up ahead, she made out the shimmering rectangles that marked the four moon pools on Sirenica's bottom level. A glittering steel grate lowered from one, trailing bubbles as if in welcome. She clicked a button labeled *AUTOMATED ROV RETRIEVAL PROGRAM*.

Jordan's chair made another plaintive squeal as she slid out of it and dashed down to the lower levels. She took the short, steep metal stairs two at a time, heart pounding in her chest by the time she arrived at the moon pool room.

While the circular space wasn't particularly large, it was cavernous by the standards of any undersea habitat. Wavy turquoise reflections danced across a domed ceiling. The sharp scent of salt mixed with the heady fumes of motor oil. A minisub lay beached on the far side of the room, parts scattered like fresh guts across the floor.

Wheezy rattles came from the dive platform motor as it pulled up a quartet of chains from the pool. A jumble of black, yellow and red shapes appeared in the water below. They surfaced amidst a cascade of foam.

The ROV sat in the middle, its unblinking eye staring as if in amazement. The two divers that accompanied it lay crumpled and bleeding on the steel grate on either side of the vehicle. Sawyer stepped onto the closest segment, Dive Master Hanick right beside her. The big man's bald pate gleamed in the pool's bright lights as he lifted Peterson's head out of the water and removed the man's face gear.

"Eyes open," Hanick said. His German accent cut his words into harsh commands. "Stay awake, *verdammt!*"

Peterson's eyes refused to focus. His voice sounded slurred, as if drunk.

"Couldn't get away, Otto. Couldn't get back…"

The man's eyes closed. Hanick looked up in alarm at the dark-haired woman who joined them on the platform. Without ceremony, she jammed her fingers into a gap of the suit at the base of Peterson's neck.

"Still getting a pulse," she said. "Barely. He's bleeding out."

"Tell us something we don't already know, Doctor Lici," Sawyer said, as she managed to lift Peterson's wrist from where it still wrapped around the ROV's arm.

Lici ignored the jibe. She pointed from Sawyer to Peterson's biggest wound. A deep, pulsing gash on the left calf.

"Put pressure on that. Now! Hanick, grab the largest bandage you can find from the emergency cabinet and wrap it as best you can. Then carry him up to sickbay, I can infuse him there."

Hanick grunted assent. He set Peterson's head down and lumbered over towards the cabinet. Lici beckoned to Jordan with a wave of one hand.

"There's another one over here."

Jordan stepped onto the ankle-deep platform. It swayed slightly under the jostling of a half-dozen people. Her skin instantly goose-pimpled as her shoes absorbed a chilling dose of forty-five-degree seawater.

The two women trudged around the side of the ROV. Richter lay sprawled out on his back, one diving fin still caught in the vehicle's clench. Blood oozed from more than a dozen deep cuts. The wounds turned the briny foam around him a sickening shade of pink.

Lici moved to raise Richter's mask and then touched her fingers to his neck. Satisfied, she next looked down to the man's thigh. A strange bulge protruded from the suit's black rubber. Jordan moved up next to her. She stared as the bulge gave a strange *pulse*.

"I need to see what that is," Lici said. "Can you roll him over a bit?"

Jordan knelt and wedged her hands under Richter's body, shifting it to one side.

Lici pulled a utility knife from her belt and squatted at

Jordan's side. She felt around under the foam to make sure that she'd cut suit and not flesh.

"Ouch!" the doctor exclaimed, as she pulled her hand back. A drop of blood welled out from the ball of her index finger.

Jordan looked up, alarmed. "Are you all right?"

"Just poked myself." Lici returned to her work. Satisfied, she made a single slash with her knife.

The bulge exploded in a meaty *splat* of iron-rich blood.

Lici fell back with a gasp of surprise. Richter's leg simply fell apart like a roll of raw beef. Now released from its rubber-sealed pocket, the pressure of the femoral artery continued to spurt its liquid red cargo in ever-weaker pulses.

Jordan recoiled from the sight, her eyes wide and staring. Shock turned to horror as she felt a heavy hand grip her shoulder. She tried to scream, but no sound came out.

No, no, no! I don't want to see, I don't want to see!

She heard shouts from Sawyer, from Hanick. They sounded impossibly distant as the grip on her shoulder turned her inexorably around.

Richter had been a handsome man, with chiseled, even features. The blood that cascaded down those same features made him look like a statue that vandals had hosed down with scarlet paint. His eyes weren't blurred like Peterson's. They blazed with a dying, incandescent glory as he spoke.

"I saw..." he whispered. "Down there. It was full...of *stars.*"

That final energy flickered out. With a shudder and a splash, Richter fell back against the grate. His eyes stared sightlessly at the ceiling above and into the void beyond.

CHAPTER TWO

Whitespire Laboratories
Reston, Virginia
Medical Isolation Gowning Area

Leigh Austen heard the ambulance coming before she saw it.

She peered into the gowning room's mirror. Her shoulder-length auburn hair had been pinned into submission under a cloth surgical cap. The area under her eyes looked dark compared to her normally pale complexion. The price paid for doing extra evening shifts.

Barely-visible shivers ran down her wrist, making her fingers twitch. Taking a deep breath, she adjusted her spearmint-colored scrub suit. Her heartbeat picked up as the distant siren drew closer.

She took a series of deep breaths and repeated her personal anxiety-busting mantra to herself.

God grant me the courage to handle the things I can. And to not push my luck on the things that I can't do a damned thing about.

The shivers vanished as she donned a powered air-purifying respirator, a glorified helmet with a clear face shield. An air hose ran from the back of the helmet down to brick-shaped fan unit that hung from the scrub suit's thick belt. It looked ungainly, but it delivered pathogen-free filtered air to her lungs.

She pushed through a set of self-closing doors which operated like the airlocks on a spaceship. The area in between smelled like a brand-new automobile that had been doused in a vat of rubbing alcohol. Cool blue UV lights bathed all surfaces, obliterating any viral particles that managed to slip inside.

The ambulance siren cut off just as she pushed through a second set of self-closing doors. Austen heard the muffled sounds of people talking. Then the squeak of wheels as a Whitespire orderly and a harried-looking doctor pushed a gurney into the waiting area. Both men wore gloves, surgical masks, and clear face shields.

The gurney's headboard had been raised so that the patient could recline in a half-sitting position. A boy with a drained, ashen appearance looked up at her. His lanky form was all but swallowed up by the mass of white sheets surrounding him. An oxygen mask enclosed his mouth and nose.

The doctor let out a relieved breath as he spotted Austen. He began talking in quiet, urgent tones as the orderly brought the gurney to a stop.

"Leigh, thank God for you and Whitespire," he said. "Our county hospital doesn't have all your fancy tools."

"We'd never turn away a case like this, Doctor Ybanez," Austen assured him, as she took the emergency medical record from the orderly. "And the only thing we have that you don't is a dedicated isolation ward."

"We figured that's what was needed. If we've got the right diagnosis."

She scanned the record. There wasn't much. Zachary Greenfield was a healthy ten-year old who'd had all of his immunizations. Six stitches across one knee from a bicycle accident and a cracked ulna from falling out of a tree was about all the medical treatment he'd needed in the past.

Until now.

Zachary had been admitted with a high fever, dry cough,

and difficulty breathing. What's more, the hospital's test samples showed positive indicators for Salem Valley Fever. SVF, or 'rabbit warren virus' was rare, but it qualified as one of the deadliest diseases found on the Eastern Seaboard. She handed the record back and made sure to smile as the patient's eyes fixed on her.

"Hi there, Zack," she said. "I'm Leigh. How are you?"

"Hey," the boy said, in a hoarse croak. "I'm sick."

"That really stinks," Austen said sincerely. "We'll try and make you feel better. Can I listen to your heart and give you a quick check up?"

"Sure."

She grabbed a stethoscope and pressed the specially modified earpieces against her helmet to help conduct sound. Austen listened to the heart and then a couple breath cycles from the lungs. The former was sound, but the latter rattled and wheezed with mucus. She pressed a finger to the lymph nodes at the boy's neck. They were swollen and as hard as miniature ball bearings jammed under the skin.

Lymphadenitis meant a serious exposure to some pathogen. The pneumonia had been thrown in as an added bonus. But they didn't directly point to the presence of *Coclia Salemovirus*.

Austen considered. Her eye went to a distinct tan line that ran along the boy's shirt collar. That made her stop and pause.

"Have you been outside a lot recently? Maybe hiking or camping anywhere?"

"Uh-huh. Been outside some." Zach coughed weakly. His inhales sounded like death rattles. "Went out on my own. Watched 'em knock down the Sandhills."

She looked over to Ybanez with a puzzled frown. But the name 'Sandhills' sounded familiar.

"That's what they call the sandy downs just north of Bull Run," the doctor explained. "Near the old Civil War battlefield. They're bulldozing them to put in a new development."

Now the name clicked into place in her head.

"That place is riddled with rabbit warrens," she breathed. "The Department of Game and Fisheries was looking for someone to test the animals out there, see if SVF was resident in the wild populations."

"Testing was done. It came back negative."

"That doesn't rule out anything. An infectious dose of this virus can be ridiculously small. If you kicked up enough dust from old rabbit warrens and inhaled it…" Austen looked back to her patient. "Zach, this is really, really important. When did you go watch them knock down the Sandhills?"

The boy screwed up his face in thought. "Just the other Saturday."

Three days ago, Austen thought, with a flutter of fear. *The minimum incubation time for SVF.*

She turned and spoke to the orderly. "I'm going to alert the Centers for Disease Control. We've got a likely case of pneumonic Salem Valley Fever on our hands. Can you decontaminate the ambulance? The driver too."

"On it," the man said. Ybanez looked worried as the man hurried back outside.

"What do you need me to do?" he asked.

Austen pointed to the side doors. "Decon area is that way. Use it. After that, page Doctor Widerman. SVF's a slippery bug, and a pneumonic case makes it trickier. You'll want Joseph working with you to make sure the county hospital and its staff don't accidentally spread the disease any further. And we need to get that construction site shut down."

Ybanez swallowed, hard. He turned and made for the doors.

"I'm on it," he murmured under his breath. Austen went to the rear of the gurney and began pushing it further along a corridor that led deeper into the building.

Zach let out another pitiful-sounding cough.

"Where are we going?" he asked, in a quavering voice.

She couldn't blame him for sounding scared. High fever, rock-hard lymph nodes and cloggy lungs were bad enough. Being taken somewhere scary-looking made it worse. The corridor up ahead fit the bill as it shaded from linoleum tiling into sheets of stainless steel.

Austen thought quickly. She latched on to what she'd seen in Zach's medical records. Here was a kid that rode bikes, climbed trees, and hiked around the neighborhood on his own. Clues that just might point to a love of adventure.

"We're going into our isolation ward," she said. "You're getting the celebrity treatment. Ever been on board a submarine before?"

Zach shook his head. The wide-eyed look he'd worn was starting to disappear.

"Well, this place has got a few things in common with a sub," Austen continued, as she pushed them through a final security door. This one actually did have nautical looking portholes ringed with hexagonal rivets. "Do your ears feel funny at all? You might want to swallow to clear them."

"Sorta." Zach gulped. "Feels better now."

"Just like on a sub, this ward is kept under a different pressure. That's because we're operating in…well, in new territory now."

"Like aquanauts?" He reached up and tapped the side of his oxygen mask. "That's why we wear these things. To breathe, right?"

"Slightly different reasons, but yeah, I never considered it that way. This would be like you're visiting a sub's sickbay for a little while."

A pair of nurses garbed in similar Level-3 gowns arrived to gently transfer the boy to a waiting hospital bed. From there, they could attach the array of monitoring devices every patient needed to survive a trip to the ward.

"I've got to turn you over to my fellow aquanauts now," Austen said. "They have to hook you up to the ship's sensors. Stay strong, okay?"

Zach smiled and gave her a weak thumbs-up. The boy still looked terribly fragile.

But at least he didn't look nearly as scared as before.

Austen hoped that would help. Though she'd done her best to sugarcoat things, the isolation ward wasn't a place of exploration. It was a place dedicated to containment. The change Zach had felt in his eardrums came from the negative pressure regimen that kept pathogen-laden air from flowing out into the environment.

Everyone at Whitespire Labs called the ward 'Stoney Lonesome'. Exposure to any particularly dangerous pathogen won instant admission and 24x7 care from nurses and doctors wearing the best protective gear money could buy. Patients who died received a HEPA-filtered incineration as an automatic death benefit.

A *chime* broke her out of her darker musings. She moved over to the door and picked up the isolation ward's single phone line.

"Austen here."

As with the stethoscope, the phone had a specially shaped receiver that conducted the sound easily through her helmet. Joseph Widerman sounded as if he was standing right next to her.

"Leigh, I've been talking with Doctor Ybanez. I agree with your findings, we've definitely got a case of pneumonic SVF. I got hold of the CDC chapter at Falls Church, they're already moving into action."

"What about our current case?"

"The CDC's going to have its hands full already. We're going to put our scheduled tests on hold to assist where we can. That includes helping Stoney Lonesome's latest resident."

"Sounds good. I'll stay down here."

"No, you won't. I want you up in my office as soon as you can degown."

"Are you sure about that? The patient—"

"Let the nurses do their job. They'll stabilize the patient and make him reasonably comfortable."

"What about the follow-up? I'm not sure about his prognosis."

"As it happens, I'm this state's resident expert in Salem Valley fever, pneumonic or otherwise." Widerman's words didn't sound like a boast. He simply stated the facts. "I'll be taking it from here."

Austen frowned. "What do you want me doing, then?"

"That depends on how you interpret the video I just received from an old friend," Widerman said. "I've got a hunch that this'll be right up your alley."

Michael Angel

CHAPTER THREE

Joseph Widerman's office was a picture-perfect example of how to impress would-be investors. The man's diplomas and family photos adorned his desk, while the walls held row upon row of pictures underscoring his connections.

In one, Widerman beamed as he shook a former President's hand. Another had him posing in a hard hat along with the CEO of a national construction firm. A third picture showed him deep in conversation with Senator Wallace Bainbridge.

Austen had noted that one the day she'd arrived for her interview. Bainbridge was Virginia's senior senator. He also happened to be her uncle.

"Ah, there you are," Widerman said, as he finished tapping at his laptop's keyboard. He waved a hand, indicating that Austen should take the plush 'client's seat' in front of his desk. "I just got a video message from an old friend of mine. Made my ears perk up, I'll tell you that. I haven't heard from Sasha in almost a decade."

That got a raised eyebrow. "Sasha?"

"Just to her friends. Her full name is Alexandra Ilyichna Kirov. We were in college together. She was brilliant, even back then. Me, the only way I could tell a chemistry class from a biology class was whether the experiment wriggled or not."

"Good thing you finally figured it out," Austen said, with a straight face.

"I went on to pre-med. Sasha switched to marine biology. After we got our degrees, I lost track of her for a while. A long while."

Widerman's voice had a distinctly wistful tone she couldn't help but wonder about.

"Were you two platonic friends? Or, ah, something more?"

"That would've been problematic. I was already seeing Elaine then. As for Sasha, she had a long-time girlfriend of her own."

"Two big strikes, then. Was that the last you heard from her until today?"

"Not quite. And that's where it gets interesting. Eight or nine years ago, Sasha finished her degree program and became an Associate Professor at the National University of Lisbon. She sent me a letter telling me how excited she was, that she was sending me a copy of her latest published research…"

Austen leaned forward. "And?"

"And it never came." Widerman's jaw worked back and forth for a moment. "When I did an online search for it, the article she referred to had been pulled. For some unknown 'setback'. My emails to her bounced. When I contacted the university, they said that she'd left. At least I think that's what they said. I'm not exactly fluent in Portuguese."

"And now, all of a sudden, she's back."

"Back, and in a big way." He pulled out a data drive the size of a fingernail and plugged it into a port on his desk. "Sasha's on a billion-dollar research station called Sirenica, somewhere in the Med. Here, I transferred it to the office projector."

Austen shifted to one side to view the screen and video lens that descended silently from the ceiling. She'd seen her boss sweet-talk people into investing millions by using this equipment to project slideshows with skyward-pointing revenue curves. The office lights dimmed as the picture winked on.

A rich, midnight blue filled the screen, framed by a circular rim of metal. Beyond lay a mottled, tumbled seafloor. Stingrays swam by in the middle distance with steady beats of their wing-like fins.

"How do you like my office view, Joseph?" came a high-pitched female voice. "Pretty impressive, I'd say!"

The screen jostled a bit as a hand readjusted the camera. Alexandra Kirov slid into view in front of a rack of lab equipment stacked neatly on a shelf behind her. She had an understated prettiness that came from a lack of makeup and a head of damp-looking black hair. The bluish cast of the light made her cream-colored skin appear stark white.

"Welcome to Sirenica!" Kirov continued cheerily. "It's just your average billion-dollar undersea research center. And guess who they wanted to run the marine biolab? They made it so that I just couldn't say 'no' to coming here!"

Widerman paused the video. His voice was unnaturally quiet. "What do you think, Leigh?"

Austen bit her lower lip. Kirov's pale features were set off by her hair and a pair of steel-gray eyes. But the color of the woman's irises wasn't what caught her attention.

"Her pupils are abnormally dilated. And I can see the whites of her eyes very clearly. If she's working in an artificially pressurized environment, I suppose that could account for it. Otherwise…"

"Yes?"

"She's scared. Very scared, Joseph."

"That's what I was thinking. Also, she sounds off. The Sasha I know isn't quite so…would 'perky' be the right word? Sunny?"

"Might be. Let's see the rest of the video."

Kirov went into motion again. "I know it's been a while, but I couldn't let a day go by without letting you know that I took the lemons life gave me and made some excellent lemonade. And speaking of that, you need to see my setup."

The view turned to reveal an impressive array of equipment. A set of half-filled test tubes gleamed from where they sat under colored lights. Austen recognized a pair of specially modified centrifuges costing in the high five figures to one side.

The center of the screen was dominated by a laboratory table. It was tilted up towards the screen like a drafter's workstation. Kirov tapped a remote and the tabletop sank back down to the horizontal.

"I've got all the bells and whistles I want now, even if I have to share." She gestured offhandedly towards the now-flat surface. "Can you believe that one of the other scientists spilled lemon juice all over that? We don't have the room for extra staff, so guess who had to spend half an hour scrubbing the damned thing down before it got sticky?"

Kirov shook her head as if laughing at her own inside joke. Then her expression turned more serious as she pulled out a chair and took a seat. She spoke into the camera lens casually, but her eyes looked as hard as flint.

"I wish I could say that this was just a social call. But it's not. We've just come across a strange case of necrosis down here. It's troubling, because it involves a member of our dive team. If this is some bug that could be resident down here – inside the station, or God forbid, in the open ocean – then it could mean that we have more challenges to face.

"This isn't an emergency, not exactly. But I thought you might be able to help us figure this out. I've gotten the Conte's approval to invite you and an assistant out here to Sirenica. At worst, it'll be an all-expense-paid summer trip to the Mediterranean. Joseph, you're the best at handling these kinds of things, and you're the only one I trust. So please take me up on the offer! Fingers crossed that you do."

The screen flicked over to black as the video came to an end. Widerman turned the office lights back up and looked over to Austen with an expectant smile.

She didn't return it. Instead, she crossed her arms and followed that up with a frown.

Widerman cleared his throat. "In case you're curious, the 'Conte' she refers to is an actual Sicilian nobleman. I received a voucher to use for a pair of plane tickets shortly after the video arrived."

Austen let out a resigned sigh. "Come off it, Joseph. What are you asking me to do?"

"Well, I was wondering whether you'd be interested in helping out my friend."

"By 'helping out my friend', you're really saying 'go down to Sirenica'."

"If necessary, yes."

She stared at him for a moment before shaking her head.

"No way," Austen declared. "Absolutely not!"

Michael Angel

CHAPTER FOUR

Widerman sat back in his chair. Austen's resounding *Absolutely not!* hung in the air between them for a second or two. Finally, he leaned forward and put his elbows on the desk like a card player getting ready to reveal their hand.

"All right," he said. "Why not? I'd think that you'd jump at the chance to solve a mystery like this."

"Why not? Where do I begin?" Austen began counting on her fingers. "First off, I've gotten into more scrapes involving rare diseases than I care to think about. Second, we've just taken in a patient with a disease that could easily kill him, so you'll need medical support. Third, that same disease could have infected any number of people in Fairfax County – especially the construction crew bulldozing the local rabbit warrens."

"Are you done?"

"Not even close." Austen got out of her seat and began to pace. "Waterborne illnesses are especially lethal and easy to catch. When it comes to the ocean, we've classified maybe ten percent of the dangerous pathogens out there. And speaking of the ocean, I can get seasick in a backyard inflatable pool. I took a scuba course in Oahu once, and that was bad enough. This

'Sirenica' must be hundreds of feet below the surface–"

"I looked up Sirenica's information online. It's only three hundred feet down."

"That's *not* helping."

"Okay, I've heard you out," Widerman said reasonably. "Now I'd like you to hear me out in turn. Is that all right with you?"

She sighed and looked out the window. "You're the boss."

"Why, I am, aren't I?" He chuckled at that. "Let's take your objections one at a time. If you get seasick easily, I can't think of a better place to be than below the waves. Yes, there are a lot of unknown and dangerous bugs out there in the water. But you and I know that if it was that easy to catch, then everyone in an enclosed environment like Sirenica would already have it."

Austen didn't like it, but she had to admit he was right.

"Go on," she gritted.

"As for who handles what crisis...the CDC has already been alerted. And the fact of the matter is that I wrote my doctoral thesis on Salem Valley Fever. After all the dead rabbits I dissected, I can't even look at bunnies in a pet store without breaking into a sweat. How many cases of SVF have you treated, from diagnosis to completion?"

"Damn it, that would be zero."

"And that's why you're unnaturally worried about our new patient. Once properly diagnosed, SVF has a fatality rate of only five percent. We've already got the young Mister Greenfield on a regimen of antiviral medications. He'll pull through, I'll stake my reputation on it."

"Joseph–"

"Leigh, the fact is...you're right. You've been in a couple of close scrapes recently, and that's not counting the one right here in our Level 3 facility." Widerman spread his hands as he continued. "But that also means you've got the most recent field experience of anyone in this company. I can get someone to cover your work in the lab for a couple of weeks. You've risen to challenges like this before. I'm confident you can do it again."

She shook her head.

"That makes one of us. I know you want to do your friend a favor, but this is asking a lot of me. Too much, I think."

"Then I'd like you to take the rest of the day off." Widerman pulled the data drive out of its slot on his desk and held it out to her. "Go home, get some lunch. Review the information on here. Think it over. That's all I'm asking. What could it hurt?"

Austen looked away from the window, stretching her hand out for the drive.

"I'll think about it. That's all I'm going to do."

"That's all I'm asking."

Austen jammed the drive in her pocket and turned on her heel. Mind awhirl, she made her way to her office and collected her belongings. A quick wave of her security badge at the building's exit and she strode out into the humidity of a Virginia summer.

Only one thing had kept her from slamming Widerman's office door on the way out. Unbeknownst to him, she had a secret inside line to information most people would never have. And it had come as the world's most unlikely birthday present.

Thank God for DiCaprio, she thought, as she started up her car and pulled out onto the Reston Parkway.

DiCaprio was a subject she'd revealed to perhaps three people in her life. He – or she, for all Austen knew – was a special inside source of information given to her by her uncle, Senator Bainbridge. The only way she could contact DiCaprio was from a military-grade secure server back at her house.

Her best guess was that DiCaprio – who she'd named after her favorite actor from the film *Titanic* – was an intelligence operative. One who worked in what D.C. insiders called a 'Gray Zone'. Austen sensed that inquiring any further along that line would run into a wall of red tape, and a lot of people asking too many questions she'd rather not answer.

But there were three constants about DiCaprio that came in

handy. First, she could ask him any question at all – whether she should take a job, invest in a stock, or make a major life change – and he would answer within twenty-four hours. Second, he usually answered in a style so cryptic that a fortune cookie looked straightforward by comparison.

Third, and most importantly, he was always right.

Austen pulled into her driveway and walked up to her front door. The sound of the neighbors mowing rattled her ears, and the smell of cut grass filled her nose until she made her way inside. She set aside her handbag, went into her study, and sat at the computer she used to contact DiCaprio.

After a moment's consideration, she slipped Widerman's drive into a data port. A couple of clicks, and she faced a blank screen of shimmery gray-black. Her words appeared as simple white letters as she typed.

Joseph Widerman wants me to visit someplace called Sirenica. His friend Sasha Kirov sent him a message with a vague hint of trouble. The message is on a data drive I just plugged in here. What do you think?

A click of the 'return' key, and her message sailed into cyberspace. She stared at the screen as if she could will it to respond. Sometimes – it was rare, but it happened – DiCaprio would answer her directly out of the electronic ether. Other times, it could take hours.

The computer let out a low *beep*, making her jump. The data drive had a little green light on the end. It began flashing on and off as someone accessed the contents.

A *ping* came from the screen. DiCaprio had responded in record time. And for once, he'd responded to a question with a question.

What can you use lemon juice for?

Austen frowned. That wasn't at all what she'd been expecting. But DiCaprio had reasons for the way he did things, and she'd learned to trust him.

"What could I use lemon juice for?" she asked aloud. "In recipes, I guess. Lemonade. French Meringue. Or cleaning things. Making the garbage disposal smell better. In chemistry, I could use it to change the acidity of a chemical mixture."

Wait, she thought. *That's not a random question, is it? Professor Kirov had specifically mentioned someone spilling lemon juice on her brand-new lab table. Was that why she looked so scared in her video? That seemed unlikely, unless—*

She sat up straight in her chair. *Of course!*

Throughout history, people had used lemon juice to write secret messages. You could only view the words written in lemon juice under strong light or a UV lamp.

A couple of pecked commands, and the video appeared on screen. Austen clicked *PLAY.* As Kirov began talking about how excited she was about being on Sirenica, Austen adjusted her monitor's gamma correction so that the image was unnaturally bright and tilted towards the purple-violet end of the color range.

"We don't have the room for extra staff," Kirov was saying. "So, guess who had to spend half an hour scrubbing the damned thing down before it got sticky?"

She clicked *PAUSE* as the camera focused on the strangely tilted table. It was canted at an angle perfect for a draftsman — or someone trying to get a message out under watchful eyes. She made out two fuzzy lines of text written in broad strokes, as if someone had used a paintbrush instead of a pen.

> *DANGER BELOW.*
> *HELP ME JOSEPH.*

Austen felt as if a block of ice had materialized in her stomach. This wasn't some vague request to assist. It was a plea for help. And Kirov had even bypassed this 'Conte' to get the message out.

She thought about alerting the authorities for a split second at most. Aside from the nebulous nature of the message, what could any authority based in the United States really do? She wasn't sure where Sirenica was, or even if it was in international waters. And if Kirov were that worried about her message being intercepted, then alerting anyone could be a death sentence for her.

Austen blew out a breath. She hadn't been exaggerating all that much to Widerman. She didn't like the idea of visiting anywhere under three hundred feet of water. But she'd take those two vouchers. She wouldn't leave someone in harm's way, particularly if there was a killer pathogen involved.

And it's the right thing to do, she concluded to herself.

She pulled out her phone to call Joseph Widerman, but paused.

Setting her jaw, she made one more decision.

There was another number she was going to call first.

CHAPTER FIVE

Briar Patch Complex
Boiler House District
Durham, North Carolina

The last thing Austen expected to smell in this part of town was the aroma of fresh-baked bread.

She'd parked her car along a road split by industrial warehouses on one side and a set of townhouses on the other. A security camera zeroed in on the intercom button by the entry gate as she tapped in a code. The distant thunder of passenger jets taking off from the nearby airport tickled her ears as she waited for a response.

The speaker clicked on, resonating with a familiar male voice. Nicholas Navarro's masculine rumble still held its usual hint of Western twang, leavened with a dash of surprise.

"Well, I'll be. I must be seeing things, or you're someone who looks like Leigh Austen."

"I better look like her," came the reply. "I just drove four-and-a-half hours to get here."

"Problem is, Leigh Austen doesn't have my address. And there's security around these parts for a reason. If you're her, then you can prove it by answering one question."

"What is it?"

"What was the color of the underwear you showed me the last time we had dinner?"

Her eyes went wide. "I never showed you my damned underwear!"

The gate's lock buzzed as it clicked open. "You're her, all right. Come ahead."

Austen felt her cheeks burn as she passed through the gate and made her way to the townhouse at the far end. She'd first met Navarro on an overseas mission to Kazakhstan. As part of the global security firm Motte & Bailey, he and his men had gotten her out of more than a couple of scrapes. She'd returned the favor on more than one occasion.

Navarro had a quirky sense of humor and a deep, unwavering loyalty to his men. She'd found it easy to trust the man, even revealing the existence of DiCaprio. But the real surprise was that she'd found herself thinking about Nick more as a man than a hired gun.

Their last dinner together had simply been a meal snuck in between Congressional hearings over a recent shared mission to Suriname. Other people might've found it quiet, even formal. Navarro had been uncommonly quiet and even gentlemanly. She'd been as cautious and halting as any woman who was unfamiliar with how things worked outside of a laboratory.

And yet somehow, despite the fact she couldn't remember a single thing said, she'd had a good time.

Austen put it out of her mind as she rapped her knuckles on Navarro's front door. A faint 'come in', and she went inside. She looked around, surprised at what she saw.

The Motte & Bailey man's place was a sparsely furnished, neat-as-a-pin bachelor pad. Everything from the television set in the corner to the bookshelves and coffee table had the faintest coating of dust, the sign of someone who was away from home a lot. Her mouth watered as she smelled the unmistakable scent of cooking steak.

The doorway to the kitchen lay a little further down the dwelling's main corridor. Navarro leaned out for a moment. "Make yourself at home for a spell. You caught me just as I was putting dinner in the pan."

"Sorry I interrupted," she said. "Incidentally, I got your home address from your boss, Niles Bailey."

"I'm impressed that you got hold of him." She heard Navarro switch on the blower over the stove. "Normally, he's the one who calls *me*."

"Bailey said he would let you know that I was on the way."

"That explains a lot," Navarro called back, over the fan's motor. "I chucked my phone out the back window last night. Bailey put me on 'administrative leave'. Something to do with giving Geoffrey Chadwick a surprise nose job."

Austen bit back a laugh. Chadwick was also under Congressional investigation. The man had richly deserved a punch in the face from Navarro.

"I guess I did show up out of nowhere, then."

"No worries, I've got enough on the stove for two. Then you can tell me what you came all the way down here for. Whatever it is must be important for you to want to dine with me again."

"As long as I don't have to show you my underwear, I'm good."

Austen looked around the room as Navarro's chuckle was drowned out by the clatter of plates. Most of the furniture was made of dark wood and leather. A pair of cowhides was all that softened a blond hardwood floor. Eggshell colored walls sported pictures of migrating geese and close-ups of buffalos snorting steam into the air of a winter landscape.

Of the bookcase's four shelves, the top two were packed with dog-eared paperbacks. The bottom two were stuffed with videotapes meant to be played by a machine that was practically an antique.

She knelt and picked up the only dust-free tape at the top of the pile. Curious, she turned it over. Her lips curled up as she recognized the movie.

So Old Yeller *is one of your favorites? That's a throwback to 1957.* She put the tape back, considering. *Navarro, you're more of a sentimentalist than you let on.*

Austen made her way back towards the kitchen just as the fan was silenced. To the left of the doorway sat a monolith of a refrigerator and a stove covered in now-emptied pans. To the right, Navarro had set out two steaming plates of food at a table made out of a single slab of beechwood.

"Soup's on," he said, as he pulled out a chair for her.

She took it gratefully. Austen watched Navarro for a moment as he pulled up a second chair to sit opposite her. The man had the kind of shoulders that made any shirt look a size too small. As long as she'd known him, he'd kept his coffee-colored hair buzzed short enough to reveal the outline of his skull.

Watchful hazel eyes sat deep in a lantern-jawed face. That face was pleasant enough to look at, but calling it 'handsome' would've stretched things too far. Among other things, a mass of scar tissue wended down the left side from hairline to below the cheekbone.

Austen set a cloth napkin on her lap and picked up a fork. The blue-speckled plate laid out before her held a small mound of mashed potatoes, green beans topped with fried onion bits, and a palm-sized piece of flank steak cooked to a perfect medium rare pink.

Together, they dug into their dinner. She took a couple bites from each section of her plate and was pleasantly surprised. The potatoes might have come out of a cardboard box, but everything else tasted fresh from the garden or butcher.

"My compliments to the chef," she said. "The only thing that surprises me is the lack of bread. That's what I smelled on my way in."

"There's a national bakery chain that has its ovens a block over," he said, between bites. "Gives this whole neighborhood a homier feeling than you'd expect."

"I can believe that." Austen peered into the glass he'd

placed by her plate. Amber liquid swirled between a mass of ice cubes.

"Unsweetened iced tea," he said. "Leastwise, that's what I recall you like."

She smiled. "You do have an eye for detail, Nick. What're you having?"

"About what you'd expect." Navarro reached to one side and pulled out a tallboy-sized beer can. He popped open the can and took a long sip. "Every man has a few weaknesses. The occasional oat soda is one of mine."

"Another being classic books...and classic films? Like *Old Yeller*?"

Navarro finished another bite of his steak and set his fork aside for a moment. "Guilty as charged. That's the one where the boy's dog gets rabies. At the end, he has to put Old Yeller down."

She gave him a look. "Given your line of work with Mott & Bailey...were you ever put in a position like that?"

Michael Angel

CHAPTER SIX

Were you ever put in a position like that?"

Austen's question hung in the air for a moment between them. Navarro looked away for a moment. Letting out a breath, he finally spoke.

"No, thank heavens. The movie's a bit more personal for me. I had a dog like Old Yeller. He was a mutt named Hubcap, and he was a damned good friend for a ten-year old with an unstable drunk for a father."

Austen stayed quiet at that. Navarro's father had given him only two things that had lasted the test of time. His last name, and the wicked scar that ran down the side of his face.

"He got the name because he brought back a hubcap he found at the dump. We used it as a food dish for him. After that, he'd carry it around in his mouth, hoping we'd feed him extra. Unfortunately, he also picked up a case of rabies. We had to lock him up in the shed behind the house. The virus boiled his brain and he started snapping at anything that moved."

"I didn't mean to bring up bad memories, Nick."

"It's not a bad one, not exactly. It's just that I couldn't do what I had to. I couldn't put him down. A neighbor with a rifle came over. With a single shot, he took care of Hubcap for me. But my parents darn sure made me bury him. So I promised myself that I'd do what needed to be done from then on." Navarro considered a moment. "It's my turn to apologize, Leigh. That wasn't exactly good dinner conversation."

"Would you be surprised if I had a similar story?" she asked quietly. He nodded, encouraging her to go on. "I started college thinking I was going to be a big animal vet, so I interned at a wildlife sanctuary. This one place had trapped a coyote that had been attacking local livestock and pets. It showed signs of rabies, but I argued that we had to observe it longer before making the decision to put it down. I was very convincing."

Navarro took another sip from his can. "Some things about you haven't changed."

"Well, my decision bit me in the ass. Literally. That very night the coyote got out of its holding pen. Two handlers and I got bit trying – and failing - to corral it again. Thanks to me, all three of us had to get a series of rabies shots in case the damned thing was infectious. Like you, I made up my mind to do what needed to be done from then on."

"We're both slow learners," Navarro pointed out. "We'll have to see if the lesson stuck for either you or me. And that brings me to the big question: Why did you go through my boss to find me?"

Austen shrugged as she crunched down one of the green beans. "It's because I wanted to hire you. As my personal bodyguard."

Navarro almost spilt his beer. "Are you serious?"

"Serious as a case of Salem Valley Fever. Niles Bailey said that you're on administrative leave, so you can't be brought on as part of a 'professional services force' for any public agency. But you can be hired under Article 23, Subsection 7-B of your employment contract for 'consulting services' by a private individual. Which would be *me*, in this case."

"Bailey did you a favor, then."

"If he did, it came with a hefty price tag. Basically, I had to give back what he paid me for that last trip to South America. But I think you're worth it."

Navarro grinned. His front two teeth had a slight gap, which somehow melted twenty years of hard living from his face.

"Flattery gets you a long way with me. So, let's hear the rest of the story."

The steak, green beans, and potatoes disappeared in stages as Austen explained the situation. Navarro listened patiently, asking questions only when needed. Finally, he pushed away his plate and moved his lower jaw as if physically chewing over the situation.

"I've got three questions before I agree to sign on to this rodeo," he finally said. "First, what kind of hardware am I going to be able to bring along?"

She gave him a wry look. "We may end up heading down to a pressurized tin can three hundred feet below the surface of the ocean. What do you think?"

"I think that firearms are out."

"Will that be a problem for you?"

"A small one." Navarro held up his hands and bunched them into fists. "I still have these. I'm also pretty good with using knives, broken bottles, sharp sticks—"

"—In other words, you should be able to handle anything someone throws our way." Austen concluded. "What's your next question?"

"You said you had two 'open-ended' tickets originally sent to Widerman. How soon can we get airborne?"

"Well, it helps that you live in Durham International's back yard."

Navarro nodded. "That's intentional. You'd be surprised how many security contractors live around here. Even in this very complex. You probably got scoped by a half-dozen ex-snipers on your walk up to my door."

"That's comforting," Austen said, in a wry voice. She checked her watch. "We can catch a connecting flight in the next three hours. I've already got my suitcase in the trunk of my car."

"Final question, then. You're funding *me*. Who's funding *us*? That is, who's running the ball game and handing out a pair of tickets to attend?"

"I looked it up before I headed down here. The head of Sirenica Aquanaut Explorations and the man who's paid for our tickets is one and the same. His name is Count Fiorenzo Diamante. Judging from the articles about him in the financial pages, he's a rather colorful fellow."

Navarro sat back in his chair for a few seconds. Finally, he nodded, as if settling something in his mind.

"I'll go pack," he said.

Austen felt a weight lift from her chest. "You're coming, then."

"You've got a rather interesting situation brewing here," Navarro acknowledged. "And as for this 'Fiorenzo Diamante'…well, with a name like that, he probably doesn't like to be kept waiting."

CHAPTER SEVEN

Aeroporto Falcone Borsellino
Provincia di Palermo
Pozillo, Sicily

A bleary-eyed Austen set her bottle of mineral water aside as she slumped against the airport café's countertop. She fished a plastic bag out of a jacket pocket, pulled out a chunk of something spicy-smelling, and popped it in her mouth. Navarro joined her after claiming their luggage off the cart on the runway.

"Candy? At this time of the morning?" He took a spot next to her, though he half-turned to keep his eye on the outer terminal. "Seems a little out of character for you."

"It's crystallized ginger. My stomach's been a little queasy since our plane hit turbulence last night."

"We did? Hadn't noticed."

Austen swallowed the ginger slice and then took a swig of mineral water. Of course, Navarro hadn't noticed. The man had sacked out in the seat next to her as soon as they'd taken off. Then he'd barely moved until they'd arrived in Rome, just before dawn. One transfer to a propeller-driven puddle jumper and an equally bumpy ride later, they'd arrived in Sicily.

"Shouldn't you have noticed?" she grumped. "You're supposed to be my bodyguard, aren't you?"

He shrugged. "Not much I can do about air turbulence. I'm sure you would've woken me up if the plane had been hijacked, though. As for noticing things around here...I'd say that our ride just showed up."

Austen turned to see a short, well-dressed man approach them. He wore a pair of driving gloves and a gray suit jacket complete with an embroidered coat of arms at the breast pocket.

He made a short bow to them before speaking.

"*Mi scusi, per favore*," he said. "I am driver for Conte Diamante. Shall we go?"

Minutes later, Austen and Navarro sat across from each other in the back of a limousine as the driver took them through Palermo's urban core. The vehicle's air conditioner blasted out a dull roar as it tried to keep the interior cool. Buildings slid past on both sides, looking both ornately decorated and yet shabby and decaying in the blazing sun.

Austen did her best to overlook the fact that the limo ignored most of the traffic lights. The driver alternately gunned the motor or slammed on the brakes, rattling both her nerves and her body. Noticing her wide eyes, Navarro cleared his throat to get her attention.

"No need to worry," he said. "This is how everyone drives around here."

"Maybe, but I'd feel better if this limo had seat belts."

Navarro leaned towards her, his voice barely audible over the din of the air conditioner.

"This limo may be lacking certain things, but the air vents are creating a lot of white noise. Should be safe enough for me to ask: Did you ask DiCaprio anything about this mission?"

She replied in a voice as quiet. "I did. So far, no reply."

Navarro considered. "He's always gotten back to you within twenty-four hours, right?"

"Yes, and that time limit isn't up yet."

"Great," Navarro sighed. "Right now, when we could use an edge, our personal crystal ball is taking his sweet time."

The limo climbed out of the city proper and up the steeply sloping hills to the north. The vehicle navigated several switchbacks as it climbed up towards the walls of a castle that sat atop a peak overlooking the city. The driver pulled to a stop where a pair of elaborate iron gates had been thrown open.

"*Siamo arrivati*," he announced, after he came around and opened the passenger door for Austen. "Follow the red tiles, please."

After exchanging a curious glance, Austen and Navarro went through the gates, following the diamond-shaped patterns of red tile inlaid in the walkway. Inside lay a bright courtyard surrounded by a forest of slender stone pillars. A handful of small tour groups meandered around the outer edge. The interior echoed with the sound of a half-dozen different languages.

The red tiles led past the groups and up to a broad flight of stairs. A small sign sat next to the stairway. Four words in Italian were re-written below in English.

NON ENTRARE, SOLO PERSONALE
DO NOT ENTER, STAFF ONLY PLEASE

"I doubt that applies to us," Navarro said. Austen nodded and led the way up the stairs. Their steps echoed off the high stone ceiling.

The top of the stairs ended in a wide-open area illuminated by a skylight far above. The murmur of a man's voice came from behind a set of carved wooden doors, from which hung yet another sign that read: *Cinque minuti per favore*.

"Five minutes, please," Austen said, after a moment. "I guess we don't rate a formal appointment. So we wait."

"We've come far enough, and on his dime," Navarro agreed. "And speaking of dimes…it seems that the Conte has enough of them to be an art collector."

Austen stepped over to where Navarro gazed up in

contemplation. The skylight had been angled to fall upon a nearby wall. Thousands upon thousands of little squares of colored glass had been set in patterns to create a stunning mural.

Geometric lines of turquoise and azure made up a storm-tossed sea. A Homeric galley surged through the waves, propelled by muscular men working long sets of oars. Yellow glass cubes meant to represent wax dotted their ears. They bent to their task, ignoring the pair of women who perched either on the bow or foredeck railings.

The women were nude, with the litheness of youth. But they had feathered wings on their backs, cruel talons for feet, and soulless eyes. One held a horn, the other a lyre. Together they appealed to a man who strained, wild-eyed, against the ropes that bound him to the ship's mast.

"What do you think?" Navarro finally asked.

Austen shuddered. "It's more than a little disturbing."

A cultured male voice spoke from behind them.

"All the best art is, my dear."

Austen turned to find that the wooden doors had slid apart without a sound. The man who stood in the opening reminded her slightly of Niles Bailey. He was moderate of build and height, but carried himself as if he were a foot taller.

An immaculately tailored gray suit outlined his form like a knight's armor. His Roman nose shaded a mustachio that could have graced the upper lip of a barbershop quartet's lead singer. Jet black eyes matched the color of a well-oiled helmet of hair.

"*Ti saluto*, my friends!" He inclined his head for a moment before extending his hand. "I have the honor of being Count Fiorenzo Diamante. But Conte will do, if you so please."

Austen hesitated for a moment, taken aback by the mixture of formal greeting and the informality of the proffered handshake. She took it, half expecting the man to kiss the back of her hand. Instead, Count Diamante gave it a pair of imperious shakes and then repeated the gesture with Navarro.

"Ah, thank you, Conte," Austen finally said. "I'm Leigh

Austen, from Whitespire Labs. Perhaps Joseph Widerman spoke to you about my coming in his place."

"He did, he did. Quite a tragedy how that fever popped up at the last minute. Dreadful thing, these little bugs," Diamante tut-tutted. His eyes shifted to her companion. "He spoke quite highly of your accomplishments. However, he did not tell me much about *il tuo associato*."

"*Scusami*, Conte," Navarro demurred. "I'm just Ms. Austen's assistant."

"If so, then she must use test tubes made of concrete. I don't believe I've ever seen muscles like yours on any 'lab assistant'." The Conte's attention returned to Austen. "As for the art, I take it that you know what you gaze upon?"

"It's from the *Odyssey*. That's Odysseus and his ship, the *Argo*," Austen finally said. "I'm trying to remember the name for the bird-women with the musical instruments. Harpies, I think."

"They're sirens," Navarro put in. "As I once read: *The siren sings so sweetly that she lulls the mariners to sleep; then she climbs upon the ships and kills them in their slumber.*"

Conte Diamante's eyebrow rose in surprise. "Da Vinci was the one who wrote that. *Così molto interessante!* You are more than you seem at first, my friend!"

Navarro merely inclined his head at the compliment.

"Yes, these are the Sirens," Diamante went on. "They who sing a song that no man can resist, unless he's bound to the mast or has his ears stopped up with wax. One of the most powerful images in ancient literature, immortalized in this mural."

"I'm sorry if I sounded like I didn't like it," Austen said lamely.

"Nonsense! *Ridicolo!* I can always forgive a beautiful woman anything!" He turned on his well-polished heel and beckoned them to follow him into the inner chamber. "Come, follow me. I have a thing to show you which I think you will find of interest."

Michael Angel

CHAPTER EIGHT

The room beyond opened up into a brightly lit mixture of display studio and conference area. To one side, a bay window looked to the north, overlooking the winding road that led down to the city and the sea beyond. An architect's table dominated the center, complete with a king-sized diorama meant to represent an undersea plateau. Beyond lay a second broad staircase curving up to a set of closed doors.

Diamante stepped over to the window. Absently tweaking a corner of his mustache with his forefingers, he stared out as if considering a weighty matter. Finally, he let out a sigh before speaking to them again.

"To arrive at my family's *castello sulla collina*, you had to pass through Palermo. Might I ask what you two thought of the city?"

"Well, it's got…a great number of historical buildings," Austen hedged. "To be honest, some looked rather…run down. In need of a little work."

"I've seen worse in a couple parts of the United States," Navarro said. "But Leigh's right, it's seen better days."

Diamante chuckled and shook a finger at Navarro. "Well put, well put! And you are both correct. For two whole millennia, Sicily was at the center of multiple civilizations in the past. Today, is it on the *bordo*, the periphery of the economic map. Even the noble families like mine are rather poor."

"I find that a little hard to believe," Austen said. "From what I've read, your family's net worth is in the high eight-figure range."

"*Ay, magari!* If only that were so. The people who write about money are short-sighted. They do not understand the difference between net worth and *liquidity*. I learned when I was nine. I was training to join the local team for football — what you Americans call 'soccer' — by kicking the ball around one of the courtyards below this very office.

"I was practicing the inner scissor when I sent the ball sailing off one of the pillars, bouncing it against one of the inner walls. The outer layer of paint crumbled away with the blow. I remember what I saw next. It sent me running, screaming, and it gave me a nightmare later!"

"What did you see?"

"*Eyes.* Hidden eyes, staring back at me from that crack in the paint!" Diamante made his way towards the diorama as he continued talking. "And when my mother the Contessa found out...*oh, dio ce ne scampi e liberi!* I received a good *sferzata*, a lashing, and not with her tongue!"

Navarro bit back the start of a chuckle. "That happened to me once too, I took a hiding from my mother for sending a baseball through the kitchen window. Had to pay for fixing it, too."

"Ah, but our situations were different, Mister Navarro," Diamante said with a disarming smile. "The Contessa was not angry at me for breaking something that needed to be fixed. I had uncovered a classical mosaic, a brand-new historical piece of art. Under Italian law, we had to pay to *restore* it to its former glory."

"You've got me there, Conte."

"As it happened, I was better managing computers than playing football. I created the first software program to track freighter shipping and sold it to a group of investors with more money than sense. I brought the mosaic up here to look at and inspire me. To inspire this."

Diamante waved his hand like a showman. A bank of track lights in the ceiling lit up the table. Four shades of blue, set out like a contour map, drew the viewer's eye along a broad canyon.

Bright yellow minisubs looked like just-unwrapped Christmas toys against the simulated seafloor. Smaller burnt-orange box shapes with arms represented the Remotely Operated Vehicles.

Stiff threads from the ROVs led back to a central structure. That structure, which sat on multiple pairs of stilt-like girders, towered four stories above the seabed. The platform resembled a regular stack of four dinner plates sitting on a wire rack. The level of detail, right down to the LED lights that shone from the portholes, made it seem impossibly futuristic.

"This is *Sirenica*," Diamante's chest swelled as he said the words. "The ultimate in aquanaut habitats. The one I've lured the best minds to work on. Four separate decks made of exotic metal alloys and tempered glass. All lowered a hundred meters down to the seabed. Up to twenty people can live on board at the same time, so long as the umbilical remains in place."

"Umbilical?" Austen asked.

"It is not shown on the model, but there is always a support ship sitting on the surface that provides Sirenica's lifeline. It provides air and power via a set of hollow cables that make up the umbilical system. Were that severed, the habitat could still operate for several days on its own. But there is a three-week hard limit on how long one can visit."

"Why three weeks? I mean, it seems like you have this set up to run as long as you wish, so long as the support ship stays in place."

A shrug. "The deep can be an intoxicating place, Miss Austen."

"It can be," Navarro said flatly. "But I think it's more likely the nature of what the people down there are breathing. That has to be an exotic gas environment."

Diamante gave that same disarming smile again.

"It seems that someone has knowledge of this," Diamante said. "You are correct. As one descends to the depths, pressure increases. As pressure increases, so does the corrosive effect of gases like oxygen, as well as the narcotic effects of nitrogen."

"I've done technical diving," Navarro explained. "You use something called trimix for those dives. That's oxygen, nitrogen, and helium. What do you use, Conte?"

"Sirenica exclusively uses hydreliox." Diamante's chest stuck out even further, if that were possible. "We are the first aquanaut habitat in the world to do so."

"I'm not familiar with that one."

"Hydreliox is a patented combination of helium, oxygen and hydrogen. We manufacture it at a land-based center and transfer it to the support ship. From there, it's pumped down to Sirenica."

"Oxygen and hydrogen? That's a rather flammable combination."

"We've been able to eliminate the risk on an underwater station. Truly, it's the safest place below the waves. Hydreliox is a miracle gas mixture. It limits voice distortion, reduces decompression time, and cuts down considerably on high-pressure neurological syndromes. Hence, a three-week window of operations is made available to us."

A chime came from the phone next to the diorama. Diamante picked up the receiver.

"*Scusi,*" he said. "This shall only take a moment."

Navarro looked to Austen as soon as the Conte turned his attention to the call.

"I don't know anything about extended living in exotic gas environments. But if no one's been affected by it yet, it should be safe enough. What do you think?"

"We can't rule anything out before I see what's causing the necrosis out there," Austen replied. "But I think I'm starting to see why the Conte named it 'Sirenica'. He says he's lured the best minds there. Perhaps he's lured them there the way the Sirens did. By singing an irresistible song to bring in anyone who hasn't lashed themselves to the mast."

Finally, Diamante hung up the phone. His voice fairly shook with excitement.

"My friends, that call told me that we are ready. Ready to receive the help that you've brought me. Because all the great things I've done are at risk of being washed away, and by something so small that it cannot be seen. That is why I need you. To save Sirenica, so it can continue to be used to explore. To study."

"To study what, exactly?" Austen asked.

Diamante laughed. "If you want to know, then come with me!"

The doors at the far end of the room slid open. A sleek white helicopter sat atop a concrete pad. The engines started up with a cough that echoed in the enclosed space. Austen saw their limo driver placing the last of their luggage onto the aircraft.

"*Andiamo!*" Diamante declared. "We go now!"

Michael Angel

CHAPTER NINE

Tyrrhenian Sea
Provincia di Palermo
Aeolian Islands

Count Diamante's helicopter flew low, blazing northeast at full speed across the Tyrrhenian Sea. The brown and green bumps of the Aeolian isles broke up the flat, blue monotony of the horizon. Clusters of little pink and white houses clung to the steep sided islands like limpets to a boat's hull.

Austen and Navarro watched the postcard-worthy landscape slide by. The noise and thumping vibration of the helicopter's blades was blunted by headsets, allowing Austin to listen as Diamante continued their previous conversation.

"You asked what there is to explore, to study. Something big, something *bellissima!*" Diamante enthused. He moved his hands as if to place items on a board hanging before him. "This ancient body of water we fly over is called the Tyrrhenian Sea. In the north and west, it is bounded by Sardinia and the 'shin' of the Italian boot. These places sit on the Eurasian continental plate. In the south it is bounded by my home island of Sicily, which sits on the African plate. And they are in *collisione*, or 'collision'."

"I'm familiar with plate tectonics," Austen said. "The African plate is sinking, or 'subducting' under the Eurasian one. This melting and compressing are why Italy has major volcanic activity when places like England or Germany don't."

The helicopter drew close to the last island in the Aeolian chain. The sharp relief of a volcanic cone revealed they were about to pass over the volcano of Stromboli. A cloud of vapor rose from the crater inside, as if from a sleeping dragon. The faint smell of brimstone seeped into the cabin, like a promise from Hell.

"Ah, you know much. But what you may not be aware of is that subduction also produces oceanic trenches. At that point, where one plate plunges back into the mantle, it forms a subterranean magma plume. If the rock above is porous enough to allow seawater to percolate down and vaporize against this liquid rock—"

"You get a hydrothermal vent field," Austen sat back and touched a finger to her lips in thought. "That's why you placed Sirenica on a plateau, at the edge of a much greater depth."

Navarro considered. "That makes sense. It can be used as a base of operations for deep-water expeditions. The only question is, how deep?"

"Sirenica sits at one hundred meters. The aquanauts there have constructed a second habitat called 'Base Camp' at three hundred meters. We've been exploring the area around base camp to find the safest way to approach what we think of as the Final Frontier. Or the Point of No Return."

"How about the Holy Grail?"

"Bravo, Mister Navarro! As they say in America, you 'get my drift'. From just beyond Base Camp, it is one thousand meters down to the Palinuro Vent Field. There are dozens upon dozens of what are called 'black smoker' or 'white smoker' vents. Each one gushes minerals dissolved in thousands of gallons of superheated water.

"The Palinuro field emits enough raw geothermal power to light up Italy's boot from toe to garter! And that's not counting the incalculable mineral wealth being discharged into the water…if only we can figure out where to collect it!"

Austen noticed Diamante's choice of words.

"You said 'where'. Not 'how'. That's surprising, since you seem to know where this vent field is located."

"*Per favore*, Miss Austen! We are not timber barons from a century ago! At best we will harvest, not exploit what is found. A whole ecosystem of newly discovered life exists down there, and I have no wish to harm it."

"I've heard things like that before." She crossed her arms. "Temptation can undo a lot of nice words."

"If you shall not believe words, then perhaps you shall believe in the laws of physical matter. Consider that the water-mineral suspension has been superheated to four hundred degrees Celsius – easily twice as hot as a kitchen oven at full blast!"

Diamante gestured for her to look down and to the right as they passed over Stromboli's throat. A gray pancake of rock smoldered as it glowed red through a series of cracks. "Also consider that we are dealing with fields of molten magma bubbling away on the seafloor that can melt metal. And then there is the problem of bringing it almost a full kilometer back to the surface…"

Austen nodded. "I see what you're getting at, Conte."

"That is why I say 'where', not 'how'. We shall only harvest minerals from where the vents are cold and have petered out. The life forms that thrive near the active vents will have moved on now that their source of heat and food is gone."

"My apologies, then. Usually there is less thought put into these ventures."

"Believe me, I have had much time to ponder this. Multiple international organizations have wanted to shut me down already. For that alone, I've needed both legal and physical firepower."

Navarro's ears perked up at that. "Wait, what do you mean by–"

But Diamante had grown more animated, not hearing the

question. "And now, *piove sul bagnato*! When it rains, it pours. Three divers go out to explore, to find the place we can tap the priceless resources of the Palinuro. One returns, only to die. One missing. One placed in a medical coma. And now, I hear that another may be sick!"

Stromboli faded into the distance behind them as Austen sat up in turn. She'd been waiting to turn the conversation back around to the illness that had brought her a third of the way around the globe.

"What else can you tell us about that?" she urged. "All I heard about was some strange necrosis."

"It is an infection, a life-threatening one, and that is enough! What might we have to do to combat this thing?"

"I don't know yet, Conte. Maybe you'll have to disinfect part of the station. Isolate those with the sickness. And that's if it's not waterborne."

"But what if it is?"

Austen's voice remained matter-of-fact. "Then we face one of two choices. We figure out a way around the microorganism – a vaccine, cleaning regimen, or barrier method. Or, you abandon your underseas project."

Diamante went a shade pale at that. "*Povero me*! That is just what Orcus would want!"

Before Austen could ask what he meant, Navarro spoke up. His face had taken on a stormy scowl.

"I've read about them. They're not the best sort of people, to put it mildly."

"Ah, so you understand why Sirenica needs multiple levels of security." Diamante jerked his head towards the cabin's window. "We're drawing close. You can see what I mean by 'physical firepower'."

Far below, three ships bobbed on the waves. The middle one was wide and fairly flat, like a cargo container ship. The remaining two moved in an elliptical orbit around the first. They had sharp, aggressive outlines and bristled with anti-aircraft missile launchers and 127mm marine artillery launchers. The tricolor flag of the Italian Navy fluttered from their sterns.

"They look armed for bear," Navarro observed.

"If the bear is flying or swimming, they shall get a hot welcome," Diamante declared. "Those are a pair of the *Marina Militare's* best destroyers. But our destination is that ship at the center, the *Acheron*. She's a Deepwater Cable Vessel."

The helicopter came about to circle in towards the *Acheron's* helipad. The ship's bulk grew as they descended, revealing the true size of the vessel. Austen looked from one side to the other, impressed.

"Wow! She's got to be wider and longer than a cruise liner."

"I purchased her from one of your country's oceanographic research institutes. As her designation implies, she used to lay underseas cables. I suppose it's rather fitting, since she's still paying out a cable. Only that leads to Sirenica now."

"Fitting or not, she's quite a ship."

"Oh, she may look like a ship, but she's not," Diamante said, with a chuckle. "She's really a *portale*. A door to an elevator that shall take you to straight to the bottom of the sea!"

Michael Angel

CHAPTER TEN

Orcus Teleconference
Harstaad Island
Dårlig Mann Fjord

Victor Lawrence Wakelin heard voices in his head every day.

That didn't bother him.

These days, he practically lived with a miniaturized speaker in his ear canal and a bone-conducting sonic microphone attached to his jawline. It came with the job.

Wakelin's forebears had come from many places on the European continent. The marble and glass cubist fantasy that made up his house on the hill above had been in the family for generations. So had the private island it sat upon.

They'd been paid for, of course. Paid by sales of gunpowder and sugar and dynamite and enriched uranium. The efforts of Wakelin's father had hacked down much of Bolivia's rain forest and turned it into swampy, malarial grassland for soybean profits.

Wakelin himself had done one better. He'd used currency manipulation to reap five times the amount. Several Asian countries had been plunged into multi-year depressions as a result.

That didn't bother him either.

No, he only wished that he'd chosen to come out of retirement for a better role. Playing glorified teleconference leader for a gaggle of people myopically focused on the day-to-day was tiring. It played on the nerves.

Right now, two of the Orcus members were busy arguing with each other. Metaphorically trying to show who had the larger set of male genitals. He put it out of mind for a moment.

Wakelin stood at the edge of an open green below the house. The smell of the pines at the far end tickled his nose along with a dose of brine from the ocean. He rested the butt of a shotgun that cost more than a pair of his vintage automobiles against his shoulder.

He waited.

A pair of inverted saucers meant to represent pigeons were launched in an arc from a trap downslope. He tracked them and pulled the trigger twice in quick succession. The gas-actuated semiautomatic weapon coughed more than boomed in his ear. Still, the earbud system had to electronically suppress the noise so that the teleconference wouldn't be disrupted.

That would be impolite, after all.

The pair of pulverized limestone 'birds' disintegrated on contact. He considered a moment, and then lowered his gun. With a wave, one of his long-time servants approached. Wakelin moved his hands fluidly to communicate his concerns to the man.

This ceases to amuse me, he signed. *It's not close enough to the real thing.*

The servant replied in the same style. *What are your wishes, sir?*

Wakelin considered. *I wish a changeup in targets.*

The man bowed and went to handle the request. Meanwhile, the sparring going on in Wakelin's ear sounded as if it were over now. He returned his attention to the conversation.

"That may be, but it don't amount to a hill of beans," one of the voices in Wakelin's head drawled. "I want to know how we're going to shutter up Sirenica."

"*Druz'ya moi*," said a Russian woman. "I too wish to know, Moderator."

"Everyone, I must counsel patience," Wakelin said. "Things are well in hand for now. Sirenica's run into problems that none of us have anticipated. Their work shall slow to a crawl."

"Crawling may be good," a third voice grunted. "Stopping is better."

"I must agree," said another. "I want things stopped now. We have the Tarantus brothers. I say we finally use them."

A chorus of agreement echoed in Wakelin's ear. He cursed to himself. Wakelin shook his finger as he spoke, as if he could visibly lecture the participants.

"The point of our organization is to keep our lantern covered. Some of us have been too high profile for a while now, and our existence has gotten out into the intelligence community. I brought the brothers in under protest, and only if they performed surveillance. Not to act further."

One of the conference members laughed. "That island has made you soft."

"They have a reckless streak," Wakelin insisted. "And they encourage it in their own men."

"I say we vote on it, then."

Once again, a chorus of agreement. To no one's surprise, they voted unanimously in favor of taking 'more aggressive' action with the Tarantus brothers.

Wakelin's grip tightened on his shotgun as he spoke. "Very well. I shall contact the brothers and tell them they need to move more aggressively against Sirenica. But only if it looks like the researchers there are moving ahead with their plans again."

There was some grumbling, which he ignored. His servant reappeared, this time downrange by the traps. The man waved to him, signaling *READY*.

One after another, the Orcus members bid farewell and cut

their secured connections from around the globe. Yet one client remained on the line. The man's words fairly dripped from the earbud with honeyed words.

"Shucks, I wouldn't get your suspenders in a twist over this," the man assured him. "The way I see it, with the Tarantus folks on the job, you can spend less of your brain-space thinking about all of us."

Wakelin brought his shotgun back up.

"Oh, I doubt that," he said, as the trap released a live pigeon into the air with a flutter of soft grey wings. "I can't help but think of you people all the time."

He tracked the bird's flight and pulled the trigger.

CHAPTER ELEVEN

Tyrrhenian Sea
Deepwater Cable Vessel (DCV) Acheron

The harsh sunlight of the central Mediterranean glared through the windows on the *Acheron's* enclosed bridge wing. Austen watched the pair of naval destroyers go through their perimeter patrol. They circled the converted cable laying ship like a pair of sharks.

Count Diamante and Navarro emerged from the bridge proper and came to stand next to her. Diamante swayed back and forth on the balls of his feet, like a child waiting to unwrap a birthday present. Navarro simply looked unconcerned. But Austen knew that was more often than not a cover for the way he really felt.

"*Fantastico*, is it not?" Diamante said, in bubbly tone. "These two magnificent warships are at our beck and call!"

Austen considered. "That's one way to put it. Overkill is the word that comes to my mind."

"Oh, I wish it were so! There is a race on below the waves, and some take it more seriously than others. Either to win it, or to keep others from the prize."

"The Conte has a point," Navarro put in. "Motte & Bailey keeps tabs on all the players around the globe who like to play dirty pool. Orcus is one. A big one."

"What *is* this Orcus, exactly?" Austen asked. "Which country are they based out of?"

"That's just it. As far as anyone knows, they're a consortium of companies operating across a whole bunch of countries. But their cash cows are primarily energy exports. That, and minerals critical to defense or technical manufacturing. Tungsten, platinum, chromium. That sort of thing."

"All of which can be found at undersea vent sites," Diamante said. "They surely would like to see us shut down, to protect their profit margins if nothing else!"

"Have you seen anything threatening out here yet, Conte?"

"*Che macello!* If you only knew! Sirenica's in international waters, but we've had numerous ships encroach within our safety zone."

"That doesn't sound all that bad to me," Austen frowned. "I mean, navigation mistakes do happen on the high seas."

Diamante's lips curled up in amusement. "Would those navigation mistakes extend to combat jet aircraft? Several weeks ago, our destroyers came close to shooting down a pair of Sukhoi Su-30s launched, as best as we can tell, from Tripoli. We've also had a couple of sonar contacts that looked suspiciously like attack submarines, though God knows from under what flag!"

Navarro rubbed his chin. "That's serious. Deadly serious."

"I have done the calculations in my spare time, Mister Navarro. The potential mineral wealth from the Palinuro field is worth upwards of six billion dollars. The geothermal energy could be worth three or four times that. That's why the *Repubblica Italiana* has committed two warships to me!" Diamante patted his shirt just below the neck. "It's also why I personally hold the records to all of our research."

The door to the bridge creaked open. A man with a naval officer's uniform and a nattily trimmed beard stood in the doorway. Count Diamante looked up, his face aglow with anticipation.

"Capitano Benetti," he said, "What news do you bring?"

"*Siamo pronti*," came the reply. "She is on the way."

"Excellent. Is the boat ready for us to complete the transfer?"

"*Ovviamente, Conte.*"

"Transfer?" Austen looked between the two men. "Transfer of what?"

"Your first patient, so to speak," Diamante said, with a wisp of a grin. "We are picking him up with our inflatable motorboat in a few minutes."

"Then I'd like to come along! This could be important."

Navarro opened his mouth as if to object. At the last moment, he kept his opinion to himself. He stayed at the window and watched as Diamante led Austen and a trio of crewmen down to a platform bolted to the waterline. A Zodiac-style inflatable boat with an outboard motor waited for them.

Austen boarded and found a bench-like seat. She held onto the cord grips next to her as the motor grumbled to life with a puff of gasoline fumes. That was washed away by the tang of salt spray as the boat jounced its way across the waves. Austen felt the first stirrings of seasickness. It wasn't intolerable, but she swallowed hard and tried to keep her eyes fixed to the horizon.

"We need to keep a sharp lookout," Diamante said, his voice raised to be heard over the buzz of the motor. "The coffin should come up within a twenty-meter radius of our boat."

That stopped her. "Wait, *what*? The coffin?"

"It is merely what we call them. There is no need for alarm."

A bright orange object appeared ahead of the boat with a loud *bloop!* The crewman at the tiller reduced speed and slewed the boat slightly to one side. Austen leaned out to get a better look at the item as they approached.

"Undignified, but there wasn't much in the way of choice," Diamante continued. "The 'coffins' are our *soprannome*, our nickname for Sirenica's waste containers."

"You're kidding me!" Austen said, surprised.

"They are filled with the station's garbage and human waste, for the most part. It is sent up in containers attached to inflatable bags for collection and land disposal. Much easier than pumping it back up to the surface. Or worse, releasing it raw into the undersea environment."

Two crewmen came up on either side of Austen. They extended long wooden poles with hooks at the end to bring the container up against the boat. To her surprise, the container did roughly resemble a plastic coffin in size and lozenge shape.

Austen leaned out a little further. A transparent slit about three-quarters of the way up towards the top of the container gleamed at her. She peered inside.

A pair of sightless gray eyes stared back at her.

Startled, she fell back in her seat. The crewmen and Count Diamante let out a hearty laugh at her reaction. Austen felt her cheeks redden. So did Diamante's, though his change in color came purely from merriment.

"That would be Carl Richter in there. As I said, you can consider him your first patient. Don't worry about bedside manners, Miss Austen. He is quite beyond offending now, I should think."

Suddenly, another orange coffin surfaced on the opposite side of the boat with an even louder *bloop!*

The crewmen hooked this second package and tugged it in. Diamante joined Austen this time to peer through the slit. Inside, another set of dead eyes stared out into oblivion. The Sicilian nobleman's flush vanished, along with his easy good humor.

"*Per amor del cielo!*" he whispered, and his legs wobbled as he took a seat of his own. "What the hell is going on down there?"

CHAPTER TWELVE

Austen commandeered one of the *Acheron's* refrigerated storage rooms for her makeshift morgue. At Count Diamante's direction, the crew removed the food to a different location and disinfected the room for medical use. Soon, only the ghostly smell of fresh vegetables and lemon-scented cleaner lingered in the air.

A team of sailors brought in two double-wide steel tables and locked them to skid-proof panels in the floor. While this was being done, Austen retrieved her hard-shelled luggage case and pulled out a pair of pre-packaged protective gowning sets. She threw one to Navarro.

He gave her a look. "Tell me you're not serious."

"Serious as an autopsy," she replied. "Which we may end up doing."

"Why do you need me for this?"

"Two reasons. First, I need another set of eyes looking for clues. Second, I don't have all the tools I need to fully open a body – in particular, a rib-cutter. If all I can get is a pair of kitchen shears from the mess, then I need someone with strength to cut through bone."

"Right."

Austen rummaged in her case and came up with two face shields. "Here, put this on over the face mask. If what we're dealing with is highly contagious, then it's a good insurance policy."

They completed the rest of their gowning up in silence. Relative silence, anyway. Austen shook her head and muttered under her breath a couple of times. Navarro watched her from the corner of his eye as she grasped one hand in the other to keep her fingers still. Finally, after they'd pulled on their nitrile gloves, he spoke quietly to her.

"You sure you're all right? This kind of stuff...it should be second nature to you."

She paused a moment before answering. "I've got it under control now. This whole thing rattled me a bit."

"You weren't the only one. I was watching from the bridge wing through a pair of binoculars. You should've seen Diamante's face when that second coffin bobbed to the surface."

"It's just that I wasn't expecting to arrive and perform autopsies. This is what happened in Africa, during an outbreak of Black Nile hemorrhagic fever. I showed up to help sick people and ended up dealing with dead ones. The virus had already burned through an entire field hospital, and there was nothing left to do but pick up the bloody pieces."

"Locking the stable door after the horse has bolted is never a good feeling," he agreed. "What about our friend, Edward Preble? Think we might give him a call?"

She shook her head. "I thought about it, but no. Ted's specialty is in industrial toxicology. Whatever these divers ran into down there, it wasn't man-made. I just want to get on with the examination. Don't know why Diamante hasn't sent the coffins down here yet."

"Decompression process. Normally, that takes around eight hours when you come up from Sirenica's exotic gas environment. They're performing an accelerated version of that right now, since the two men in question aren't worried about the bends."

There was a creak as the doors to the room rolled back. A seaman handed Navarro a dispatch while four others wheeled in the coffin-shaped waste containers and placed each atop a steel table. Navarro scanned the paper as the men left and slid the doors shut.

"Here's some info we were missing," Navarro said, as Austen set out her examination tools next to the closest coffin. "Yesterday, Sirenica lost contact with a three-man dive team comprised of Lead Diver Jonas Peterson, Carl Richter, and Moritz Lang. Forty minutes later, Peterson and Richter were spotted attempting to return to the station, though they were only able to make it back via an ROV-assisted rescue. Richter died shortly thereafter. Lang's body was recovered earlier today from someplace between the station and a spot marked on the map as Site 1725."

Austen pulled down her clear face shield. Navarro set the dispatch aside and followed suit.

"Lang's in this coffin," she said. "He's been out in open water, so there's going to be more organ decomposition. We've got to look at him first."

Together, they unlatched the seals on the waste container and levered it open. The tang of brine layered with the faint smell of gone-off flesh scoured itself onto Austen's nose and tongue. Navarro wrinkled his nose but didn't flinch away from either the smell or the sight of what lay within.

At first glance, it looked like Moritz Lang had tried to swim through a wood chipper.

Slashes and tears crisscrossed the man's body from head to toe. Whole sections of his dive suit lay in tatters. Austen peeled back the edge of one chunk at Lang's hip. A set of gouges in the pale pink-white flesh went as deep as the bone. She picked up one of her examination tools and probed a little further.

"If these wounds didn't kill him outright," she muttered, "then the blood loss did. He's been completely exsanguinated."

Navarro looked over her shoulder. A nub of bone gleamed from deep within the muscle. He let out a breath before voicing his thoughts.

"Odd pattern to these marks. Almost like he tangled with a propeller. Could've been a submarine accident."

Austen shook her head. "This was no sub accident!"

"What, then? It wasn't any shark. These wounds are star-shaped, like the pattern you'd make if you sliced up a pizza with a round cutter."

"Some of the wounds are star shaped, yes. Others are straightforward slashes or even puncture wounds. In fact, I'd even say–"

She paused.

Austen grabbed a scalpel from her tool set. She sliced along the deepest part of the wound, which followed the path of the largest hip adductors. Instead of healthy red muscle fiber, she found clots of blackened, dead tissue. The smell of rotting flesh grew stronger.

"That can't be normal," she said, in a voice just above a whisper.

"What is?"

"That's *necrotic* tissue. The inside of the muscle's reached an advanced stage of decomposition."

She moved on to a wound higher up on the body, under the arm. A quick slice and probe along the triceps showed the same pattern. So did two more probes in different areas of the body. Austen took samples at each point and handed them to Navarro for labeling.

She considered a moment. "What do you think this man's health was when he died?"

"You can't work as an active deep-sea diver without being in good condition," Navarro replied, after looking at Lang's pale face. "The work burns calories off you, too. I'd be surprised if he had more than ten percent body fat."

"And yet I'm seeing signs of localized, but advanced necrosis. That would indicate some underlying chronic infection. Something that a compromised immune system couldn't quite overcome."

Navarro shook his head. "He'd never be let off station, not if they have a competent dive master on board. Which I'm sure they do."

"I agree. After spending a billion dollars on setting up Sirenica, I doubt they'd skimp on personnel." Austen found a secure container for her tissue samples and swapped out her gloves. She went over to the remaining coffin, unlatched the lid, and opened it. "Let's see what secrets Carl Richter can tell us."

The gangrenous stench that rose from the opened container hit them like a tidal wave. Navarro winced and took a step back. Austen's eyes watered as she did her best to look at Carl Richter's remains.

Dark fluid pooled in the star-shaped wounds and deep slashes. Where Lang's body had been bone dry, this corpse looked as if it had been left out to decompose in a swamp. Veins of black ichor stood out against puffy white skin. An entire chunk had been bitten or torn out of the man's thigh.

"Good Lord," Navarro coughed. "This can't be normal either."

"It sure as hell isn't."

When Austen went in to use her probe, the flesh felt spongy. Again, the muscle tissue at each site showed advanced necrosis. Only here, the rot had run along the fascia of the major muscles, turning them into mushy slime.

She took her samples and mercifully closed the coffin-sized case.

"Advanced necropsy like this in two different people isn't just rare," Austen said, as she sprayed disinfectant on her soiled gloves. "It's one in a billion rare. It's a pathogen, and it likes to eat flesh."

"You mean, aside from whatever it is that cut these men into mincemeat."

"That's right. The presence of the pathogen at the site of the wounds might mean that whatever caused the wounds is the source of the pathogen. At least, we can hope that's the case."

"You *hope* that's the case?"

"If the pathogen is spread by other means – such as contact

with seawater – then anyone taking a swim is bound to come down with flesh-eating necrosis."

Navarro shuddered as he let the thought sink in. "But Lang was chopped up much worse than Richter. If you're right, why wasn't Lang in a half-dissolved state, or worse?"

"I don't know!" Austen clenched her fists and turned away to stare out one of the room's portholes. "In fact, I don't even know if my samples will show anything! It's possible that the pathogen didn't survive the accelerated decompression. Or the transition from an exotic gas to a normal atmosphere. This bug's one of the worst things I've seen, and I don't have enough information to even take an educated guess about it!"

"Okay, then I'm afraid I'm the slow learner today. What do you think we need to do next?"

"I need to look at something more than corpses, Nick. I need to look at an in-progress infection."

"The only person that fits the bill right now is the third member of that ill-fated dive team. Jonas Peterson. And you know what that means."

She nodded. When she finally turned to face him, her eyes were hard as flint.

"Yes. We're going to have to go down to Sirenica. *Now.*"

CHAPTER THIRTEEN

With a *whoosh* of compressed air, the doors to the *Acheron's* sub platform admitted Austen and Navarro. A series of elevated walkways made up of metal grating led down to a cavernous room buzzing with activity. Austen placed her hands on the railing, leaning out to look at the sights below.

The space at the very bottom of the *Acheron* centered around four large rectangles that had been cut out of the hull. Seawater sloshed about inside each rectangle, though a knee-high lip prevented the ship's floor from being soaked. The bright blue of the water cast bands of turquoise that snaked their way across the ceiling.

Two spaces were empty. The remaining pair each held a bright yellow minisub that rocked ever so slightly with the motion of the seawater. Between that tiny movement and the high stacks of storage crates in the background, the submarines looked like children's toys bobbing in a bathtub.

Diamante stood next to one of the pools. He held a clipboard as he shouted orders to a crane operator. The operator nodded and began lowering a shrink-wrapped bundle of crates into the rear compartment of the nearest sub. The Sicilian nobleman spotted Austen and Navarro and waved for them to come join him.

As the two made their way down the steps, the illusion that the vessels looked like toys vanished. Up close, each was an elongated comma of heavy steel roughly the size of a large delivery van. The smooth hulls were punctuated by enclosed xenon lamps and razor-sharp propellers mounted in four rotatable housings.

Foot-thick hemispheres of clear acrylic made up the subs' front ends. Each was held fast to the hull with bolts as thick as Navarro's wrist. Sled like runners hung below, holding tools and a pair of spidery grasping arms.

A smaller acrylic dome formed a separate viewing bubble at the top of each sub. Austen noticed that just below the dome on the sub next to Diamante, someone had affixed a tiny Italian tricolor. Underneath that, painted in bold black lettering, was the name *DEV-2 MCCARTNEY.*

"Ah, now you see why I was so happy to hear that you wanted to set off immediately," Diamante enthused. "These submarines are designed to hold a maximum of three people, and yet Sirenica needs supplies sent down. So, I must make a sacrifice and make a supply run myself."

"You don't sound too disappointed," Navarro observed.

"In truth, they don't let me drive nearly enough!" Diamante handed his clipboard over to Austen. "Your *capitana* shall be here shortly. In the meantime, this is the list of the science staff aboard Sirenica. It would be worth your while to study it."

"And what will you be doing in the meantime?" Austen asked.

"As you Americans might say, I am 'on the clock'." He stepped on a sensor plate next to the pool's lip. A ramp extended from the floor up to the entrance hatch atop the submarine. "*Addio per ora!* I shall see you next aboard Sirenica proper!"

Diamante clambered aboard and shut the hatch behind him with a *clank.* A few moments later, his face appeared behind the windshield-like dome of tempered acrylic at the front of the sub. Lights surrounding the pool flashed red as the ramp withdrew. A spray of seafoam bubbled up from below as the submarine sank out of sight.

"You have to admit," Navarro said, "the Conte has a way with his entrances and exits."

"I'm more interested in the information he left us." Austen held up the clipboard so they could both read it. The listings were short and to the point.

Sirenica Science Staff, Rotation Q3-2 - Q3-3

Dr. Miguel Gimenez - Field Geologist
Dr. Iona Lici–Petroleum Geologist / DMT
Dr. Alexandra Kirov - Marine Biologist
Dr. Neely Madrigal - Volcanologist

Austen pursed her lips. "Look at the designation next to Lici's name. Any idea what a 'DMT' is?"

"That's a Diver Medical Technician. Someone who can do basic to intermediate first aid. Suturing, setting fractures, giving anesthetics·or antivenins."

"Let's be generous and say that a DMT's in line with an Emergency Medical Technician. I doubt they would be doing exploratory surgery or bacterial cultures."

Navarro nodded. "Safe bet. If they had an epidemiologist down there, they wouldn't have contacted Joe Widerman."

"And don't forget, 'they' didn't contact him. That was done by Alexandra Kirov, and even she had to pass on a warning in code."

"The question remains: Why?"

She shrugged. "You read people better than me, Nick. Do you sense anything unusual about our new best friend, Count Diamante?"

"He's not telling us everything. But in a way, he's just a kid playing with new toys. And if he had something to hide, why not keep us off Sirenica entirely?"

The soft sound of approaching steps stopped Austen from replying.

A woman wearing a curve-hugging blue jumpsuit walked

out onto the main floor. She wore her hair in a series of cornrow braids that linked up into a bun at the nape of the neck. Her dusky complexion lit up with a flashbulb-bright smile as she joined them.

"Good afternoon! I'm Neely Madrigal, or just 'Madrigal' to my passengers," she said. Her voice had a light, musical accent. "And it does seem that you two are my fares for the day."

"That we are," Austen said, as she extended a hand. "I'm Leigh Austen, and this is my assistant, Nicholas Navarro."

Madrigal shook the proffered hand, though she eyed Navarro suspiciously before taking his.

"Goodness! You look like a Bad John. Do you bite?"

"Only when provoked," Navarro replied. "The expression you just used…sounds like something you'd hear on Trinidad."

Madrigal let out a laugh. "Hole in one, I'm a Trini. How did you know?"

"I've done some work out that way, up north to the Virgin Islands. You pick up an ear for the lingo."

"You'll hear it from my husband too, then. Doctor Gimenez, he's from the next island up in Saint Croix. Good man, but can't make a macaroni pie worth a damn." She nodded towards the remaining submarine. "Let's go, my chariot's waiting for us."

"So you handle subs too," Austen marveled, as they walked over to the vessel. "The few volcanologists I've met barely know how to drive a car. They prefer to hike in on foot."

"Everyone on Sirenica has to be a jack-at-all," Madrigal found the sensor plate in the floor and stamped on it. The ramp extended up to the open hatch. "Mister Bad John, bring up the rear, if you would. I'd feel better with an extra-strong pair of hands dogging the hatch behind us."

Austen clambered aboard in Madrigal's wake after a quick glance at the sub's name. Inside, it was more cramped than she'd expected. She slid into the passenger-side seat at the front of the vessel.

The seat felt like it had been swapped out of a family station wagon, complete with springs that squeaked as she shifted her weight. But the view through the half-sphere acrylic windshield in front took her breath away. It was like sitting right next to a floor-to-ceiling aquarium window.

Madrigal took the driver's side seat and began powering up the sub's various systems. A *clank* came from behind them, followed by yet more squeaks as Navarro closed the upper hatch. Joining them, he took the remaining seat behind the two women.

"Belt yourselves in," Madrigal ordered, and her two passengers followed her lead as she buckled up. "Thank you much. Please keep your arms and legs inside the vehicle for the remainder of the ride."

Austen looked around as the hum of motors joined the *psssht* of venting air. Red light glowed through the main window as the entry ramp retracted. The water at the edges churned to foam as the propellers started to spin.

"I have to ask," Austen finally said. "I noticed that the name of this vessel is the *DEV-1 Lennon*."

"That it is. 'DEV' stands for Deepwater Exploration Vehicle."

"Since this is the *Lennon*, and the other sub was the *McCartney*, then I'm guessing that you have four subs in total. And that whoever named them is a big Beatles fan."

"You nailed it. As for naming them after the Beatles, that was my doing." Madrigal's lips curled up into a grin. "After all, we may not all live on them, but they're definitely yellow submarines."

Austen and Navarro's groans were blotted out by the gurgling rush of water as they sank below the surface.

The red of the surface lights faded to the greens and blues of open water. Austen watched through the top bubble dome as the oblong shape of the *Acheron's* hull shrank in the distance. A school of sardines swam by, glittering silver against the teal-colored backdrop until they too vanished overhead.

Green-blue faded away to pure blue, then to ever-darker shades. Rays of sunlight became muted. Then they too began to fade away in turn.

Austen heard a teeth-rattling *pop* followed by the moan of tortured steel. Goose bumps ran up and down her arms and legs. To her annoyance, both Navarro and Madrigal looked completely unconcerned as the pressure built on the vessel's metal sides.

"How often does a sub like this fail?" Austen ventured. "I mean, how often do they just…implode?"

"Oh, not often," Madrigal reassured her. "Usually only once."

Austen stayed quiet after that. Madrigal hummed quietly to herself for a few more minutes, gently nudging the control stick from time to time. Suddenly, the sub jerked forward, as if kicked in the rear by a giant, unseen force. The sensation of forward speed picked up.

Madrigal nodded her approval. "There you are. We just entered the prevailing thermohaline current. That's a kind of river in the ocean that separates two different temperatures and salinities. It gives us a bit of a free ride as we descend through it."

A chill crept into the air inside the submarine. At first, it was refreshing after the dry heat at the surface. Then after another couple of minutes, it began to get uncomfortable. Austen rubbed her hands to distract herself as well as to keep warm.

"You weren't kidding about the temperature change," Navarro remarked. "That's what, a forty degree drop?"

"Roughly. The water's about forty-five degrees down by the habitat."

"Sounds awfully cold to dive in," Austen said.

"Oh, it's quite comfortable. The dive teams use special suits that circulate warm water in tubes next to the skin."

That's nice, Austen thought wryly. *At least Richter and Lang were able to die without freezing to death.*

Navarro let out a low whistle as Sirenica finally came into view.

The quadruple-tiered structure sat on a steeply sloped section of seafloor. The clean lines of Diamante's model had been blurred by the growth of seaweed along the sides, but a panoply of lights from inside made the place look heavenly compared to the surrounding depths.

Madrigal maneuvered the *Lennon* around Sirenica's perimeter. They passed a mound of piled cases, also fringed with seaweed, before lining up with an open moon pool. A few more touches of the control stick, combined with bursts of the propeller, and they were in position under the habitat.

The sub rose slowly. As they broke the surface, the water around them cascaded down the sides of the window, but didn't break into foam. The pressure one hundred meters below was just too high to allow that.

Lights shone in, revealing a much smaller space than above on the *Acheron*. A dull *thud* and a higher-pitched *clank* came from the entry hatch above and behind them.

"Airlock passage." Madrigal explained, as she unsnapped her seat belts. "We still need to adjust our bodies to handle the pressure and exotic gas atmosphere down here."

She made her way past Navarro and waited until she heard a two-tone chime. A quick twist of the hatch, and it opened to reveal a set of rungs leading to a chamber above the submarine.

"You'll see," Madrigal said cheerily. "Sirenica's just like home. That is, so long as you grew up in a fallout shelter. Come on, let's get pressurized so that you can press the flesh with everyone down here."

Austen suppressed a shudder as she joined Madrigal to climb up and out of the submarine.

Michael Angel

CHAPTER FOURTEEN

Sirenica Research Station
Depth: 100 Meters

Austen adjusted her robin's egg blue jumpsuit before returning to her seat inside Sirenica's Pressure Equalization Chamber. The cramped cube of space looked like the waiting room at a down-and-out dentist's office. Only the hiss of gas vents, a stack of dog-eared paperbacks, and a poster of a dangling kitten advising them to *Hang in there!* broke up the monotony.

During the hour-long wait, Madrigal had scrounged up a pair of jumpsuits for the two newcomers to wear. Navarro shifted his shoulders as he got used to the form-fitting clothing. The light shade of blue looked faintly ridiculous on him, but he didn't complain.

At least the uniforms provided proper insulation. Sirenica's exotic gas environment wicked away significantly more body heat than a normal atmosphere. It also pitched everyone's voice a full octave higher. When she spoke, Austen felt like she'd regressed to being twelve years old again.

"Don't let it bother you," Madrigal advised her, in her own

higher-pitched voice. "Give it a couple minutes, and you won't notice it – or the smell of the station – ever again."

Austen blinked. "The smell of the station?"

A two-toned chime echoed in the bare little room.

"You'll see what I mean," Madrigal said, as she undid a pressure latch and opened the exit door.

Sure enough, a mixture of scents hit Austen as she stepped out onto the station proper. The air had a strange heaviness to it. Her first breath took her back to just before high school swim class. The sting of chlorine, followed by the earthier smell of sweaty clothes. And underneath it all, a vague hint of rust and mildew.

"Not what I'd have expected," Navarro remarked. "At least not on a billion-dollar aquanaut facility."

That got a shrug from Madrigal. "It's a regular jumble, is all. High moisture means a constant struggle to keep things disinfected or free from rust. Hold up one sec."

She opened a door on the opposite side of hallway. The tang of brine mixed with motor oil wafted up to them as they looked back down to the moon pool room. A man with a tangled mass of curly black hair looked up from where he was working on a half-disassembled minisub labeled *DEV-3 HARRISON*.

"Hey, spouse-man!" Madrigal called. "I've got visitors."

"Give them a cookie and some milk, then!" came the faint reply. "Can't you see I'm busy, woman?"

"No can do. Got to take 'em to the boss. You better be there too." She closed the door, cutting off his string of protests. "That's my *bazodee*, my husband. In the meantime, you'd best follow me. Conte Diamante said he wanted me to bring you to Topside as soon as we pressured up."

Madrigal led the way. The silver-gray hallway curved slightly to the right, punctuated only by the occasional side door or corridor-constricting pressure hatch. Each hatch they stepped through reinforced Austen's impression that they were on a structure built to contain hull failures.

That didn't make her feel any better, so she asked about

something else.

"By the way, what's Topside?"

"It's what we call the open meeting area on A-Deck. It's also the dining area, so hopefully someone left the kettle on."

"What do you eat down here, anyway?" Navarro asked. "I'd think that the exotic gas environment would make cooking with an open flame explosively difficult."

"We use an induction cooker for some things. Re-heating with a microwave for most." Madrigal answered, as she brought them up a steep stairway to the next level up. Their feet made a noisy patter on the stainless steel grates. "The Conte does his best, but don't expect too much. Everything ends up steamrolled by the pressure here."

"You're serious, aren't you?"

She let out a laugh. "Hope you like flatbread pizza. The pressure down here squeezes gas bubbles out of carbonated drinks and collapses the open spaces in bread or Swiss cheese. Sasha Kirov figured out a way to make a meringue once, but that's about it."

"Speaking of Kirov," Austen said, as they went up another flight of stairs, "Will she be there in Topside?"

"When the Conte calls an all-hands meeting, she's usually there. Maybe. Lately, she hasn't poked her head out of that lab of hers." Madrigal made a circling motion next to her ear with an index finger. "If you ask me, I think she's gone a little cray-cray."

"What about the patient in sickbay? Is Doctor Lici still treating him?"

"I think you'd best ask the Conte about that. And speak of the devil, I think I hear him in mid-fulmination."

Sure enough, Diamante's voice echoed down the curved passageway. Austen thought she heard a woman's voice reply. But what struck her first as they left the hall were the sights above, as well as the curious glances thrown her way by the assembled onlookers.

Topside was about the same size as the moon pool room, but with one big difference. The domed ceiling was made up of a huge hemisphere of transparent acrylic. While they were too far down to make out the surface, the view straight up was a deep vault of midnight blue, pierced by the occasional stray sunbeam.

Austen had to tear her eyes away from the hypnotic sight. She focused instead on the people who stood or sat among the clusters of unopened boxes and modular steel-framed furniture. A small-framed woman with chestnut colored bangs sat closest to the door. Her fingers twitched spasmodically as she acknowledged the newcomers with a bob of her head.

Next to her, a group of four men huddled together around a table. They had wiry bodies, heads shaved to near-baldness, and hard-bitten expressions. They reminded her of the dead Moritz Lang.

But the woman in spirited discussion with the Count was the one who commanded attention.

She had short white-blonde hair that clung to her scalp as if she wore a skullcap. While she wore the same light blue jumpsuit as everyone else, the effect it had on her figure was markedly different. With Neely Madrigal, the material emphasized her curves. On this woman, the jumpsuit outlined hard planes of raw muscle.

Her face was pretty, with prominent cheekbones and eyes the color of cut emeralds. The set of her jaw hinted at a bulldog stubbornness. And those hard eyes flashed at Diamante's next words.

"*Questo è sufficiente!*" the Count thundered, as he jabbed a finger at her. "That is quite enough! You are my Station Chief, it is your job to know everything!"

Finally, the woman answered in a voice that had a handful of grit thrown in.

"As you wish, Conte."

Diamante glowered at her a moment longer. Then, he turned to where Austen and Navarro had joined them. His anger fell away, to be replaced by the same smiling showman they'd seen since arriving in Sicily.

"Ah, it looks like our guests have arrived! At long last,

welcome to Sirenica." The man's face showed a flicker of his remaining anger as his eyes roamed across the room. "At least, I hoped to make it a full welcome. We are missing a couple of people."

"Hold on, I'm here," came a man's voice. Austen stepped aside as Madrigal's husband came up behind them to stand next to his wife. "Sorry, I was trying to rouse Sasha. She said she'd be along…well, eventually. And Lici's still in sickbay along with Peterson."

"*Che cariño*," the Count grumbled. "Everyone, this is Doctor Leigh Austen and her assistant Nicholas Navarro. They'll be helping us overcome our latest obstacle to success."

Austen nodded at the acknowledgement. Navarro followed suit. Diamante went on to perform the rest of the introductions.

"I believe that you've already met Doctor Gimenez and his wife, Doctor Madrigal," the Conte said, as he gestured grandly to each person. The shorter woman with the bangs straightened up when it came to her turn. "This is Reece Jordan, our Dive Monitor and main ROV operator. The four gentlemen sitting next to her are our remaining divers – *signores* Kurtzmann, Wolfe, Ersler, and Ossberg."

The men didn't do so much as nod. They ignored Austen and looked to Navarro like a quartet of convicts sizing up a newcomer across the prison yard. Diamante then indicated the blonde woman next to him with a theatrical flourish.

"And the expert I have chosen to run this installation is the incomparable Dylan Sawyer. She's run security and operations for all sorts of expeditions, from Greenland to–"

"They're already aware," Sawyer said, before nodding towards Navarro. "Or at least, *he* is. How's it hanging these days, Nick?"

"As always, Sawyer," Navarro said. "Low and a bit to the left."

Austen looked between the two. "You know each other?"

Sawyer raised one blonde eyebrow.

"You could say that. We were seeing each other for more

than a year." She paused for a moment as the room went silent. "What, didn't he ever mention that to you?"

"It never came up," Navarro said tightly.

"Hm." Sawyer's lips curled up in a mirthless smile. "Now that *is* interesting, isn't it?"

CHAPTER FIFTEEN

Count Diamante cleared his throat to break the increasingly awkward silence.

"Well, that is convenient. Since we all know each other, or have been *introdotto*, then I shall allow everyone to return to their tasks."

The group broke up, with multiple conversations echoing off the domed ceiling. Gimenez and Madrigal embraced and then left the room. The four divers moved off as a group, one letting out a crude laugh as he did so. Reece Jordan went over to Diamante and handed him a sheaf of documents.

"Conte," Austen called, "I'd really like to visit the sickbay ASAP. It's why I came down here, after all."

"You have free run of the station," Diamante replied. "I only need find you a guide."

Sawyer stepped forward. "I'll take her there."

Austen only hesitated for a second. "That would be fine."

Navarro turned to her. "Want me to come along? If you need someone who can cut through a rib cage with kitchen shears…"

"Thanks, but I think I've got this."

"Okay. I'll see what other information I can dig up. I want

to talk to their Dive Monitor, for starters."

Sawyer walked over to them. Her eyes flicked back and forth between Austen and Navarro. "Am I interrupting anything? I thought you want to get to the sickbay as soon as possible."

"Of course." Austen gestured towards the exit. "Lead the way."

Austen did her best to keep a regular schedule of jogs around Old Dominion Lake next to her house. Yet although Sawyer was an inch or two shorter, Austen found herself having to lengthen her stride and quicken her pace to keep up with the blonde woman.

"It sounded like Diamante wasn't happy with something," Austen ventured, as they continued along one of Sirenica's curved hallways.

A roll of those sea-green eyes. "The Conte rarely is. His bluff good cheer is reserved for those who don't work for him. He was annoyed that he hadn't heard about the second body we sent up. Not much we could do about that. The communications system between here and the surface is dodgy as hell."

"Who retrieved the second diver?"

"I did. We have a minisub more-or-less permanently housed at Base Camp, down at three hundred meters. I took it out and performed a search pattern until I found Moritz Lang. Or what was left of him."

"I'm surprised you were the one driving the sub."

Again with the eyebrow raise. Sawyer's voice took on a curt edge.

"Oh? Why?"

Austen felt dull heat creep into her cheeks. She sensed that she'd just stepped on someone's toes and backed off in a hurry.

"I mean...I thought Madrigal was the sub driver down here, that's all."

"Ah. Well, you're way off on that." Sawyer nodded towards a set of stairs. The two women's steps echoed off the walls as they descended. "Several of us can do it in a pinch. These aren't complicated vessels. I run the station, handle security, communications, one of the mess shifts, and I still found time to train up on the minisubs. Down here, you have to wear a lot of hats. Luckily, I like hats."

Austen nodded at that. They continued down a second flight of stairs in silence for a couple seconds. This time, Sawyer was the one who spoke first.

"I'm surprised."

"About what?"

Sawyer gave Austen a sidelong look. "You don't seem to be Nick's type."

The flush doubled in intensity. Austen blurted out the first thing that came to her mind.

"I never said I was his type. What about you?"

The woman's lips twitched at that. "I'm my own type."

Sawyer stopped at the next door, helpfully labeled *SICKBAY*. She rapped her knuckles on the door with a tinny clank. A dim reply came from within, so she pushed her way on through.

Austen's first impression was that the sickbay looked like a miniaturized field hospital. All-too familiar odors greeted her. Antiseptics, rubbing alcohol, and an off-putting sweet smell she thought of as the scent of sickness.

Shelving crammed with medical supplies blocked part of her view. From what she could see, a tall, gaunt man covered in bandages lay on a nearby bed. His eyes were closed, and a breathing mask covered his nose and mouth.

"Well, here we are," Sawyer gestured towards the shelves. "See anything you can use?"

"Gowning equipment," Austen said immediately, as she went to grab a face mask and a package of scrubs. "This place doesn't have nearly enough barriers in place. Who's running this place? Where's Doctor Lici?"

A faint voice answered. "That would be me. I'm over here."

Austen shouldered her way past Sawyer and moved around the shelving. Lici reclined on a second bed, one that had been hastily set up and bolted to the wall. She was an olive-skinned woman with cropped dark hair. Her face looked flushed and feverish.

Like everyone on the station, she wore a light blue jumpsuit. But the outfit's left arm had been cut away to leave the skin exposed. Austen heard Sawyer's intake of breath.

A horrid black streak ran up Lici's arm. At first glance, it resembled a stain of India ink that someone had injected into the woman's veins. Austen snapped on the face mask and a pair of nitrile gloves before coming any closer.

"Good Lord," Sawyer whispered, as she looked into Lici's fever-bright eyes. "This is...you weren't like this earlier today."

"No," Lici agreed. "It progressed faster than I thought it would. I passed out on the bed a little while ago. Only came to when you knocked."

Austen gingerly turned over the diseased arm. Close up, she made out a trio of abscesses. One at the elbow, one at the wrist, and one at the ball of the index finger. Red and yellow fluid mixed with grains of black, like coffee grounds, oozed from all three points.

"Looks bad," Lici observed, in a detached voice. "Nothing hurts, though. Don't know if that's a good sign. I heard they were sending someone out to look at it. Leigh Austen, right?"

"That's right," Austen agreed. "Doctor Lici, this is very serious. Your life, and your patient's life is in serious jeopardy."

A dazed nod. "Do what you have to. I can't assist you anymore. I'm sorry."

"Just relax for right now." Austen turned back to Sawyer. "How soon can you get these two to the surface?"

Sawyer pursed her lips for a moment. "The two minisubs need a few hours to recharge their batteries. By then, it'll be nightfall. The Conte doesn't like performing descents or ascents in the dark."

"We may not have a choice. This bug moves fast."

"Wait, I've got a better idea." The Station Chief snapped her fingers. "I'll run down to the moon pool room, get Gimenez to swap out the battery on the *Harrison*. That sub's still half-disassembled, it won't be going anywhere. It'll take maybe an hour to perform."

"Good," Austen said, as she stepped away from Lici's bed. "As soon as you do that, I'll need you back here."

"Me? What for?"

"I'll need your help to do a complete exam on these patients. So we'll know what we're dealing with before the sub's ready. I'm sure as hell not sending an underwater plague to the surface if I can help it."

Sawyer stared at her for a moment. The woman's take-charge, confident demeanor faltered for a second.

"But...I don't know anything about how to do a medical exam!"

"It'll be fine," Austen reassured her, with a wry grin. "Just pretend that we're out together, trying on hats."

Michael Angel

CHAPTER SIXTEEN

Navarro straightened out his jumpsuit once Austen and Sawyer exited Topside. He went over to the side table where Reece Jordan and Count Diamante went through a sheaf of documents with the help of a brightly lit recessed lamp. The dim light that filtered through Topside's acrylic dome just wasn't enough for easy reading.

"Excuse me, Conte," Navarro said. "I was wondering if I could speak to the Dive Monitor when you're done."

Diamante's face brightened. "Mister Navarro, I welcome any excuse to get away from the dullness of daily paperwork. Whatever you wish, you merely need to ask it of my people."

"Uh, right. Well, that's actually what I want to get into. The dull paperwork."

"You are one for punishment, aren't you? What is it you wish to see?"

"Sirenica's security schedule. I'm not talking about the destroyers you have circling above. I mean whatever you have snooping around down here."

"For that, I give you Miss Reece Giordania." Diamante brought his hands together and then gestured as if to pass a plate over to the younger woman. "*So tu volessi.*"

Her cheeks colored a bit. "I, ah, just go by 'Jordan'. It's easier if I show you the rotation plans in my latest update."

"Does it cover the period when your dive team ran into trouble at that Subsite Field?"

"It does." Jordan brushed a couple strands of her chestnut bangs out of the way as she flipped through the printouts. "Sirenica has a system of passive sonar sensors on our perimeter. They relay data to the ships above as well as to us. It's pretty low-resolution. Not much use in spotting objects less than three or four meters in size."

"I wouldn't be so dismissive," Diamante huffed. "The navy assured me that this would be perfect at picking up the approach of hostile submarines."

"Surely it is, Conte," Navarro said politely. "However, it's less than perfect at picking up the approach of human divers."

"That's why it wasn't of any use when Peterson and his men went missing," Jordan agreed. "The other form of detection we use is our squad of remote-intelligence ROVs."

Navarro nodded. "Underwater versions of aerial drones. Only yours can manipulate or retrieve objects. Of course, they have to stay leashed on cables, right?"

"Actually, ROV tech is advancing right along with the drones," Jordan corrected him. She found the sheets she needed and slid them across the table into Navarro's hands. "We have up to four regular ROVs and two extended-range ROVs doing patrols. Those are the schedules programmed into both types of drones from last week, going through the end of the month."

"Interesting." The paper was ever-so-slightly damp, as everything seemed to be in the habitat. But at least they didn't smear as he ran a finger over them. "What happens when the drones spot something out of the ordinary?"

"They send out an alert. Then they use what we call an 'intelligent orbit' program. When an ROV spies anything moving that's over a meter long, it will automatically go into orbit at a safe distance until we identify it."

"It's surprisingly effective," Diamante added. "Nothing but

false alarms so far, of course. But we did discover three new species of deep-water shark unknown to science."

"That's all well and good, but..." Navarro rubbed his chin in thought for a moment. "There's *accuracy*, and then there's *coverage*."

"What do you mean?"

Navarro tapped a finger on the schedule page. His brows rose as he came to a conclusion, then looked over to the other two people at the table.

"Do either of you have a pen?"

Diamante chuckled as if the request were something faintly ridiculous. Jordan pulled one from her pocket and handed it over. Navarro took another sheet of the printout, flipped it over, and began sectioning it into a grid marked by ROV number and hours of the day.

"You have each ROV on a rotation that's off-set by a couple hours from the next," he murmured. "But you've got to pull them offline every sixteen to eighteen hours."

"Yes. They run low on battery power, and need recharging. The run time depends on the depth and total distance travelled."

"That's what I thought." Navarro finishing sectioning off his makeshift schedule grid and circled blank three columns. "The schedules create a gap in your ROV coverage. Every ten days, you're blind for almost ninety minutes. As it happens, the last time this happened was yesterday morning."

Diamante sat back, aghast. "*Porca miseria!* Mister Navarro, I must know: How did you spot this so quickly? You are no lab assistant, or I'm *Giuseppe Maria Garibaldi!*"

"With all due respect, Conte, I never said I was a 'lab' assistant."

"No, you did not. That was my mistake, indeed. Given that my Station Chief knew you, likely in the Biblical sense, I can only assume that you worked in private security with her."

"I work in private security," Navarro acknowledged. "And yes, I did work alongside Sawyer. I'm with Mott & Bailey. She worked for a competing firm."

"That might explain the sparks that flew from her eyes when she saw you, then. I know of your firm. I might have hired them, had the *Marina Militare* not been offered to me. So what interest does Niles Bailey have in my undersea operation?"

"None that I know of, Conte."

"*Sei fuori!*" Diamante scoffed. "I find that hard to believe, that a veteran military contractor like you just happened to show up on my station by chance!"

"I was hired by Leigh Austen. That's all."

"Well, now that you are here, you can help Miss Austen by helping *me*." Diamante looked to one side as one of the doors to Topside opened to admit a man so wide across the shoulders that he had to turn to fit comfortably through the gap. "Ah, there's our Dive Master. Do join us, Otto! I have some hard questions for you!"

The man, who wore a blue jacket that tented over his large frame, lumbered over to the table. Like the other divers, he seemed to size up Navarro less as a newcomer and more of a newly arrived threat. A face seared into a permanent scowl glowered beneath the shaved dome of a head.

"*Was ist das*, Conte?" he asked bluntly.

"Mister Navarro," Diamante said, "This is Otto Hanick. He's the resident Dive Master."

Navarro nodded. Hanick didn't return it. Like a muscular plank of wood, the man just stood by impassively until the Count spoke up again.

"Otto, we're discussing the circumstances around the loss of the dive team. Did you have anyone else on perimeter looking for them when we lost contact?"

"*Nein.* All off mapping other sectors. By the time they were called back, Petersen and Richter returned."

"That's only sort of true," Jordan pointed out. "One of the ROVs managed to catch sight of them. I took manual control to do an ROV-assisted rescue. Otherwise, they'd never have made it that far."

"That might be true. Or not. All three were good divers.

Very good."

Diamante scowled. He banged a fist on the table. The sound rippled off the dome and rattled the steel cabinets.

"Those facts are irrelevant! We were blind when we needed to see. We couldn't save them when they ran into trouble. Our visitor, Mister Navarro, is from the security firm of Motte & Bailey. He spotted a gap in the ROV schedule – a gap which both my Dive Monitor and my Dive Master *failed to spot or plan for!*"

Hanick just glowered at no one in particular. Jordan looked down at her lap. Navarro noticed that she ran a finger back and forth across her lips before speaking.

"We were only following the schedule given to us, Conte."

"I'm sure this can be easily fixed," Navarro added, before Diamante could go on. "No schedule can be perfect. Something unexpected must've happened. Hanick wouldn't send an inexperienced diver out there."

"There aren't any inexperienced divers on the team," the nobleman insisted angrily. "They're all Germans or Danes, handpicked by Mister Hanick for cold-water operations. Extra-special ones, at that!"

"Conte–"

Diamante pushed back from the table and stood. He wiped the sudden sheen of perspiration from his forehead.

"No, Mister Navarro, I've heard enough for now. The final authority for approving this *idiozia* of a schedule is Dylan Sawyer. I'm going to my quarters to have a bit of *vino*. Then, if I manage not to vomit, I'll ask her how she could screw up this badly!"

With that, the Count stalked off, disappearing through the exit. Hanick gave Navarro a last sour look before turning to stomp out through the opposite door. Jordan remained where she was, looking downcast. She rubbed her lips once more.

Navarro debated whether to say anything for a few seconds. Finally, he made up his mind.

"For me, it was Jimmy Beam," he said. "I used to call a rough time a 'three shots of Jimmy-B' kind of day."

Jordan glanced at him, startled. "How'd you know?"

"My father," Navarro sighed. "He didn't stay sober much. When he was trying to hang onto the wagon by his nails, he'd get sullen. And he'd rub his finger across his lips, like he was trying to get 'em wet."

Jordan swallowed, hard. "Jack Daniels was the one that got me. Still tries to, when things get stressful."

"Well, don't stress out any more than you have to. I won't say anything to the Conte."

The young woman let out a bitter laugh. "When it comes to Diamante, that's the *last* thing I have to worry about."

"Tough one to work for?"

"You have no idea. Sawyer's tough too, but she seems to know what she's doing. At least I thought so. Something must've caused her to slip up and leave that gap in coverage. The divers…they just had the bad luck to run into a situation at the wrong time."

"Maybe." Navarro leaned forward so that he could speak more quietly. "But you know what I'd like to ask?"

She shook her head.

"Jordan, what kind of situation do *you* think the dive team found themselves in?"

CHAPTER SEVENTEEN

Dylan Sawyer finally managed to pull the nitrile glove over her hand with a rubbery *snap*.

"That would've been easier," Austen remarked, "if you'd powdered your hands like I recommended."

"Fine, whatever. What do you want me to do?"

Austen pulled up her mask and led the way over to Jonas Peterson. Once again, she noted that the small room's equipment was better suited for quick treatment of trauma, not extended rest and examination. The lead diver lay limp and unconscious, his heels extending an inch or two beyond the foot of the bed.

"Grab the pen flashlight from the side counter," Austen instructed, as she moved around the bed. Her gloved fingers gently pulled back the eyelids. "Shine it in here."

Sawyer did as she asked for one eye, then the other. Peterson's pupils were widely dilated. The intense LED beam from the flashlight did nothing to shrink them.

Not a good sign, Austen thought, and Sawyer echoed that in her words.

"I've seen that before. That can't be good."

"The dilation might be from the drugs used to put him into

a medically induced coma," Austen observed. Without looking over her shoulder, she threw out a question. "Doctor Lici, are you still with us? What medication did you use on Mister Peterson here?"

"I'm here," Lici called over from her bed. The slurring of her voice was more pronounced that before. "Pentobarbital is all we had. Had to stop the swelling of the...of the head trauma."

"I see why you used that."

Austen grimaced as the light played over a deep slash that ran across the top of the man's head. The skull would've been visible had it not been for the mass of tarry black clots that filled the wound site.

"Would that drug also be why the pupils aren't contracting?" Sawyer asked.

"There's a lot of reasons," Austen hedged. "I'm sorry, but none of them are good. Here, hand me the light and put both of your hands under the back of his neck. Lift just a little."

Peterson's mouth fell open easily. Austen shone the light to check the back of the throat. She next checked the nose and ears. Except for one ear canal that had been filled with dried blood from the head wound, everything looked clear. A quick check of the lungs and heart revealed nothing out of the ordinary, save for the extremely low and weak respiration cycle.

"All right, I need to check the lymph nodes next."

"I think there's something going on there," Sawyer said, as she moved her hands around from where she'd held up Peterson's neck. "I felt a lump on the side."

"You got that right," Austen agreed, as she felt one lump, then a matching one on the other side of the neck. She pulled back the bed's blanket and found a similar condition on the man's inner thighs. "No doubt about it, he's dealing with a raging infection."

"Same as Dr. Lici, looks like."

Austen touched several spots on the man's abdomen. The upper left section was warm to the touch. What's more, it was firm as a bag stuffed with some unknown noxious substance.

Steeling herself, she examined a couple of the man's worst wounds, the slash across the skull and the heavily bandaged left calf. She set her jaw as she examined and took samples from each area. Sawyer's eyes watered and her hands shook. But she helped Austen turn the man's body and handed over tools and plastic bags whenever asked.

The faint smell of putrescent flesh grew as they worked. Dark granules mixed with strangely sticky masses of half-coagulated blood. Worst of all was the broad band of black that ran up Peterson's leg like the smoke marks from a long-dead fire.

Sawyer breathed a sigh of relief as they changed out gloves and moved to repeat the examination on Iona Lici. Save for the obvious state of her arm, the only thing the doctor had in common with the diver were badly swollen lymph nodes.

"Interesting," Austen observed. "The abscesses at the elbow and wrist are slit-shaped."

"Scalpel mark," Lici gritted. "Had to…relieve the swelling."

"Anything else? Medications, other surgical self-help?"

A hard swallow. "Ciprofloxacin. Local shot of anesthetic to the wrist. All I had around."

"This stuff just blew right through the Cipro," Sawyer murmured. "Like it was tissue paper."

"The mark on your finger," Austen looked Lici in the eye. "That's not a slit mark. It's a round puncture wound. Where did you get it?"

"Moon pool room. Pricked myself as I turned Richter over to check a wound. Didn't think much of it at the time."

"What did you prick yourself on?"

"Not sure. Found it later. When probing Richter's body." Lici moved her good arm weakly to one side, trying to uncurl her fingers as she did so.

A rap came from the open door.

"Okay, battery's been swapped," Madrigal announced. Her eyes went wide as she saw the condition of the two patients. "*Oui, Pappa!* What has happened here?"

"We're about ready to get these patients on your sub,"

Austen said. "But not without taking some precautions."

"First, I want to hear your best guess as to what this crap is," Sawyer insisted. "I don't want to put my best sub driver at risk if I can help it."

Madrigal nodded vigorously. "Make that a double-triple from me!"

"Fair enough," Austen said, with a sigh. "This is a highly pathogenic organism that acts like a bloodborne infection. It could be dangerous if brought into contact with the human body in any way – on the skin, though the mouth, or nasal membranes. On the other hand, it could be something that's harmless on the skin but lethal if it gets into the bloodstream."

"You mean like lockjaw," Madrigal said.

"Or staph, maybe." Sawyer added.

"Neither of which survive for long in saline environments," Austen pointed out. "No, this is from a class of organisms that people call 'flesh eating' bacteria. There's a distant cousin of cholera that does this – *Vibrio vulnificus*. You normally get it by consuming contaminated mollusks. Oysters and the like."

"I'm allergic to shellfish," Lici groaned. "I can't eat the stuff."

"I don't think anyone tried the local seafood buffet. But there were some recent cases from along the Gulf of Mexico. Hurricane victims who suffered abrasions and were then exposed to water where shellfish had been farmed. They ended up with similar symptoms."

"So you think it's in the water?" Sawyer asked, in disbelief. "Then all of the divers would've come down with this already."

"I don't know for sure," Austen hedged. "Not yet. I need more to work with. But I don't think it's spread through the air, or everyone would have it by now. I don't know the original source of the disease, but I'm betting that it could still be spread via person-to-person contact."

"Well, that's great news," Madrigal groused.

"There's an onboard airlock section in the rear of the sub," Sawyer said, picking up on that thought. "That's so you can leave the sub directly when you're out in open water. It'll be cramped, but Peterson and Lici could share that space for a trip to the surface if needed."

"And if we relay that information to the *Acheron*," Austen said, "they could have a medical team pressurized, gowned, and standing by to retrieve them."

"If that gives me the best chance," Lici said, "then I'm up for it."

"It will," Austen assured her. "I'll let the ship's doctors know what medications to try for a *Vibrio* infection. But...I'm not sure that they can save that arm."

"Given a choice, I'll lose the arm if it saves my life. I'm a righty anyway."

"Once we get you moved, we've got a lot more to do." Austen turned back to Sawyer. "How are we fixed for cleaning supplies?"

"It's a constant fight against mold down here. What do you want?"

"Form a cleaning crew, make sure they have hand and eye protection. Use spray bottles and wipes to coat every possible surface in a line from here to the moon pool." Austen pointed up to a vent in the ceiling. "Is that a HEPA filter?"

"Every filter we have down here is."

"Good, that's a lucky break. Set this segment of the station to slight negative pressure. Five millibars will do. That'll help prevent spread if there's an airborne component to this bug."

Sawyer nodded. "All right, then. Neely, go prep the airlock."

"On it!" Madrigal took off at a run.

"Shall we begin?" Sawyer gestured towards a supply closet. "There should be a fold-up stretcher in there."

Austen took a step towards the closet. She suddenly froze as something tickled her at the back of her mind. She let out a breath through her mask.

"Just one moment." She went over to one of the sickbay desk drawers. The one that Lici had tried to point to.

Austen's hand shook as she reached out to pull the drawer knob.

What did you prick yourself on?
Not sure. Found it later when probing Richter's body.

Her fingers closed around the knob and pulled the drawer out. Something rolled inside, making a sinister little noise. She looked inside.

Austen let out a startled gasp as she did so.

CHAPTER EIGHTEEN

Harstaad Island
Dårlig Mann Fjord

Victor Lawrence Wakelin sighed as he listened to the ice cubes in his drink sing to him.

He set down a pen and pushed away from his marble-topped writing desk. He took a contemplative sip as he watched fog curl its way up the fjord. It was one thing to drink some of the world's most expensive scotch.

Wakelin, on the other hand, liked vanishingly rare *ice*.

The pentagonal cubes floating in his drink came from deep within a glacier located far beyond the Arctic Circle. The ice had been so tightly compressed over thousands of years by the weight of the glacier that they took forever to melt. What's more, they hissed and popped as they melted, singing as they released air trapped from a time when humans hunted mammoth.

He smiled as he thought of the irony. Hundreds of tons of hydrocarbons had been released into the present-day atmosphere by tractors, trucks, and jets. All to bring him water that was exceptionally pure – because it came from a time before those machines existed.

But his rare good mood shattered like glass with the sound he'd been dreading.

The multi-chord ring of his secure video phone line. That meant the Tarantus brothers were finally reaching out. Finally contacting him to pick up the job he dreaded giving them in the first place.

Wakelin went to the videophone booth and took a seat. He smoothed out the crease in his pant leg as he flicked the screen on. The image flickered a moment before showing him a cramped gray-green room that looked as if it had been built from industrial piping.

The faces of Tomaz and Sebastian Tarantus swam into focus. Both wore gray diving suits that looked oil-slick with dampness. Tomaz had a sharp chin and a sharper nose that protruded from below a mop of blond hair. Sebastian's features were rounder, and yet somehow harder looking.

"We got your message." Tomaz said, in a voice clogged by static. "You realize that this could be messy. We like messy."

"Yes, that I understand," Wakelin replied. A second passed. Tomaz said something else, but the sound faded out and the image danced crazily before recomposing itself. "Say again? Can't you improve the connection?"

"No can do," Tomaz apologized, with a toothy, insincere grin. "Best we can do without getting too close to the surface before dark."

That was probably true enough, Wakelin thought.

The Tarantus' submarine, the *Umorjen*, was a converted Soviet-era diesel boat. The torpedo tubes had been removed to add space for smuggling cargo. A three-person minisub had been secured to the vessel's afterdeck for smaller, deadlier excursions.

The *Umorjen* also had an ultra-long-range antenna set up to send a signal to a weather satellite hovering high over the Western Mediterranean. A hidden array bounced the signal off three more birds in succession to mask the origin and destination of the signal before it arrived on Wakelin's screen.

"I just received some disturbing news," Wakelin said. "It looks like Sirenica's called in an expert in identifying exotic diseases. There's a better than seventy percent possibility that they will resume exploration of the vent field, even with the loss of their first team."

Tomaz exchanged a glance with his brother. Wakelin suppressed a shudder as Sebastian simply nodded in return. The silent Tarantus brother had eyes that were cold and devoid of expression.

"Are you in a position to intercept if they make another attempt?" Wakelin finally asked.

"We will be. By early tomorrow morning."

"Then I'll leave you to it. Only…"

"What is it?"

Another haze of static blurred the screen. Wakelin waited until it passed. He didn't want to his next statement to be lost in the ether or misunderstood.

"Whatever you do….make it look like an accident. Do you understand? An *accident*."

"Don't wet your spun-gold bedsheets," Tomas said. "We're professionals."

"You're terrorists." Wakelin's mouth settled into a hard line. "Your whole family traffics in blood."

Sebastian laughed before he spoke for the first time.

"Yet, you still hire us. Pay us with pallets of cash and gold bars. What does that make *you*?"

"I didn't contract you to kill innocents. Especially children."

A shrug. "Still worried about that, a year on? Breakage happens in our line of work, Mister Wakelin. We all do what we must."

"As far as I'm concerned, you're a pair of mad dogs."

The insult didn't faze the two in the slightest.

"We prefer the term 'entrepreneurs'," Tomaz corrected him. "And no matter how crude our methods, there's always someone like you willing to pay."

Wakelin cut the connection.

He downed the rest of his drink. Rising, he went into his personal office washroom. He held his hands under the motion-sensors for the sink's soap dispenser, and then the faucet.

Wakelin plunged his hands into the warm water, scrubbing his palms over and over again.

CHAPTER NINETEEN

Sirenica Research Station
Deck B – Crew Quarters

Austen closed the little hard-shelled case in her hand and took three short steps to cross her cramped sleeping quarters. She pulled open the room's single wall drawer with a *squeak*. Inside lay shrink-wrapped packages containing more pale blue jumpsuits, pale blue underwear, and a single zip-locked plastic bag labeled *Feminine Hygiene Products*. Austen didn't open it, but she'd bet a month's pay that everything inside was pale blue as well.

She appreciated the fact that space on an underwater station was at a premium. But it didn't make Sirenica's accommodations any lusher. The best a billion dollars could buy for comfort was a bed slab that folded out from the wall. A built-in gel pad at one end of the slab made for a quivery, gelatinous pillow.

At least she couldn't complain about the view. She pocketed the case and pushed the drawer back in. Then she sat down on the bed slab to look out the flattened oval of acrylic that made up the porthole window.

Even in the fading light, the scene looked like something out of a Jules Verne novel. Shades of rich, cobalt blue swirled outside. She didn't see any fish, but fronds of red sea fern branched up in bunches from the rocky seafloor around the habitat. That same floor sloped away and down towards unknown depths.

For a second, she thought she saw a glittering mass at the edge of her vision. A sprinkle of starlight from the depths beyond. She got up and squinted out the window, but whatever it was had vanished in the gloom.

Austen rubbed her tired eyes. She still hadn't recovered from the loss of sleep on the bumpy transatlantic flight. She perked up at a metallic rapping at her door.

"Come in," she called.

The door opened with a squeak to reveal a similarly tired-looking Navarro. He stuck his head in, looked around, but didn't enter. She got the sense that he wanted to speak privately.

"Tight quarters, I know." Austen shifted positions to recline on the slab. "Here, that gets my legs out of the way."

"Thanks," he said. "That helps."

Navarro stepped inside and closed the door. It *clanked* like the closing of the hatch on Madrigal's sub. Abruptly, with her prone and him standing, she became aware of how crowded the room suddenly felt.

It wasn't a suddenly intimate feeling, however. If anything, Navarro's expression took on a more downcast shade. In the cramped quarters he looked like a gloomy English Mastiff shoved into a too-small kennel.

Perhaps it was the fatigue, but the image came precariously close to making her giggle. She reined in the temptation. After what she'd seen today, laughs weren't foremost on her mind.

"Is your place this nice?" she asked.

"Sort of. It's a mite larger, but it's also right across from the port-a-potties. Makes the space outside my door smell like a stack of urinal cakes."

"You're kidding me. They use portable toilets down here?"

"A variation of the phone-booth kind, yeah. They're all hooked into a central drain system that fills up one of the floating coffin things. Can't complain, though. This is five-star luxury compared to most aquanaut habitats."

She shook her head and felt her damp hair flop against her neck. "Great."

"Well, luxury or no, did you learn anything down in sickbay?"

"A couple of things. I'm pretty sure we're dealing with a form of flesh-eating bacteria, one that's related to *Vibrio vulnificus*."

Navarro took a half-step back at the news, almost thumping his head against the descending curve of the ceiling. "That's...pretty damned awful. How contagious is this stuff?"

"If it's *Vibrio*, then it's highly contagious. All you need is contaminated water touching a scrape on the skin."

"I was afraid you were going to say that."

"The problem is, if it's primarily transmitted through the water, then all the divers should be sick by now. Everyone working outside is going to get a scrape sooner or later."

"Well, I met both the Dive Master and the Dive Monitor a little while ago. The Dive Master's name is Otto Hanick, and he's healthy as a horse. Big as one, too."

"Well, maybe the samples I took will tell us something."

"I heard that you sent Madrigal topside with both patients and samples."

"Yes, but the samples I took from Lang and Richter on board the *Acheron* were flown to a lab in Naples. They should have the results back by now."

Navarro's face brightened a bit. "Maybe I have some good news for you then. Sawyer told me that you've received two new emails on Sirenica's server. Maybe one of them is from that lab."

That made Austen sit up. "Maybe it is! But...how am I going to retrieve them from here?"

"Ah, then I have something else new to share with you," Navarro said, as he pointed towards one of the black-sheened raised sections of station wall. "Wherever you see one of these, that's a touch-sensitive terminal. Give it a try."

Austen got up, she and Navarro moving around each other so she could get to the panel. He ended up sitting towards the foot of the bed as a screen lit up at the touch of her palm. A virtual keyboard glowed underneath the screen, allowing her to locate the Whitespire site and log into her mail account.

"You called it," she said, in a happy voice. "The first message is from the lab. The results are a big attachment, though. It'll take a minute to download."

"What's the second message?"

She blinked. "It's from DiCaprio."

Navarro perked up in turn. "What does our dime-store Nostradamus have to say?"

A pause. "It's another riddle."

She stepped to one side so that Navarro could read the screen's contents.

Diamonds make prisons harder than the strongest jail
A corporeal film keeps the outside from the inside.
An ethereal film keeps the depth from the surface.
Do not breach the prison of Hades.
A flicker of starlight may yet save you.

Navarro groaned and pinched the bridge of his nose.

"It's getting too late in the day for this kind of stuff. Why does he do this?"

"It may be the only way he *can* do this," Austen reasoned. "If DiCaprio's embedded at the top levels of government, he's going to have to be cryptic. Otherwise, it might be too easy for someone to track the message back to the source."

"Cryptic riddles aren't any easier or more difficult to track along a network than a plain 'Here's the skinny on X' message," Navarro grumped. "What I want to know is how he's always right. It's just plain spooky."

"It's not spooky, it's useful!"

A metallic *rap-rap-rap* came from the door a moment before

it was pushed open. Sawyer peered inside, eying where Navarro sat on Austen's bed. She chuckled.

"Normally, this is the part where I'd tell you two to get a room. Seems like you already have one, though."

Navarro frowned. "What do you want, Dylan?"

"Have some news for you both," Sawyer said. "I'm afraid that Peterson didn't make it. He died in the depressurization room on board the *Acheron*. Lici made it out. They amputated her arm at the shoulder. They're administering the medications you recommended. Her condition is rated as 'serious', but at least it's stable. They're flying her to a hospital on the mainland before nightfall."

Austen looked away. "That's something, at least."

"Also, Diamante's calling an all-hands meeting over dinner. This time, the Conte says that failure to attend will get you keel-hauled."

"That would be quite a feat," Navarro observed, "considering that we're on an undersea habitat, not a sailing ship."

"It's the spirit of the thing."

"We *get* it," Austen said, with a roll of her eyes.

"Good." Sawyer nodded. "The meeting's in fifteen minutes. So, whatever you two are up to, make it a quickie."

Sawyer closed the door before Austen could sputter a reply.

Michael Angel

CHAPTER TWENTY

Neely Madrigal hadn't been kidding about the flatbread pizza.

Several of Topside's tables and unpacked box crates had been pushed together to form a central serving area. The summery scents of warm tomato sauce, roasted artichoke, and melted cheese hung in the air. Each entree sat in a nest-like wrapper on single portion sized microwave plates.

Austen found that her appetite came back with a vengeance. She grabbed a tray and snatched up portions labeled *Pizza Capricciosa, Insalata di Tapenade,* and a tea-like mixture called *rooibos.* She took a seat next to Navarro at a handy side table.

Navarro had opted for an entire carafe of rooibos and a stack of flattened white and pink triangles. He munched his way through them as she plowed through her food in turn. The pizza was the source of the tomato sauce and artichoke aromas. Just as Madrigal had warned her, the crust was solid and cracker-thin.

The salad fared similarly in the high-pressure environment. The lettuce leaves, olives, and nibs of salami had been squashed almost flat. To Austen it looked as if each ingredient had been smashed between a pair of bricks.

"Well, it's not bad for microwave food," she ventured, after a bit. "What did you pick up?"

Navarro turned a wrapper around to read the label. "*Panino prosciutto e formaggio*. Not bad. Tastes like ham and cheese."

Now that her hunger had been sated, Austen looked around the room. The transparent dome above had shaded to black. The darkness threw the room's lamps into sharp relief, making the lighting dramatic and moody.

A bald man with massive shoulders was seated at a table with the four remaining divers. Based on what Navarro had said, that was Otto Hanick. Sawyer and Jordan sat conversing with Diamante as he picked at a plate of food. Gimenez was busy carrying a precariously balanced pile of wrappers and trays to the trash receptacle.

As he passed a table at the edge of the room, Austin noticed a pale, dark-haired woman sitting alone. Moving her fork mechanically from plate to mouth, her eyes darted back and forth, scanning the room. When she caught sight of Austen and Navarro, only one emotion registered clearly.

Disappointment.

"That's Kirov," she whispered to Navarro.

"I was waiting for you to spot her," he whispered back. "She's a flighty looking one."

Before Austen could reply, Diamante stood and went over to one of the black-sheened sections of station wall. A wave of his palm, and the hidden screen lit up. He tapped in a few commands and then walked over to the center of the room. He waited a few moments before the conversation and clink of silverware on plates died down.

"I have news from the surface," Diamante began. His voice rang with a slight echo off the domed ceiling. "Doctor Lici is in stable condition. But I'm afraid that our friend and comrade, Jonas Peterson, died aboard the *Acheron* this evening."

A chorus of low murmurs rose from the diver's table before Hanick ended them with an annoyed glance. He raised one beefy hand and spoke in turn.

"The doctors. Do they know how he died?"

"Heart failure. His death was painless, *Grazie Dio.*"

"Heart failure? How can this be possible?" one of the other divers demanded. "He had the strongest heart of us all!"

There were more dark mutters from the table. Austen looked between the group of angry divers and Diamante. The Count cleared his throat, trying to figure out something to say. Austen leapt to her feet.

"It's *very* possible," she said firmly. Instantly, every eye was on her. "When I examined Peterson, his body was riddled with a bacterial infection. One that attacked the tissues in his muscles, tendons, and large blood vessels. Bacteria that do this throw off toxins directly into the bloodstream. When those toxins reach a critical level, they can cause even a perfectly healthy heart like Peterson's to fail."

Her answer didn't win any smiles. But at least the muttering had stopped. Diamante paused and motioned as if to tip his hat to her before speaking again.

"*Grazie,* Doctor Austen. Do you have anything else to share with us about what the late Mister Peterson contracted?"

Austen paused. A series of creaks echoed in the room as everyone sat up expectantly. "I just finished downloading a report on the samples taken from Lang and Richter. The toxins in their bloodstream closely resemble those thrown off by *Vibrio vulnificus.* That's one of a number of organisms the press likes to call 'flesh eating' bacteria."

"You said it closely resembled *Vibrio,*" said a quiet female voice. Everyone's head turned in surprise towards Sasha Kirov. "But is it an exact match?"

"No, it's not," Austen admitted. "I think it's a new strain, one that works a hell of a lot more quickly. At least in some instances."

Kirov's brows knitted together. "I'm familiar with *Vibrio.* It doesn't spread easily. You typically have to ingest it."

"Austen says that people have gotten it other ways," Sawyer pointed out. "They were exposed to water from an oyster farm."

"Well, that's rather inconvenient," Kirov shot back. "Nobody's farming oysters three hundred feet below the surface. *Vibrio* needs an active mollusk population to survive."

"All good points," Diamante said. "But the loss of the dive team has put us behind schedule in mapping the periphery of the vent field, and I want to know what we can do about it."

He waved a hand above his head. A glass lens folded out from the rear wall and projected a mural-sized picture next to Diamante. The image resembled an abstract version of a dart board, complete with rings marked by little white lines.

The outer rings were blue, followed by sections of darker blue and green further in. A mass of fiery red made up the center. Two black dots punctuated the periphery, and a long, curved rectangle lay closer to the reddish mass. Most of the rectangle was also black, though a sliver at one edge was shaded gray.

"Allow me to explain for the sake of our guests," Diamante announced. He tweaked one end of his mustache before pointing to the black dots. "Sirenica is here, at the *periferia*. Further in and deeper down lies Base Camp. The rectangle is the currently unmapped area remaining, while the shaded section is 'in progress'."

"That would be Subsite Field 1725," Navarro said. "Where you lost contact with the last dive team."

"That's right, Mister Navarro."

"What do the lines and colors represent?" Austen asked. "I'm guessing that the lines are like those on a contour map."

"Very much so," the Count replied. "On land, the lines would measure altitude. Here, they measure depth. The colors mark temperature changes. As a general rule, when you move closer to the vents, temperature increases. And I want to take extra precautions in completing the mapping of 1725. I don't think the first team sliced themselves up over a disagreement. There's still something else down there."

Hanick snorted. "Twinkling stars, maybe. If there is a monster, we will kill it!"

"Miguel," Diamante called, and Doctor Gimenez perked up

at his name. "Do we have one submarine ready to go, or two?"

"Just the *McCartney*," came the sheepish reply. "The *Harrison* is still under repair."

The Count made a dramatic sigh.

"Then it looks like I shall be gracing you all with my presence a while longer. Doctor Madrigal should be back late tomorrow morning with the *Lennon*. Hanick, I want a team of two sent down in the *McCartney* at first light."

"*Ja*, Conte. Wolfe, Ossberg. You shall be the team." The two men nodded in turn as Hanick mentioned their names.

"Good." Diamante looked over to the pair. Wolfe was shaved bald like Hanick, while Ossberg sported a shock of reddish hair. "No going off to check anything on your own. If you have to plant sensors manually, stay close to your submersible."

"I've still got a pair of long-range ROVs," Jordan put in. "I'll send one down with you to try and provide as much coverage as possible."

Diamante rubbed his hands excitedly. "This is what I like to hear. Problems being overcome and plans being made. My only remaining question must go to our resident epidemiologist: Do you think that my men will be safe?"

Austen blinked for a moment as she was put on the spot.

"I know that I haven't convinced everyone that we're looking at a strain of *Vibrio*," she said, just as Kirov crossed her arms. "And yes, it's just a working theory based on symptomology and some basic testing. But there is a bacterial threat of some kind out there, possibly waterborne. If you're going out, be sure to keep your suits on."

"*Natürlich, Doktor.*" Hanick agreed. "In case you hadn't noticed, it's cold enough out there to shrink our balls without some protection!"

The divers laughed coarsely before Austen spoke again.

"All I'm saying is that I wouldn't go out if you have a cut or a scrape."

"Then we would have to stop work. Everyone gets a scuff or two. Our suits are heated, not watertight."

"Doctor Austen," Diamante said, "as you have pointed out yourself, if this bacteria was in the water, then all the divers should have gotten it by now. So, it can hardly be *that* much of a threat."

That got a few more rough laughs out of Hanick's men.

"Make light of it if you want," Austen said, nettled. "But if we can't figure out what this pathogen can do, it could spread beyond this marine basin. From then on, anyone going into the ocean with the tiniest scratch is as good as dead!"

The laughter stopped.

"Well then, on that happy note, everyone is dismissed," Diamante declared, before the silence dragged on. "Save for Chief Sawyer and Mister Navarro."

Sawyer frowned, while Navarro looked surprised. He nodded to Austen as she left the room, following in Sasha Kirov's wake. Sawyer came over to join the Count and Navarro as the room emptied.

"Conte," she began, "I don't see why you've asked Navarro to remain here. If you have a problem, I'm sure that I can–"

"You don't know?" Diamante asked, incredulous. "You are my Station Chief; it is your job to know everything! That includes gaps in our security coverage!"

"I reviewed your objections already. Yes, mistakes were made. I told you that it wouldn't happen again."

"It shouldn't have happened in the first place! *Mortacci tua,* what happens when the news gets out that entire dive team has been killed – just as we lost contact with them for over an hour! That gap in coverage could have made all the difference between their living or dying!"

"Conte, there's nothing to prove that."

"So far, Miss Sawyer. So far. Perhaps I should have hired people from Motte and Bailey instead. At least they seem to know what they're doing!"

With that, the Count stormed off. Sawyer whirled to glower at Navarro.

"Well, Nick, it looks just like old times. You're trying to upstage my work all over again."

"Hold on there," he said, as he held his hands up. "Yes, I told the Count what I saw. It was a mistake. I didn't do anything to–"

"Save it, Navarro!" Sawyer spat. A tremor ran through her hands as she spoke. "I don't make scheduling errors. I just *don't.*"

She turned and stamped out in Diamante's wake.

Michael Angel

CHAPTER TWENTY-ONE

Alexandra Kirov's door shut with a *clank* just as Austen came down the corridor. She jogged up to the steel-framed slab labeled *Laboratorio di Biologia*. She paused for a moment as Madrigal's words about Kirov came back to her.

If you ask me, I think she's gone a little cray-cray.

Austen pushed that aside and rapped her knuckles on the hard surface. It opened slightly with a squeak. Kirov peered suspiciously through the gap.

"Yes? What is it?"

"I'm Leigh Austen, from Whitespire Labs–"

"You're not Joseph Widerman. Goodbye."

A *squeak* as Kirov began to shut the door. Without thinking, Austen jammed her foot into the gap. A jab of pain made her grimace.

"Wait, wait!" She looked up and down the hall, which had remained empty. "I got your message."

"Yes, I'm sure Joseph showed you my video. He's generous that way. Good day."

Austen dropped her voice. "Not that message. The other one. In lemon juice."

Kirov hesitated a moment, and then stepped back. Austen

pushed her way inside and then closed the door behind her.

The biology lab had a deep blue-green cast from a bank of lamps Kirov had clipped to the edge of several fluid-filled tanks. Austen spotted the lab table and circular window from the video. A fold-out desk piled high with notes and personal belongings lay crammed into a corner.

"So," Kirov said, "did Joseph send you after he saw my message?"

Austen shook her head. Kirov's delicate complexion went a shade paler, if that were possible.

"Of course he didn't see it," Austen said quickly. "If he had, don't you think he'd have come in person?"

The marine biologist sagged visibly as she nodded. She went to her desk and practically threw herself into her chair. She ran her fingers through her dark hair with a faint moan.

"You're right, he would have. I'm sorry. I'm just so...tired." With a sigh, she gathered herself together. "So. Why are you here? You're out of luck if you want to betray me to Diamante."

"I'm not here to betray anyone, I'm here to help!" Austen snapped. "You said there's danger down here. Are you referring to this necrotic pathogen?"

"In part. There's been a...let's say, a number of suspicious deaths down here. I'm not sure who or what's responsible."

"From this disease? Or other things?"

Kirov looked away and remained silent for a moment. "I'm sorry. I just don't know who to trust anymore."

"Doctor Kirov," Austen said, "I haven't known Joseph Widerman as long as you, but I consider him one of my best friends. I found your message on my own. Well, pretty much on my own. I didn't share it with Joseph because I knew that he'd insist on coming. Even though he's handling a health crisis back in Virginia."

"So you brought that man with you in his stead? The one with that awful-looking scar?"

"That's Nick, yes. He's more than what he seems. And frankly, if there's going to be trouble, he'll be more apt to deal with it than a concert pianist. Hopefully, that proves my good intentions. You can trust me as much as the people who've chosen to be here to work on Sirenica."

Kirov let out a sour, bitter laugh.

"No one here is working purely out of choice. This place is no better than a prison. A prison with little hope of escape."

"Talk to me, Alexandra. Please."

She looked longingly at one of the raised shelves on her desk. Austen saw that she'd propped up a wire frame there. The frame held a picture of Kirov, who was embracing another woman. The two were on a sunlit beach together, and they were smiling.

"We all have secrets we keep close," Kirov finally said. "Even from those we care about."

A moment of silence passed. Then two. Austen couldn't take it anymore. She squelched the first three angry replies that came to mind.

No, she thought to herself. *That's not how you catch a scientist. You can't bully them. You grab them by their dominant personality trait: their curiosity.*

Austen pulled out the little hard case she'd stowed in her pocket earlier. She opened it carefully and set it on the desk so that the biologist could see it.

It was a two-inch sliver, made of some foreign substance that gleamed pearlescent in the light. The tapered ends were razor-sharp. Kirov stared at the thing with an expression stuck somewhere between puzzled and surprised.

"If you won't tell me more about what's happening on Sirenica, at least you can work with me on this," Austen declared. "I was going to ask if you know what this is."

A shake of the head. "I'm not sure. Where did you get this?"

"From Iona Lici's desk drawer. She pulled it out of Carl Richter leg after pricking herself on it. Lici came down with an infection at her wound site. So far, it's cost her an arm. Maybe her life. I'm not sure that this thing's been sterilized, so be careful when you examine it."

"I'll be damned careful," Kirov agreed, as she peered at the sliver more closely.

"Do you think it could be from a weapon? If something's going on aboard this station, could the men have turned on each other?"

"Unlikely. The dive team's as thick as thieves, they wouldn't do that. Out of fear of Hanick, if nothing else. Also…this looks organic to me. Maybe it's a tooth fragment from some kind of fish. Or not. It looks familiar, but also very odd."

"Doctor Kirov, promise me one thing: that you'll contact me immediately, as soon as you come to any conclusion about what this is."

"Certainly, certainly. Perhaps you should let me work on this now. Alone."

Austen recognized the not-so-subtle cue to make her exit. She left the biology lab, closing the door behind her. She leaned against the wall and let out a breath.

That had been a strange and rather frosty introduction. Widerman hadn't been wrong when he said that the Sasha Kirov in the video was too 'bubbly' to be real. This woman was close-guarded by nature, and that had only gotten worse three hundred feet below the surface.

Austen set off for her quarters, mind awhirl. But something kept playing through her mind in a sing-song loop. The first line in DiCaprio's message.

Diamonds make prisons harder than the strongest jail.

CHAPTER TWENTY-TWO

Austen slept fitfully during her first night on Sirenica.

Part of it was simple physical discomfort. The bed slab was as hard as a wood plank. The gel-pillow gave little support and made a *squelp* whenever she turned her head. And the persistent humidity in the air permeated everything, leaving her hair and skin damp.

But it was the part of her brain that refused to shut down that kept her tossing and turning.

Sometime in the night, she woke with a gasp, arms flailing for a moment. She banged the side of one hand against the wall.

"Ouch!" she exclaimed, as a flash of pain ran up her limb.

Austen sat up and cradled one hand in the other as she looked around blearily. Lighter shades of blue filtered in through the porthole window across from her bed. A silver-sided fish picked its way through the bed of reddish sea ferns outside the habitat.

She gingerly touched the hard metal wall next to her. The material that made up the barrier was strong. It needed to be as strong as it was to keep the three hundred feet of water stacked above her from roaring in and drowning everything.

The second line from DiCaprio's message ran through her mind.

A corporeal film keeps the outside from the inside.

She pondered that for a moment. The walls separated the seawater outside from the atmosphere inside. The bruise developing on the outside of her hand proved that those walls were material. Corporeal.

Was that what DiCaprio meant? What other kind of corporeal barriers could there be?

For the hundredth time since she'd been gifted with the strange advice-giver, she wished that DiCaprio spoke in something other than riddles. Getting up, she put on a new, pale blue jumpsuit. As she pulled on the clingy outfit, she decided on a course of action.

She needed someone she trusted to bounce ideas off of. And that meant she needed to go see Navarro.

Austen opened her door, cringing at the rusty squeal. Peeking out the door, she was surprised to see him already there. Navarro reclined in a fold-out fabric chair placed only a few feet down the corridor. While his presence blocked more than half of the passageway, he didn't seem all that concerned.

"Mornin', sunshine," he said, with a tired grin.

She sputtered a moment as her brain tried to compose words. "Nick? How long have you been out here?"

"Long enough to make sure no one disturbed your rest."

"Then…how did you get any sleep?"

"A few catnaps and I'm right as rain. I'm supposed to be your bodyguard, aren't I?" Navarro patted a compact leather holster that he'd hung at his jumpsuit's waist. "It's not a gun, if that's what you're thinking. Collapsible stun baton."

"You really thought I was in danger last night?"

"Well, you've got DiCaprio to predict the future. I've just got my instincts. And something down here is odd…like it's not quite jelling for me."

Austen chewed that one over. "You're good at reading people, Nick. Even better than me. Who're you getting bad vibes from?"

"Honestly?"

She nodded.

"Everyone." he quickly added, "I'm not saying everyone here poses a danger. But I don't think a single person here is what they seem to be. It's like a nest of hornets...and the deaths of the dive team was like a kid giving that nest a good *thwack*."

She sighed. "Should've known better than to ask. I was hoping to get your thoughts on a few more things. Want to head up to Topside? See if they have some coffee?"

"I'm game. They've got a drip machine up there doing an Italian brew. Good stuff. Black as tar and strong enough to float a horseshoe."

Austen headed towards the nearest set of stairs with Navarro in tow. She shook her head.

"How is it you always know where the nearest coffee is?"

He shrugged. "Survival instinct. Do enough double-shifts in a combat zone and you pick up the knack."

They made their way up two levels. The patter of people walking down other corridors echoed in their ears. Austen glimpsed the back of Reece Jordan's head as they passed the Dive Monitoring Center. When they arrived at Topside it was quiet and empty.

A shiny red-and silver coffee machine perched at the edge of the counter, emitting perking and bubbling noises. Austen picked up a disposable cup from a nearby tray, filled it, and tossed in a packet of cream.

Navarro took his black. He sat on one of the half-opened crates, took a sip, and listened patiently as Austen recounted her experience with Sasha Kirov. His lips pursed in thought as she repeated how Kirov had described working on Sirenica.

"This place is no better than a prison," he murmured. "DiCaprio referred to prisons in the first line of his message."

"Could it somehow refer to Sawyer?" Austen asked, after a long drink of her own.

He gave her a look. "What do you mean?"

"I spent some time with her, planning how to get Peterson

and Lici to the surface. She's a very driven woman. My guess is that she's tough to work for."

"Warden-like material, maybe?" Navarro snorted. "If so, she's met her match in her own boss, the Count. I found a gap in her surveillance schedule, one that might have affected how long they lost contact with that dive team. Diamante came down pretty hard on her. She didn't take it well. Blames me for opening up old wounds again, too."

"What exactly happened…"

Austen's voice trailed off. Her cheeks colored and she looked away. Navarro downed the rest of his cup before speaking.

"What happened between us in the past? That's what you were going to ask, wasn't it?"

"Forget it. I didn't mean to pry."

"You did mean to, but that's okay. You deserve to know." Navarro pitched his cup into a nearby waste bin. "Dylan and I had a thing a while back. I was running half the security detail for a DoD project in New Mexico. Sawyer ran the other half, and for one of M&B's competitors. Long hours and no one else to talk to, but I wasn't complaining. We became…well, I guess you could call it 'friends with benefits' at the start. Sorry if that shatters the lily-white image you had of me."

"Well, that's a problem," she replied, doing her best not to smile. "I'll just have to burn that altar boy picture I have of you on my desk."

"Things started getting more serious between us. Even considered having her move in with me. She asked me to pass on her resume directly to Niles Bailey, which I did happily. Thought it would be great to have a co-worker around I was falling for."

"I gather that it didn't work out."

"To put it mildly. Bailey turned her down, said that she didn't pass their background check." Navarro looked down at his hands. "She didn't take it well. Told me that she expected that I'd get her in, otherwise what use was I as a man?"

"Yikes. Not good."

"Oh, it gets better. I told her to get out, we were through, and she nearly pulled a gun on me. Then she made a mistake on the security detail and got dismissed for cause. She was off the base in fifteen minutes. Never even called me to say 'goodbye'."

Austen cleared her throat. "I, uh, have to ask something."

"Shoot."

"I was wondering why you liked her. I mean, I get that you like *me*, Nick. But isn't she more...I don't know, more your speed?"

"There's a lot of daylight between you and her, Leigh. A lot more than a jarhead like me could put into words. But in the here and now, there's one big difference."

Navarro reached into the half-open crate. He pulled out a chunk of packing foam and held it in both hands. Like everything else sent down to Sirenica, it had been squashed down into a solid mass.

"This is how you handle setbacks," he said, and he squeezed the chunk even further. He let go, and it slowly flexed back into shape. "Now let me show you how Sawyer handles them."

Instead of squeezing, he twisted the chunk. It shattered into a blizzard of white particles. His point made, Navarro tossed the broken ends into the waste bin.

Austen picked up one of the shattered bits. Even though the piece had been compressed by the exotic atmosphere and her friend's demonstration, she still could make out the individual chambers that had made up the foam structure.

They look like little cells, she thought. *Individual cells separated by cell walls.*

Aloud, she mused, "Maybe that's it. In fact, that's got to be it."

"What do you mean?" Navarro asked.

She put her coffee aside. "I mean that I've got to find out more about our mystery pathogen. And to do that, I've got to get down to where it lives."

His eyebrows went up at that. "Down? Why 'down'?"

"It's what DiCaprio was talking about with corporeal barriers keeping the outside from the inside," she said excitedly. "He's referring to the walls or membranes between cells in the body. They keep the outside from getting in. Particularly the cells that make up the human epidermis."

"But the divers have suffered abrasions before," Navarro pointed out. "None of them have gotten ill."

"Except for one group – the one who went to Site 1725." Austen stopped and inhaled sharply. She looked to Navarro, eyes bright. "Of course! That would explain it!"

"When you get around to explaining it to us normal folk, let me know," Navarro said.

"Just one second," Austen went over to the touch-sensitive terminal Diamante had used at last night's dinner. She began tapping in commands. "Do you remember when we did the autopsies on the *Acheron*? The one we did on Lang surprised me. Because his infection wasn't that advanced."

"I remember. Lang had been found several hours after the others, floating in the ocean depths between here and Site 1725."

"But Richter's body was half-decomposed already, which puzzled me. Then you have Peterson and Lici. Their infections were advanced, but nowhere as far along as Richter." The dartboard style map of the Palinuro vent field winked into existence. She pointed to the gray-shaded field and compared it with the closest mapped area. "Do you see anything interesting?"

Navarro squinted. "It's one of the warmest areas outside the vent field proper."

"It's not just warm," she concluded triumphantly. "The water out there is close to *body temperature*."

"So Lang's condition was the least advanced…because he made it into cooler water?"

"That's part of it. If this is an organism that thrives in temperatures comfortable to humans, then it continued to dissolve Richter's tissues because it made it back to Sirenica. Peterson and Lici ended up in the middle, since their immune systems were still alive and functioning to try and slow the pathogen's advance."

"Looks like you're on to something, Leigh."

"That bug is out there," Austen said firmly. "I need to find it and isolate it."

He held up a hand. "Whoa, slow down a step. Are you actually thinking of going out there on your own?"

"On my own? I'm not that crazy. You're the one with deep diving experience, so you'll be coming with me." She grabbed him by the arm. "We've got to notify the dive team heading down there of my suspicions. But we're going down there, one way or another. You're supposed to be my bodyguard, right?"

Navarro let out a long-suffering sigh.

"This has *got* to count for hazardous duty pay."

Michael Angel

CHAPTER TWENTY-THREE

Sirenica Research Station
Deck D – Moon Pool Room

Austen stared at the shimmering rectangles that marked the moon pools on Sirenica's bottom level. A glittering steel grate hung ankle-deep in the water, suspended from the ceiling above by steel chains attached to a hoist. Below that grate lay a gray-green stony seabed studded with clumps of seaweed.

The diving suit she'd slipped on alongside Navarro clung to her body like a second skin. A pair of dive fins made walking comical. To top it off, a metallic belt hung heavily at her waist while an even heavier air tank tugged at her shoulders.

At least the entire outfit's black, she thought. *Not robins-egg blue, like everything else around here.*

Navarro had coached her through the equipment's basic operation and how to put it on. Miguel Gimenez and Reece Jordan had joined them to help with gearing up. Gimenez added more details as to the suit's special deep-water features.

"These things feel like you're wearing the love child of a space suit and wet suit," he said, grinning. "There's a reason for that. Every inch of the suit from the neck down is layered with a network of tubes filled with a saline solution. That solution is warmed and pumped through the system by the heating unit threaded through the suit's belt."

"That's why it feels like I'm carrying around a pack of bricks," Austen observed.

"Well, yes," Jordan said. "And there's some weight added by a tool pack on the left hip."

Gimenez pulled out a pair of rigid helmets and set them on the seats next to the two divers. The transparent faceplates and attached flashlights reminded Navarro of the Chiron hardsuits he and Austen had worn at the bottom of a methane-filled mine shaft.

"Reinforced helmets with a voice transmitter and a small heads-up display. That's mostly for your heading and depth." Gimenez tapped the sides and top of the helmet with his fingers. "You also have miniaturized halogen lights and a camera mount at the forehead. Part of Diamante's new diving policy since we lost Peterson's dive team."

"Can't say I blame him for wanting to use better gear," Navarro said, as he flexed his arms, making his suit squeak. "Speaking of our favorite Sicilian count, did he finally give us his blessing for all of this?"

"He did not," Sawyer said, as she stepped into the room. Her voice echoed off the domed ceiling as she walked over to them. "After taking the time to chastise me last evening, the Conte retired to his room for an *aperitivo*, or after-dinner 'digestive'. For him, it's a bottle of 80-proof *Mellone Mezzeluna* that he hides in his luggage whenever he comes down to the station."

Navarro whistled. "That's a lot of digesting. How'd you know?"

"It's my job to know everything, remember? The point is, he's passed out and probably won't be up for a while. So while he can't say 'yes' to your little expedition, neither can he explicitly say 'no'."

"That's cutting things a mite fine, Sawyer."

"That might be, Navarro. Or maybe, I just want to catch

you making a mistake for once."

That exchange didn't boost Austen's confidence. Luckily, Reece Jordan spoke up before it could go any further.

"I was able to pass on your warning to the dive team before I came down," she said. "Wolfe and Ossberg are more than halfway to Site 1725 already. They're not turning back. The two claim that they're free of cuts or abrasions, and that we should 'change up our pants' already."

"Change up our pants?" Austen asked.

Jordan coughed into her hand. "It's a German euphemism. Doesn't translate well. Means that if we've pissed ourselves, to go change our pants and let the big boys do the work."

Navarro snorted at that. "Deep-water divers are all that way. They want the world to know they've got brass ones."

"I've programmed the heading for Base Camp into the suit helmets," Gimenez said. "Once you get there, you'll gain access to our last submarine. From there you should be able to navigate to Site 1725. You can't miss the spot, believe me. We call it the 'Palinuro Pinnacles'."

"Since we don't know what tore up the first dive team, we're minimizing everyone's exposure below three hundred meters," Sawyer added. "The dive team ahead of you won't be leaving their sub to plant mapping sensors unless the seabed is too hard to set them automatically. I don't want either of you leaving the safety of your sub *at all*. Is that clear?"

"As crystal," Austen agreed.

"I'll be following you at a distance with an ROV," Jordan put in. "Once you switch over to the sub, you'll be able to talk with us again. Right now, your transmitters are only good suit-to-suit."

"That's all the bases covered, then." Navarro looked to Austen. "You still want to do this?"

She looked over to the water once more. The surface gleamed back like a sheet of glass. Austen found that her throat had gone bone dry.

All she could do was nod in reply and then reach for her helmet.

The thing slipped on as if made for her. Her nose filled with a heady mix. Plastic, rubber, and the warm scent of coffee on her own breath.

A hiss sounded as the breathing gas mixture from her tank filled the helmet. Austen didn't smell anything different, but now she tasted something metallic at the back of her tongue. She stood, hoping that her knees wouldn't buckle. Navarro followed suit once he'd finished adjusting his helmet.

"Not a bad setup," he said, and she heard him clearly in her ear. "Could've used this rig a couple times before in my life."

They stepped onto the grate suspended in the moon pool. Austen gasped as the chill seawater went up to her ankles. A slight hum echoed in her helmet, and the chill vanished as the internal heating system kicked in.

Finally, Austen found her voice.

"You're right," she said. "This isn't bad at all."

Gimenez went to a nearby console and pressed a button. With a wheeze, the platform sank, lowering them into the water. Jordan gave them a thumbs-up and left for the Dive Monitoring center. Sawyer remained behind with Gimenez, her expression inscrutable as she watched them descend.

Austen felt the cold bite into her at her knees. Then her hips. Then her belly. Each time, the sensation only lasted a couple of seconds before warm water pulsed through the suit, banishing the sensation.

Now I know what it feels like to wear a body-sized hot water bottle, she thought.

The water closed over her head. The weights on her back and waist fell away. Austen felt her heartbeat pick up as she realized that they were outside the station now. Unprotected, in water so deep and heavy that by all rights it should have crushed each of her lungs down to the size of a tennis ball.

The platform stopped with a jolt. Tumbled rocks covered with red algae and gently waving fronds of seaweed stretched out before her in an alien vista. Austen didn't see any animal life, but that didn't mean it wasn't out there.

"Let's get a move-on," Navarro said, as he kicked off and

swam ahead of her. "We're not here to sightsee."

For a moment, she hesitated. The man-made brightness of the moon pool room glared down from above. It felt like standing below a skylight cut into the roof of a prison basement.

No telling what lay beyond the light.

She clenched her hands and let out a deep breath. The metallic taste tingled at the back of her throat, but she forced herself to ignore it.

Austen kicked off after Navarro, her fins raising a cloud of silt behind her as she swam out into the cold and the dark.

Michael Angel

CHAPTER TWENTY-FOUR

Deep diving was a world apart from a simple scuba trip.

The gear was more sophisticated, but it was somewhat familiar to Austen. If anything, the higher grade of technology comforted her. The enclosed helmet protected her eardrums from feeling the direct press of the water. The soft glow of an arrow in the lower corner of her faceplate reassured her that Navarro was leading her in the right direction.

But the environment more than made up for that tiny feeling of comfort. The rocky plane of the seafloor sloped inexorably *down*. Once they left Sirenica behind, the remaining sunlight rapidly diminished to a mere hint of blue in a vast field of black.

The fields of sea ferns and weeds fell away with the light. All that remained were hillocks of slime-covered boulders on either side. The cumulative effect made it feel like she was gliding down a watery canyon, en route to a sunless cavern.

"Still hanging in there?" Navarro's voice tickled her ear.

"Yeah, think I am," she said.

Austen kicked a little harder to keep the man's swim fins in view. Her own voice sounded tiny and insignificant against the sheer mass of rock and water pressing down on them. She shoved that idea as quickly out of her head as possible.

"You sound like you're breathing a little hard, that's all. If I need to slacken the pace, let me know."

"I can keep up. It's just…it's getting a little harder to breathe. Suit feels tight all over."

"You taste anything in the back of your throat? Like you're licking a spoon?"

"More like sucking on a pack of double-A batteries, but yes."

"That means we're descending a little on the fast side." Navarro stopped kicking his fins for a moment so that she could swim at his side. "We'll slow up a bit then."

"I'm all right with a speedy descent if it gets us into a submarine a little quicker. It's spooky being all alone out here."

"Beats something *else* being out here with us."

"Yeah…I don't even want to think about that. You saw Lang and Richter's bodies."

As they spoke, the lights set into their helmets had begun to glow. Their radiance was welcome, though it redoubled Austen's perception of descending through a vast, unknown space. Her breath caught as she spotted movement from above and to one side. A boxy silhouette resolved itself into the form of an automated ROV.

"Reece Jordan's been keeping that thing orbiting overhead for a while," Navarro said. "She seems to be on the up-and-up for the most part."

"Thought you said that you got an odd vibe off everyone in Sirenica."

"I did say 'for the most part'. Among other things, I worked out that Jordan's a recovering alcoholic. Luckily, being stuck in a place like Sirenica pretty much guarantees that you'll be staying on the wagon. Whether you like it or not."

"Diamante brought his own alcohol," Austen pointed out.

"As we say in the military, 'rank has its privileges for the officers, not the enlisted'. And besides, Jordan told me an interesting tidbit. One of the divers we examined, Richter, said something puzzling just before he died."

"He did?" She turned her head to look at him. Her suit lamps made his suit look as if it were made of clotted oil. "That wasn't in the report that got sent up to the *Acheron*."

"No, it wasn't. Richter said to her, "Down there, it was full of stars."

The two were silent. Then they said one word at the same time.

"DiCaprio."

"Now *that* is spooky," Navarro declared. "What was it he said in his message? Something about a flicker of starlight?"

"He said that it could save us, but I've got no idea what that means. Maybe it's just a metaphor. I mean, do you have any ideas about what could mimic starlight down here?"

"Not a clue."

A sigh. "I was afraid you'd say that."

They continued on for a while longer. Austen felt the squeezing continue to compress her body, as if she'd been caught in some strange underwater press. Just as the very last bit of blue faded away from around them, she spotted Base Camp.

Unlike Sirenica, which had a certain science-fiction elegance to its structure, Base Camp was sparse and purely functional. It consisted of a large cylindrical tank laid out on its side and supported on a set of spindly looking legs. To Navarro's eyes it looked like a grain silo that had been tipped over and placed on a couple pairs of stilts.

As with Sirenica, the bottom of the habitat had four open moon pools, illuminated from above by the habitat's internal lights. Three of the pools shone brightly, as they were empty. The final one was shaded by the form of a docked minisub.

Navarro and Austen swam up to an open moon pool next to the shaded one. A diver's platform hung at the edge. They surfaced and climbed up onto the platform before removing their helmets. Austen felt the heavy weight on her back and around her waist return.

But the air inside Base Camp was enough compensation for that. It was damp and cool, like the atmosphere on Sirenica, and it was perfumed with the smells of bleach and motor oil. But the strange metallic taste at the back of her mouth vanished like a bad memory.

"Looks like they split Base Camp into four compartments," Navarro pointed to the thick steel walls separating one moon pool from another. "Gives them separate watertight compartments, one for each sub."

"As long as the sub they've got here is working," Austen said. "One long swim in the dark was enough for me."

They removed their dive fins, belt heating units, and breathing apparatus. Navarro set his aside to spin the wheel that held the connecting hatch shut. It creaked open and the two carried their gear into the airlock separating the two halves of the habitat before shutting it behind them.

"That's our ride," Navarro remarked, as he looked through the porthole window through the exit door. A chime, and he opened it. Austen saw the yellow sub bobbing gently in the moon pool. An entry ramp already connected the edge of the pool with the entry hatch up top.

She couldn't help but grin as she saw the sub's designation stenciled high on the hull: *DEV-4 RINGO*.

"I guess we found the fourth Beatle," Austen said, as they walked over and then up the ramp. She noticed Navarro pausing to consider where to store their bulky air tanks. "Here, Nick. Let me show you something."

She knelt and pressed a button recessed into the hull. A *click*, and a second opening unlatched, just aft of the main entry hatch. It was just big enough to admit one person at a time.

"Impressive," Navarro said. "How'd you find that specific button?"

"Sawyer showed it to me. That's how you access the airlock chamber at the rear of the sub from the outside. It was the only way to get Peterson and Lici to the surface while keeping them separate from Madrigal's compartment."

It only took a few seconds for them to stash their gear inside and close the rear hatch. Then they slid down through the main entryway. Navarro dogged the hatch shut behind him and took the driver's seat as Austen belted herself into the passenger-side one.

"Hope you know how to drive one of these things," she said. "Because I don't."

"I've piloted similar things," Navarro replied.

He secured the seat and began powering up the controls. The hum of a motor powering up filled the cabin. Navarro flicked a couple of extra switches to the side, which made a section in front of her light up.

"You're going to handle the robotic arms," he said. "If you can figure them out."

To Austen's delight, the panel that slid into position in front of her seat was the exact same type she'd used in a Level 4 isolation room. When it was too dangerous for humans to physically handle a specimen, robot arms were a godsend. She slipped her hands into the glove-like servo controls and tried out a few moves.

A pair of robotic arms came into view at the five and seven o'clock positions on the acrylic window before them. She spun the claw-like appendages both clockwise and reverse. Then she squeezed the claw-like pincers open and closed. Everything performed like clockwork.

"Impressive," Navarro observed. "Didn't know you could do that."

Austen shrugged. "I've piloted similar things."

"Are there sample bags or jars on board this boat? Be kind of silly to come all this way and forget something like that."

She checked the readouts. "Plenty of both. They're stashed in a compartment below the left arm."

"Let's be on our way, then."

The *psssht* of venting air washed out the hum of the motors. Red light glowed through the main window as the entry ramp retracted. The water next to the propellers churned, but the pressure was too high down here for it to burst into foam. Navarro switched on both the lights and the radio as the moon pool room vanished from sight.

Michael Angel

CHAPTER TWENTY-FIVE

Jordan's voice greeted them as soon as they emerged from under the stilt-like Base Camp supports. The Dive Monitor's ROV kept its cyclopean eye riveted on the *Ringo*.

"This is Sirenica to DEV-4," Jordan said. "Seems like you two found our remaining submarine in working condition."

"This is DEV-4," Navarro responded, as he continued to fiddle with one of the screens at his side. "She's in excellent condition and her batteries were fully charged. Pass on my compliments to the last people to bring her home. In the meantime, I'm trying to call up the course projection to Site 1725."

"Touch the menu bar on the center screen."

"Got it. Putting DEV-4 on autopilot now." Navarro set the course and the sub's propeller units kicked up a notch, speeding them on their way. He tilted the screen so that Austen could see. "Interesting. The site's a mile further north, and almost twice as deep as Base Camp."

"Five hundred and fifty meters," Austen murmured. "I'm guessing that's…around eighteen hundred feet down."

"Eighteen hundred and change, yeah."

Austen felt her guts tighten as the numbers sank in.

That's way, way deeper than the Empire State building is tall, she thought. *That's deeper than Vatican City is wide!*

She did her best to shake off the feeling of unease as Jordan's voice came through the cabin speakers. This time, the Dive Monitor's speech sounded a little strained and unsure.

"DEV-4, you need to be aware that we're having some immediate difficulties. I can't promise ROV coverage beyond a depth of four hundred meters."

"That's coming up pretty darn quick," Austen pointed out. "That's not something I was planning on. Why the sudden change? What's going on?"

The connection crackled with interference. Then the harder edge of Dylan Sawyer's voice came through the speakers.

"Steady on, Austen. We've been having problems with a thermocline at that depth. That's a layer beyond which the ocean's temperature and salinity go sideways on us."

"Sideways meaning what, exactly?" Navarro asked.

"Hotter and more saline. Also, more metallic particles from the vents below. The top layer of the thermocline acts like a cap, keeping the particulates and the hotter water sealed in."

Austen considered. "Sounds similar to a temperature inversion in the atmosphere. That's what causes dangerous smog conditions in places like California."

"Close enough," Sawyer agreed. "But smog doesn't cause transmission blackouts. We lost communication with DEV-2 a couple minutes ago."

"I thought Jordan sent down an ROV with them," Navarro pointed out. "Just to keep an eye on things in case there's anything down here with teeth."

"Now you're catching on. We lost contact with their ROV too. This happens on occasion. Depends on how active the vent field is on a given day. But if we lose that ROV, plus the one we have following you, then we're up a certain creek without a paddle. We've got maybe one more long-range ROV, and its batteries are dry."

"Gotcha. We'll try staying above the layer for now. Out."

They continued on for a while with nothing but the hum of

the propellers driving them along the relentless downward march of the seafloor. The boulders slowly petered out, until it was replaced by a simple slope of gray ooze.

White particles of silt or organic matter fell like snowflakes tumbling to earth in slow motion. Austen caught a few glimpses of rainbow-sheened creatures that could fit in the palm of her hand. One finally collided with the foot-thick acrylic window and stuck for a moment before drifting off.

"Comb jellies," Navarro remarked. "Probably one of the very few creatures that likes it down here."

"Hold up," Austen said. Navarro switched off the autopilot and the sub coasted to a halt. "The temperature's been creeping up as we've been descending. It was forty-one degrees outside of Base Camp, but now it's fifty-four degrees. I'm going to take a sample."

She reached into the servo gloves. A whirr, and she used the claw on the right to grab hold of a fluid sample jar. A squeeze, and the miniaturized vacuum attachment slurped up a pint of the local water. She stowed the jar in a compartment on the sub's hull and motioned for Navarro to continue on.

The temperature continued to inch up as they descended. Navarro looked over to her a couple of times, surprised. Finally, he cleared his throat.

"The temperature's close to sixty degrees now," he said. "Sure you don't want to take a second sample?"

She shook her head. "We're still not all that close to body temperature. I'm going to wait to take another sample when we get close to…"

Austen's voice trailed off as her eyes went wide. Navarro snapped his attention back to his domed acrylic windshield. His hands leaped to the controls. The minisub shuddered as the propellers swiveled around, bringing the vessel to a quick stop.

The scene spread out before them in the glare of the submarine's lamps was as spooky as the first glimpse of a haunted graveyard. One which relied upon large amounts of dry ice to maintain the macabre atmosphere.

An impenetrable layer of mist rippled and undulated as far as the limit of their lights. At first glance, Austen had thought it was a heavy sheet of gray-white cloth buoyed by deep-sea currents. It rose and fell in slow waves, as if some monstrous creature below breathed deeply in its slumber.

CHAPTER TWENTY-SIX

"There's your thermocline," Navarro said quietly. He checked his screen. "Four hundred and two meters down. That's our limit if we want to keep in easy contact with Sirenica."

"A mix of the hot and cold water under pressure would cause this turbidity," Austen murmured, as if to herself. "That tells me the samples I need are below this layer. Probably not too far beyond, I think."

Suddenly, a babble of voices broke out over the speaker. Austen and Navarro exchanged a puzzled glance before one person came in loud and clear. Count Fiorenzo Diamante did not sound a bit happy.

"*Figlio un cane!* Miss Austen, Mister Navarro, I am told that you are 'on excursion' with my company's last available submarine!"

"We're not exactly out for a country drive," Austen replied. "I'm taking water samples to determine whether or not that strain of *Vibro* is resident down here."

"That may be, but I did *not* expressly approve of–" the Count's voice broke up into static, followed by a few moments of heated cross-talk. "*Mie scuse.* I may have been too hasty. My head hurts. It is likely the hydreliox affecting my brain."

More likely the bottle of 80-proof jet fuel you drank last night, Austen thought, but she kept that to herself as Diamante went on.

"Station Chief Sawyer tells me that they've been unable to contact either DEV-2 or the ROV sent to accompany them. Short blackouts are common enough. But at fifteen minutes, I cannot help but worry. Therefore, I would like to make a request of you and Mister Navarro."

A pause. "We're listening."

"It's likely that nothing is wrong with DEV-2, save for a temporary loss of contact. But if you could do a...reconnaissance for us, that would be most welcome. We are too far away to do this ourselves, you understand."

"You'll be on your own, since I've got to pull my ROV back to Sirenica," Jordan said apologetically. "If I lose contact with it, I've got no way to get it back."

"Yes, yes, they are aware of that issue!" Diamante snapped. That was followed by more back-and-forth in Sirenica's Dive Monitoring Center. "What is it? Are we holding a convention in here now?"

Diamante's loud voice was replaced by Sasha Kirov's softer one.

"Austen, I finished my analysis of the sample you left me," Kirov said. "The sliver that Doctor Lici pulled out of Richter's leg."

"We're listening," Austen said.

"Lici cleaned the sample before you got hold of it," she said, disgusted. "It's biologically sterile, and the antiseptic used degraded the surface. I can't do a genetic match with the instruments in the lab down here."

"Well, that tears it. Looks like we're back to square one."

"Not quite. I can tell you two things. First, whatever this is looks like it's made of polished metal, but it's actually organic. Second, it's not a tooth of some deep-sea shark."

"You sure? It looked like it could pierce flesh. It did a number on Richter."

"Yes, but teeth have a certain structure, a growth pattern common to almost all animals," Kirov pointed out. "I looked at it under high-power magnification. I'll bet a month's pay that this didn't come out of anything's mouth."

"That's actually encouraging," Navarro admitted. He turned to Austen. "It's your call."

She let out a breath. "Let's go. Whether or not anyone's in trouble, I need my samples."

"You heard the lady." Navarro took hold of the controls and rotated the propeller housings to send the sub down towards the layer. "DEV-4 to Sirenica, we'll see you on the other side."

"Sawyer's going to stay in contact with you as long as possible," Jordan replied. "Be careful. We'll see what we can do at our end."

The hum of the propellers grew in intensity as the *Ringo* drew close the watery barrier. Though it was only fluid, Austen caught herself gripping the arms of her chair. The thermocline seemed to dissolve into smoke as they sank through it.

To her astonishment, the layer was so thin that they could see it rise from bottom to top along their acrylic windshield. In less than five seconds, they'd passed through. Austen sat back, astonished.

"That layer couldn't have been more than a few inches thick. It took ten minutes to get through one of these when Madrigal first took us down to Sirenica!"

"That was a thermohaline current," Navarro pointed out. "Not a simple water layer. It makes me wonder how much of a barrier this really is."

"It's real enough." Austen tapped her screen in emphasis. "The water temperature's jumped twenty-five degrees! Take us down another fifty meters and then stop. I want to take another sample."

Navarro tapped the controls as they reached the specified depth. The sub's halt was jarring this time, as if it had run over a bump. Austen looked over in alarm.

"What was that?"

"Ran into some turbulence. Big disturbance in the water from up ahead." Navarro paused. Now it was his turn to look on wide-eyed. "Maybe from those things out there…"

Austen craned her neck to look out to the right-hand side of the domed window. Just out at the limit of their vision, the steep slope turned into a sheer drop-off. But where the sub's lamps failed, a faint glow illuminated what could only be described as Hell's furnace.

Far, far below, the drop-off terminated in the Palinuro sub-oceanic vent field. The surface of the field was a glossy, shiny obsidian, crisscrossed by ropy mounds of solidified lava. Punctuating the field in dozens of places were hundred-foot high cones. Some gushed black vapor in noxious-looking plumes. Others billowed sediments which were a startling shade of white.

Austen wiped away the sweat that beaded at her brow. She stared at the moisture on the back of her hand before turning her attention to the control screen.

"No wonder," she breathed. "The outside water's one hundred and thirty degrees!"

"It's a lot hotter a thousand meters deeper," Navarro said. "And some of the critters down here seem to like it. That's where the light is coming from."

She leaned forward until her nose was almost touching the transparent hemisphere of acrylic. The warmth of the water radiated from the clear surface. Sure enough, the dim light came from a myriad of organisms clustered around the base of the vents.

Scarlet-tipped tube worms extended their red fans from ten-foot long casings. Their fanlike filters glowed with reddish bioluminescence. Ghostly white shrimp waved blue-green lights from the ends of their antennae, while strange rat-like fish did the same from the tips of their fins.

"Interesting," Navarro remarked. "You'd think that light would attract a little too much unwanted attention in the ocean."

"We know almost nothing about how deep ocean

ecosystems work." Austen sat back, mesmerized by the distant light show. "It could serve as a form of identification. A lure to prey animals. But I'm thinking that it's related to chemosynthesis – where the microbes at the base of this system's food chain convert the elements pouring from the vents into usable energy."

"You want to take a sample of the water at this point, then? It's getting mighty warm in here."

She shook her head. "Too hot down here by the drop-off. Anything adapted to this wouldn't survive in the human bloodstream."

Navarro swung the sub around in a wide arc and put on a burst of speed to get away from the edge. Though they continued to descend, the temperature outside decreased to a shade under one hundred degrees. A section of the topography up in the middle distance reared up into a series of impossibly steep-sided hills.

"Those must be the Palinuro Pinnacles, the kind of dead vent field that Diamante wanted to harvest," Austen said. "The slopes are similar to the smoker vents below. Those vents must be made up of calcified mineral deposits."

The speaker crackled to life again, startling her. Sawyer's voice filtered through a haze of static.

"…still there? Sirenica to DEV-2 or DEV-4, come in."

"This is DEV-4," Navarro replied, after a quick glance at his monitor. "We're fine. Holding at five hundred and fifty meters. We're nearing the pinnacles at Site 1725."

"DEV-4, we're getting every other word," Sawyer's voice faded out entirely for a moment before coming back in again. "…no word from DEV-2."

"Sirenica, stand by," Austen said, as she spotted an orange shape appear out of the gloom. "I think we just found the ROV sent down with DEV-2."

Sawyer's voice swam in a sea of crackling interference.

"Say again, DEV-4? What about the ROV?"

Navarro slowed so that the ROV drifted only a few meters off their left. The craft appeared undamaged to Austen's eyes.

One of the probe's propellers churned sporadically, spinning it in a slow circle.

"We found the ROV sent down with DEV-2," Austen repeated. "It's getting sporadic signals from you, the way we are right now."

"Read you…will keep trying to retrieve…" A gush of static, followed by the admonition, "Proceed…be cautious."

"Don't have to tell me twice," Navarro said under his breath. "It's not like we're just—"

He jerked the controls to the right as he let out startled curse. Austen gasped as she held a hand to her lips. The sub crabbed to the side just as it passed a chunk of metal drifting in the slow deepwater current.

More bits of metal and plastic came into view before them. Red and white steel panels had been bent or broken. All looked as if they'd been scored with a rasp or series of sharp knives.

"Sirenica, this is DEV-4," Austen said, trying to keep the shock out of her voice. "We've entered a debris field."

CHAPTER TWENTY-SEVEN

A confused babble of voices came through the speaker, laced throughout with white noise. Navarro turned the sub's lights up to full power, but the ooze from the seafloor below had been disturbed. Deep-sea sediment glared back at them like dense fog, making the view worse.

"Do we have anything else we can use?" Navarro asked, squinting. "Something like fog lamps?"

"No other lights," Austen said, after a quick check. "Wait. There's different lenses for the ones we've got. Let me know if any of these help."

She flicked a few switches. The beam switched from white over to blue tones, then green ones. Finally, as they shaded past red and into yellow, Navarro spoke up.

"That seems to help. Not much, but a little."

"Oh, God." Austen said, with a sinking feeling in the pit of her stomach. "Just look at that."

An elongated mass of steel loomed up before them, slowly drifting in the direction of the drop-off. At one time, the vessel had been vaguely cylindrical. But to Navarro's eyes, it looked like the remains of a crushed beer can.

"Implosion," he said, his voice suddenly hoarse. "Madrigal

was right. These things really do only fail once."

"Look at the surface of the hull," Austen murmured, as their sub's lights played over the wreckage. "What happened here?"

Sure enough, every inch of the wreck had been scored or scoured by some sharp object. Every object attached to the hull – stabilizer fins, mechanical arms, propeller mounts – had been ripped off in an orgy of destruction. Worst of all, as they came around to the front of the submarine, they saw where the bow had completely caved in. Shards of foot-thick acrylic like their own dome poked out at jagged angles from the remains.

"Sirenica, this is DEV-4," Austen finally said, when she heard a flicker of sound from the speakers. "We've found wreckage."

The reply filtered through the static. "Have you found the wreckage of DEV-2?"

Austen's voice trailed off. In the shock of seeing a mass of wreckage a quarter mile beneath the surface, her brain hadn't picked up on an important detail. The surface of the wreck had been scratched all over, but it hadn't taken off all the paint. And that paint was white, not bright yellow, like a Beatles-named submarine would be.

"Negative! Sirenica, we've found *someone else's* submarine! We've found…"

"Bodies," Navarro said, as he continued to nudge their way through the field of debris surrounding the wrecked sub. "We're coming up to them."

Austen looked on grimly. The speakers flickered with the occasional half-word from Sirenica, then even that went silent. In the dim light, a section of someone's lower torso had landed on the seabed, legs akimbo in the muck.

Another body came into view. This one was half-crushed and missing its head. It drifted by serenely, as if showing off its raggedly torn neck stump. A loaded speargun floated alongside the corpse, attached by a restraining strap at the wrist.

Both bodies had been clad in gray wetsuits. Each wetsuit had been torn and slashed like Sirenica's first dive team.

"There!" Austen pointed. "Just up ahead! I saw something move. Could someone be alive down here?"

"One in a million chance. But we'll see."

The body that floated into view only a couple of meters before them had a battered gray wetsuit on. Blood dribbled from the end of a leg that was missing a cleanly severed foot. As they drew close, the form stirred.

It quivered as if gathering the last of its strength. Shaking hands reeled in a speargun at the end of a restraining strap attached to one wrist. As the wounded diver turned, Navarro caught a crystal-clear glimpse of the face behind the mask.

That face was male, with green eyes and a fringe of flaxen hair. What little Navarro could see of the man's expression showed nothing but determination. Determination not tempered by anything resembling reason or mercy.

The diver gripped the stock of his speargun and pointed it at the approaching sub.

"Hold on!" Navarro yanked the control stick.

The minisub lurched backwards with a scream of abused propellers.

But the diver's trigger finger was faster.

A soundless jet of compressed air sent a barbed dart hurtling through the water. It struck the apex of their acrylic windshield with a *pok!* that echoed through the cabin. The spear's barb stuck fast in the foot-thick acrylic.

That was followed by a low, ear-tickling *snap*. The snap of an ice cube in a glass of warm liquid. A hairline crack appeared at the top and bottom of the embedded spear. It crazed along the dome for two inches, then three.

Austen felt the blood in her veins turn to liquid nitrogen.

Oh my God, she thought. *The water pressure's going to force that crack open until the dome shatters!*

Michael Angel

CHAPTER TWENTY-EIGHT

As if she'd willed it, the cracks stopped. Her eyes focused beyond the spear and saw the heavy monofilament line that led from its base back to the speargun. Navarro let out another curse.

"Son of a bitch is using a line rig," he swore. "We're tugging him along with us!"

Sure enough, the wounded diver clung to his speargun with the strength of a madman. Blood streamed freely from his leg stump as he was dragged along. Worse, Austen saw him reach down to a quiver case he'd strapped to one hip. More barbed spears glinted from inside.

"He's trying to reload his speargun!" she warned.

"I see it," came the reply, through gritted teeth. "Hang on. This is going to be messy."

The propellers went silent as Navarro cut the power to them. The *Ringo* slowed, while the diver they'd been towing drifted closer to their sub. Now they could both see the coldness in the man's eyes as he pulled a second spear from his hip-mounted case.

Just as the man was about to slam into the acrylic dome, Navarro spun the sub to the right. The propellers whined as they were twisted into a new position. Austen's knuckles went white as she gripped her chair's armrests.

The diver, still attached to the speargun by his wrist-mounted strap, collided with the sub's hull on the left side. A hollow *thump* as his body bounced against the steel. Navarro continued to spin the sub to the right at full throttle. Outside, the port-side propeller's rotatable housings bit into the water, sucking in anything in its path.

That included the diver's remaining swim fin.

The blades chewed through the rubber of the fin, then right through the flesh and bone of the man's remaining foot. It stuttered in a *rat-chat-chat!* as it chopped its way up his ankle. It threw up a cloud of gore and minced flesh as it moved up the shinbones and kept on going.

Navarro finally let up on the controls. His head was awhirl from the spinning motion, and his forehead ran with sweat from the warmth of the water around them. He cautiously put the sub into reverse.

The port propeller coughed, as if spitting out something it didn't like. A cloud of blood, particles of rubber, and bits of flesh slowly turned and dissipated in the current. The remainder only vaguely resembled a portion of a human being.

Austen couldn't help but stare. She'd seen death in more colorful forms than many people. Still, she had to swallow before she trusted herself to speak.

"That had to be done."

"Better him than us," Navarro agreed. "But he did fracture our dome. I'd rather not spend too much more time down here. And I certainly don't want to go any deeper."

"No argument there."

"Wait." Austen sat up and pointed directly ahead. "Out there. Maybe thirty yards beyond the debris field. Another body on the seafloor."

Navarro goosed the throttle, trying to clear the debris and sediment kicked up by the mystery sub's implosion. Austen switched their xenon lamps back to their default white glow as they did so. Another diver lay clearly outlined in the muck.

Luckily, the body had landed face up. The man had on a badly slashed black wetsuit, though no blood oozed from the open cuts. His eyes were blank and open, his lips white as marble. A shock of rust-red hair wafted back and forth in the water like the sea ferns outside Sirenica.

"Sirenica, this is DEV-4," Austen said. She repeated herself twice more before getting an answer. Sawyer's reply was tinny and distant, but clear for the moment.

"Come again, DEV-4. We lost you after you found the unknown sub. Were you able to identify the vessel's nationality?"

She looked to Navarro for an answer. He shook his head as he spoke.

"Negative, Sirenica. But they were hostile. We proceeded further and have found another body. It's one of Hanick's dive team. Ossberg, I think."

The pause that followed was long enough for Austen to think that they'd lost contact again. Finally, the transmission came through again.

"Understood. Have you found wreckage from DEV-2?"

Navarro opened his mouth to reply just as he spotted something at the very edge of the light.

"Stand by," he said. "Leigh, can you turn our lamps up to max?"

"On it." The xenon lamps' brilliance went up a couple notches.

Now they made out the dim silhouette of yet another vessel. Another burst of speed in that direction confirmed it. A yellow hull in the shape of an elongated comma sat on the seafloor, its skids and grappling arms half-buried in the abyssal ooze.

They'd finally found the *McCartney*.

Navarro made a cautious circle around the sub. The *McCartney* looked intact, though she'd suffered some damage across the outside of her hull. Her lights were smashed, paint scraped, and her propeller housings had been bent or shorn off.

Austen did her best to peer through their cracked acrylic dome and into the one covering their fellow sub's cabin. She could make out the wavy forms of the pilot's chair and some of the equipment inside. For a second, she thought she made out the movement of a shadowy form inside.

"Did you see..." she whispered.

"Movement inside? Yes. I think so, anyway."

"Could be Wolfe. If he's badly hurt or semiconscious, he might not be able to signal us."

"Possible." Navarro squinted more closely. "The hatches to the main compartment and the airlock chamber at the rear of the sub are both closed. Yeah, there could be someone in there."

Austen flickered the xenon lamps on the *Ringo* to get the occupant's attention. Once again, she thought she spotted a furtive movement, but nothing else.

The speaker crackled to life again.

"DEV-4, we're still monitoring. Have you found DEV-2?"

"Yes, we have!" Austen replied excitedly. "It's intact! We think Wolfe might still be on board."

"Might be on board?"

"We see movement, but we're getting no response to our lights."

"Is there..." Sawyer's voice faded out for a couple seconds before returning. "...I say again, is there power to DEV-2's engines?"

"Doesn't look like it," Austen replied. "It's dark inside the cabin as well, almost as dark as the surrounding water. In fact—"

Austen's voice faded out. Navarro threw her a curious glance. Her eyes focused on the void outside, her expression stuck somewhere between perplexed and terrified.

He looked past the inert form of the *McCartney*. Pale pinnacles of rock loomed nearby, looking more like skeletal fingers than long-dead mineral vents. There was nothing but the blackness of open water above and beyond.

Navarro's breath caught in his throat.

He saw the one thing he'd never expect to find more than a thousand feet below the surface.

A glittering panoply of lights. Thousands of pinpricks glowing against the darkness like stars against the black firmament of a moonless night sky. It was wondrous and frightening at the same time.

"Sirenica, this is DEV-4," he said, his voice a mere croak. "We're seeing...a starfield."

Even through the hiss and pop of the terrible connection, he heard the disbelief if Sawyer's voice.

"Seeing a *what?*"

"It looks like stars," Austen finally said. "Richter was telling the truth."

But even as she spoke, something happened to dispel the illusion. Each little star moved on its own. It didn't break apart or explode. Instead, it shifted as if to rotate around some unseen central point. It made Navarro think of a school of fish, or a hellishly large swarm of bees in flight.

Little flickers of phosphorescence made the mass start to glimmer. The sense of unease returned as little black spots or slits emerged from the centers of the individual star-lights. Unease turned swiftly to horror as Austen finally realized what she was looking at.

"Sirenica, those aren't stars. They're *eyes!*"

Michael Angel

CHAPTER TWENTY-NINE

The undulating mass of black closed in on the submarine with astounding speed. In only a few seconds, they'd surrounded the *Ringo* in a circle of unblinking eyes. Austen made out flecks of scarlet against the starry yellow irises, tinting them blood red.

Flickers of phosphorescence began to form outlines against the darkness. Individual outlines began to appear within the larger group. Those outlines were muscular and bullet-shaped at the front, wavy and indistinct at the rear.

The images finally clicked before Navarro's eyes.

"They're *squid*," he finally said. "But I've never seen a school like this before."

"They're cephalopods of some sort," Austen finally agreed. "I don't think anyone's seen this species before."

And survived, her mind helpfully put in.

A squadron peeled off from the main body and zipped by, giving her and Navarro their first good look under decent lighting. Austen immediately saw how well the animals could blend into the background. Their look was at once sleek, aerodynamic, and nightmarish.

Each meter-long squid was roughly conical in shape and as

thick around as a roll of carpet. They glided through the water like living torpedoes, midnight black in color and as agile as any fish. A single diaphanous fin fringed the rear half of the mollusk's body, undulating as it propelled itself forward with jets of water.

But those weren't the features that made it stand out.

Normal squid possessed a spindly set of arms that radiated out from the head below the eye. This creature's arms were connected by a web of dark, velvety flesh that resembled Dracula's cape. Austen spotted another feature that this animal was missing.

"Where are its tentacles?" she asked out loud. "Squid are supposed to have eight arms, and two longer tentacles they shoot out and grab prey with. I'm seeing eight equally sized arms here."

"And they're interwoven with that webbing of skin between each limb," Navarro agreed. "So how does it grab its prey?"

As if in answer, the school swirled inward on them, making the submarine shudder. A wave of color wove its way through the mass like a slow-motion flash of sheet lightning. In an instant, the mass of creatures was upon them.

A dozen of the squid hit the domed window with fleshy *thumps!*

Their cape-like bundle of arms flared out into octagonal star-shapes as they pressed against the clear surface. Austen saw to her horror that the interior of the cape was lined with tiny stiletto-shaped spikes. Spikes identical to the one she'd left with Sasha Kirov.

Those spikes now *tapped* and *clicked* as the creatures scrabbled for purchase.

The writhing mass of arms finally grabbed hold with thumbnail-sized suction pads. Each pad was the color of drying blood. Two tentacles emerged from hidden pockets inside the flare, tipped with yet more pads studded with fishhook shaped claws. They slapped and scraped against the surface with skin-rippling *shrieks* of nails on a slate board.

But what came next drew a short scream out of Austen.

Each squid writhed forward to reveal parrot-like beaks. The beaks were corpse-white and large as a man's fist. They rotated within a ring of muscle as they snapped at the acrylic. *Clacks* and *crunches* filtered through the surface and into the cabin.

"Okay," Navarro announced, "we've officially seen enough."

He rotated the propellers and gunned the engine. The sub rose a few feet through the mass of animals, then shuddered to a halt. The top-side dome window turned into a solid panel of inky-black flesh. Lights flashed through the mass around them, even as the sub fought against a great weight to gain even a few more inches.

"This can't be..." Austen gasped. "They're holding us down here!"

One of the squid at the front window began to bite at the spear left embedded in the acrylic. The mollusk wrapped its muscular arms about the spear's handle and started to flex it back and forth. The barb stuck in the dome started to flex. A new crack began to craze along the surface.

"No you don't!" Navarro spat.

White-knuckled, he gripped the controls as he shook the sub side to side. Several of the creatures fell off the dome, only to be replaced by others. At least three more latched on to the spear.

Austen pushed her hands into the glove-like servo controls. The robotic arms came to life with a *whirr*. She brought the arms around and inward, grasping a squid in each of the claw-like pincers at the ends. They fought, lashing out against the pincers as they closed. Angry flashes of red and blue rippled through their bodies as she pulled them off and tossed them aside. Yet for each one she removed, two more glommed on their place.

They're not giving up, Austen realized, with a sick shock. *They're pressing their attack!*

Now the squid began attacking the robot arms, wrapping arms and tentacles against the devices and bending them back and forth. Austen felt the strain on the servos as well as a whine as the robotic joints were pressed to their limit. The scraping and shrieking sounds redoubled, making it hard for Austen to think.

The submarine sank unsteadily back towards the seafloor. Navarro shook his head as he fought with the controls. Jolts and grinding sounds came from the propellers on either side of the submarine.

"Shit!" he cursed. "There's too damn many of these things! I'm going to burn out the motors if I keep pushing!"

Austen looked at him, alarmed. "Can you back off the power then?"

"The spinning propellers are all that's keeping the squid from getting a grip on the housings. If I slow them down, they'll be wrenched from their sockets!"

Her mind flashed to the inert form of the nearby *McCartney*. Their fellow minisub's lights had been smashed, paint scraped, and her propeller housings had been shorn off. It was a perfect example of the fate that awaited them in a few moments.

Austen shoved the escalating panic that threatened to overwhelm her brain. By sheer force of will she forced herself to think. The squid had attacked the *McCartney*, and likely the other submarine they'd found down here as well.

But why? Sheer aggression? Blind territoriality?

She shook her head.

If so, why hadn't they remained to tear the other sub from Sirenica completely apart? Why had they retreated into the abyssal dark, only to reappear when they'd shown up in the *Ringo*?

The answer came to her with a single mental jolt.

She lunged to her side and wiped her palm across an entire series of switches. In an instant, every light on their sub – from the powerful xenon lamps to the interior cabin bulbs – winked out. Austen held her breath.

The squid detached from the spear. Several others released their suckers' hold on the acrylic. Black tentacled bodies continued to swirl around the submarine, buffeting it, but the sounds of scraping and biting had decreased by more than half.

"Cut the power," Austen said.

Navarro stared at her. "Are you serious?"

"This isn't time for jokes, Nick. Do it!"

With another curse under his breath, he did as she asked. The grinding sounds from the propellers vanished. The *Ringo* lurched as it gently sank. With a stomach-churning *bump*, it settled into the soft ooze of the bottom.

The remaining squid let go of the vessel. Austen could see out the front window once more. The darkened form of the *McCartney* lay no more than a meter away. The school swirled above them in a dense cloud. Colors flashed within the school like so much undersea lightning.

"That was quick thinking," Navarro said. "I should've thought of it too. Squid are attracted to bright lights, that's even how fishermen catch them."

"You had a lot to handle already. The question is, what are they doing now?"

"Probably still trying to figure out if we're prey. Or a threat to be neutralized." Navarro frowned. "Either way, I don't see how we're going to get past them. They can keep us down here as long as they want."

"That works for them," she said grimly. "It's not going to work for us. Not if we run out of air."

The two fell silent. They stared up into the inky mass that threatened to bury them under eighteen hundred feet of salt water. A thousand lidless eyes burned back at them through the darkness.

Michael Angel

CHAPTER THIRTY

Suddenly the depths lit up with a series of flashes. The squid moved en masse towards the soundless explosions, which resolved into a burning string of brilliant silver. The silvery mass came from higher up and far off to the left, slowly descending in a lazy spiral.

The cabin speaker crackled to life. For the first time since they'd breached the thermocline, the transmission came in loud and clear.

"*Ringo*, this is *Lennon*," came a woman's musical voice. "Anyone up for a Beatles reunion?"

"Madrigal!" Austen said joyfully. "How did you know—"

"I'd already left the *Acheron* by the time you two set out," she explained. "When I docked at Sirenica, Reece Jordan came aboard and gave me the skinny. We've been monitoring you during our descent."

Jordan's voice came over the speakers next. "We heard what you said about the squid and the lights. DEV-1 had a set of magnesium flares in its hopper, so we put that to good use."

"They're the brightest things down here, but they won't burn forever." Madrigal let out chuckle. "What say you, Bad John? You ready to get out of Davy Jones' locker?"

"Nothing I'd like better," Navarro said, as he made out the yellow comma of Madrigal's submarine descending from above. "But we need to bring the *McCartney* back with us. We might have a survivor inside."

"Roger that. You still have all your props working?"

"Let me check." Navarro flicked a few switched and the engines hummed to life again. The minisub rose from the ooze seafloor with a wet-sucking sound. It lurched a couple times as he played with the controls. "They're working. All but one on the port side."

The *Lennon* came down to gently hover next to them.

"Good Lord, it looks like they took half your paint off!" Madrigal remarked. "And it's no wonder that prop isn't working. The entire housing's been wrenched off. But we can work with that."

"What do you have in mind?" Austen asked. Out of the corner of her eye, she watched as the mass of squid circled the flares as if hypnotized. The light was already beginning to dim.

"Use your sub's manipulator claws to grab the starboard runners on the *McCartney*. We'll do the same thing on the port side."

Navarro turned their sub so that they could target the sled-like runner that ran along the *McCartney's* bottom hull. Austen rotated the grabbing 'claws' at the end of their sub's robotic arms and clamped them firmly on the length of black steel with a *clank*.

The *Lennon* rose slightly to pass over its two fellow subs. Madrigal spun her vessel around smoothly while Jordan clamped the minisub's claws on the opposite runner with an answering *clank*. Off in the distance, the magnesium flares continued to dim alarmingly fast.

"On my mark," Madrigal said crisply. "Take her straight up at full power."

"Believe me, I'm ready," Navarro said, as he saw the flares start to gutter out.

"Mark!"

The propellers burst into life with a high-pitched whine.

Austen clamped her hands on the servos, making sure that nothing would slip from her grasp. Navarro's hands went white on the controls.

For a couple agonizing seconds, nothing happened.

"Come on, you son of a bitch," Navarro gritted. "Come on!"

Finally, with an ear-popping *SMUCK!* the *McCartney* came loose from the abyssal ooze. The three craft shot upwards, trailing gray streamers of sediment. Soft *thumps* came from overhead as the subs brushed aside the few stray squid that blocked their path.

The starfield of eyes followed them. Austen's chest tightened as they drew close enough for her to start making out the flashes of color cast by each animal. Then the mass fell away as they burst through the thermocline layer into the clearer, cooler water above.

Bit by bit, the oppressive heat inside the minisub ebbed away. Soon, it was replaced with the familiar chill of the deeps. Several minutes later, Austen and Navarro spotted the sideways silo-on-stilts silhouette of Base Camp in the distance.

Under Madrigal's direction, they maneuvered the *McCartney* into one of the empty moon pools. Once Austen released the grip of their sub's robotic claw, Navarro surfaced the *Ringo* in the moon pool to the sub's left. Madrigal followed suit with the *Lennon* on the right.

Austen let out a breath of relief as she watched rivulets of water cascade down their front window. The sharp head of the spear fired at them remained embedded at the outmost point of the dome. The squid down below had torn off the shaft during their assault.

She unbuckled her seat belt and leaned forward as if to touch the trio of cracks that radiated out from the impact point. At the last second, she shrunk away. Just looking at the tiny fissures sent shivers racing down her spine.

Navarro shut down the sub's engine. He freed himself from the seat's restraints and went aft to open the sub's exit hatch. He popped it open and flipped the hatch back with a *squeak* of hinges and a *clank* of metal on metal. The welcome scents of bleach and motor oil filtered down into the sub's cabin.

"You first," Navarro said, motioning to her. "I'll be right behind you."

Austen climbed out to stand atop the minisub. The exit ramp automatically swung out to meet her. She made her way down and then around to the front of the sub to take a better look at the vessel.

The *Ringo* looked as if it had aged thirty years since she and Navarro had taken her out.

Great swathes of paint had been scraped away. The propeller mount on the lower section of the port side had been wrenched off, leaving a stub of a mount. Dents pockmarked the housings that contained the sub's xenon lamps. The fact that the housings had been made of inch-thick steel sent yet another shudder through her.

From outside, the domed windshield looked pockmarked and scored with a multitude of scratches. She could just make out Navarro in the back as he fiddled with their suit helmets. Then something else grabbed her attention.

A glistening tendril dangled from one of the sub's claw hands and trailed into the water. It *twitched*, sending a jolt through her. Then it shifted colors from blue, to green, then to brown. She called up to Navarro just as his head emerged through the exit hatch.

"Nick! Before you come down, can you find me anything that looks like a sample bag in there? And maybe something like a pair of forceps?"

He nodded and disappeared inside for a second. When he came up, he had what looked like a roll of clear garbage bags in one hand, a set of metal tongs in the other.

"How does this work for you?" he asked.

"That'll do nicely."

Navarro paused to re-seal the submarine's hatch and came down to join her. Austen opened one of the sample bags and double-checked it for thickness. Once satisfied, she leaned out over the moon pool, tongs in hand.

"What do we have here?" Navarro asked, as he knelt to get a better look. "A piece from one of our squid friends?"

"That's what I'm thinking." Austen cautiously tapped the dangling strand with the tongs. A sparkle of light radiated from the touched point, shifting from blue to red as it went. "Did you see that? This has got to be rare, perhaps even unique in nature."

"What's that? The luminescence?"

"That, plus the color change. Color shifting in squid is well known. It happens through the use of *chromatophores*, cells that contain either pigment or light-reflecting particles. Bioluminescence is also pretty common, not only in squid, but in multiple deep-water species."

"Like the worms and shrimp we saw down by the active vent field."

"That's right. The glow comes from the *photocytes*, or light-producing cells. But I don't think there's ever been a creature that contains cells that do *both*."

Austen grabbed hold of the slimy mass and tugged it free from the sub's robotic claw. The mass twitched once more and then went still as she carefully bagged it. Navarro peered at it as she held it aloft.

Up close, the mollusk flesh was dappled gray and black. Dark pinpricks embedded in the skin would visibly flex, sending a spark of light running along the muscle fiber. It was gruesome and yet fascinating to watch at the same time.

A chime sounded overhead. The airlock door connecting their moon pool room to the next creaked open. Reece Jordan brushed a chestnut-colored bang away from her face as she walked out.

"Hey, are you two going to join us or not?" she asked. "Madrigal and I are trying to figure out what's happening with the *McCartney*. Something seriously weird is going on."

"Weird?" Navarro gave her a look. "That word covers a lot of ground."

"Follow me, then." Jordan gestured for them to follow her. "Easier to show than tell."

Michael Angel

CHAPTER THIRTY-ONE

Sirenica Secondary Habitat — 'Base Camp'
Depth: 300 Meters

Austen, Navarro, and Jordan emerged from the airlock into the adjoining moon pool room. Unlike the pool they'd surfaced in before, the room surrounding the *McCartney* was packed from floor to ceiling with diving supplies.

Madrigal stood facing the minisub she'd helped bring up from below. Her hands rested on her hips and her expression seemed perplexed. Then she turned and gave them one of her flashbulb smiles.

"Good to see you two still up and kicking."

"Might not have been the case without you and Jordan." Austen said humbly. "Thank you for the assist."

"That goes double for me," Navarro said. Jordan smiled and then looked away as if embarrassed. "What's the problem with this sub? I thought we'd just open her up and see if Hanick's man Wolfe is inside."

"Wish it were that simple." Madrigal walked around to the front of the submarine. "The main hatch is jammed shut. So is the airlock exit behind it. I mean, just look at this this thing!

It's amazing that it's intact at all!"

Austen had to agree. She and Navarro joined Madrigal as they surveyed the damage. The *Ringo* seemed aged and pockmarked. But the *McCartney* looked as if it had been put through a sandblaster and torrential hailstorm.

Not a single swatch of paint had been left untouched. Save for the robotic arms, every single exterior item had been wrenched off or smashed in an orgy of destruction. Dents mottled every inch of the steel surface. Worst of all, the sub seemed oddly *misshapen* in a way that Austen couldn't put her finger on.

Navarro let out a hiss of breath. His hand went reflexively to his hip, as if reaching for a sidearm.

"Tell me you saw that!" he demanded. "Inside the sub!"

Austen shook her head. Madrigal did the same as she answered.

"No, I didn't see anything. What was it?"

"Movement. But it was quick. Like a ghost."

"Doubt there's any ghosts at the bottom of the sea, Davy Jones or no." Madrigal raised her voice. "Reece, think you can find a flashlight in one of the supply boxes? We need to see what's going on inside this cabin!"

"Sure thing, just a second." Jordan went over to the nearest wall and pulled out one of the drawers. She began to rummage around inside.

Austen chewed her lip in thought. She stepped between Navarro and Madrigal and came up to the edge of the moon pool. Up close, the sub's strangely deformed, swollen shape was even more apparent. On a hunch, she raised her bagged sample up towards the dome. It sparkled dimly as she did so.

A waterlogged *thump* came from within the submarine.

Austen's heart leapt inside her chest. Madrigal gasped. Navarro muttered a curse.

Jordan pulled out an LED headlamp and began to walk towards them. She didn't see what had appeared inside the submarine's windshield dome.

The angry red-gold eye of a meter-long cephalopod. Onyx

black tentacles flailed against the clear surface for a moment. Then it pushed off against the acrylic and vanished in a flash.

"You've got to be damned-well kidding me!" Madrigal sputtered. "What is that *thing* doing inside one of my submarines?"

All of a sudden, the condition of the *McCartney* clicked into place for Austen. She backed away from the acrylic dome even as her breath continued to race. The strangely distorted shape of the sub made sense now.

"If the squid could move like that," Austen said, "that means it flooded the cabin. The water in there is from a thousand feet deeper down."

Madrigal's dark complexion went a full shade paler as Austen's words sank in.

"Sweet Christ, this vessel's not designed to hold that kind of pressure on the inside! We just brought a damn bomb into the–"

An ear-tickling sound of grinding, loosening metal made everyone freeze.

One of the fist-sized bolts that held the base of the windshield dome wobbled in its mount for a second. Navarro's eyes latched onto it with a sick feeling of helplessness and horror.

The air rang with *POCK!*

The bolt shot across the room, propelled at bullet speed by a jet of super-pressurized water.

It struck Reece Jordan square in the face with a *CRUNCH.*

Jordan was blown out of her shoes as she flew backwards twenty feet. A spray of crimson blood and gray brain matter splattered the rear wall of the habitat. Her faceless body landed in a heap as her shoeless heels drummed against the floor.

Three more bolts sheared off with similar ear-splitting noises. One shot down into the moon pool with a comical *ploit!* Two slammed into the outer wall of the habitat. Base Camp reverberated on the inside like a giant gong, forcing Austen to cover her ears.

Then came an even worse sound. The rending squeal of

metal giving way.

A horizontal fountain of water erupted from a crack in the far wall. The force of the pressurized jet crushed a set of metal supply racks like empty soda cans. Then it rebounded against the stern of the damaged sub, spinning it as it sat in the moon pool.

For a moment, Austen and Madrigal stared in horror. The rushing tidal wave of seawater gushed forth with the thundering sound of a gigantic waterfall. It widened the wall crack every second, letting even more of the depths in.

Navarro snapped them out of it. "Dammit, *move*! We need to get back to our sub!"

But the gush of the water shifted as the crack continued to open. It hammered the closed airlock door leading back to the *Ringo's* moon pool room.

"Other way!" Madrigal shouted over the growing roar of the flood. "Get to the *Lennon*!"

The incoming seawater finally started to fill the room. The first wave to reach them was only knee-high, but it hit with a force that nearly knocked Austen over. She suppressed a gasp as the freezing cold water stabbed at her feet like knives.

Navarro reached the airlock door on the far side of the room first. He spun the wheel to open connecting hatch, then yanked it open. Madrigal made her way inside as water began spilling into the airlock. Austen stumbled as she made her way towards Navarro. She gripped her sample bag even more tightly, as if it could ward off the cold.

"Come on!" Navarro shouted. "Hurry up, Leigh!"

He reached for her as she drew closer. The water reached Austen's thighs now, numbing them. She felt her heart whamming in her chest as she fought against the swirl of the current. Navarro looked over her shoulder as he heard more squeals of metal rubbing on metal.

The rising tide had lifted the *McCartney* out of its moon pool. The damaged sub slewed to one side. Then the multi-ton steel hull lurched as if caught in an angry riptide and headed straight towards them.

"Nick," Austen gasped, as she held the bag out with her hand. "Save...the sample!"

He didn't even bother answering. He lunged forward against the waves, ignoring her hand, and grasped her by the wrist. With a mighty heave, he practically tossed Austen through the airlock door.

Navarro's face darkened as the bulk of the *McCartney* bore down on him. He dove into the airlock's opening as the minisub smashed against the outer hatch. It shoved an additional wave into the airlock, practically flooding it, before slamming the hatch shut with a *CLANG*.

The light inside flickered fitfully as Navarro got his head and shoulders above the surface. Next to him, Austen stood up and did her best to flick her wet hair out of her eyes. Madrigal practically had to tread water as she spat up a mouthful of bitterly cold seawater.

"Some help?" she gasped, as she grabbed the wheel to open the airlock door that led to the *Lennon's* moon pool room.

Navarro shoved his way over and took hold the wheel next to Madrigal. They tugged the wheel a full half-spin before it stopped. He let out a grunt as they redoubled their efforts. Another quarter-turn, a stall, and then the wheel finally turned swiftly in the right direction.

The trapped water cascaded out into the untouched moon pool room at the end of the habitat. The three stumbled out afterwards, drenched to the bone. Both women had already begun to shiver.

"Must get on board," Madrigal gritted as her teeth began to chatter. "Heater inside. Exposed to cold water. Hypothermia."

The *Lennon* floated serenely in its pool before them, oblivious to their near-death experience on the other side of the habitat wall. The entry ramp had already been extended. Navarro half-carried the two women up the ramp, opening the sub's main hatch and helping them down before climbing aboard himself.

Madrigal made her way to the driver's chair and got the engine running. Navarro dogged the hatch closed and flung himself into a seat, dripping wet and exhausted. Austen set her sample bag in a nearby compartment and found the heater controls. She set them to *MAX* and *HIGH FAN*.

"I don't think we're out of the woods yet," Austen said, as the heater began sending out waves of warmth into the cabin. She pointed towards the airlock they'd barely escaped from. Seawater had started to leak through the opening as if directed by a fire hose.

Madrigal nodded. "Not going to stay around to find out."

She took hold of the controls and spun the propeller housings around. She didn't wait for the boarding ramp to retract as she submerged the sub. Austen held her breath until they'd cleared the habitat's underbelly.

"God!" Navarro exclaimed, as they swung around to their new course. "Just look at that!"

A gout of compressed air fountained from Base Camp's outer wall. With a cacophony of rattles and moans, the moon pool room they'd evacuated collapsed in on itself. A shock wave made up of bubbles rattled the sub as Madrigal sped them back up towards Sirenica.

CHAPTER THIRTY-TWO

Tyrrhenian Sea
Enigma-Class Submarine Umorjen

Sebastian Tarantus sat in the submarine's cramped executive officer quarters, staring into space. As Victor Wakelin had noted before, his eyes were cold and devoid of expression. Yet that was only on the surface.

Beneath the exterior lay a howling storm of memory and emotion.

Sebastian's mind flashed back to two hours ago. An eternity ago, so far as he was concerned.

A time when his brother had been alive.

The plan had been for Tomaz to take the three-man minisub strapped to the rear deck of the *Umorjen*. Then he'd head out to intercept the dive team from Sirenica. As far as the two brothers could tell, it was yet another mapping survey along a ridge of underwater pinnacles. An easy target, one that was ripe for the accident that Victor Wakelin so desperately craved.

Sebastian had come to the aft airlock to wish his sibling luck. Tomaz paused after shrugging on his air tanks. They bumped fists and shared a brotherly hug made awkward by all the gear in the cramped space.

"Good hunting," Sebastian said. He pursed his lips for a moment. "This op zone…it's very far down. This is by far the deepest we've worked any job."

Tomaz made a carefree shrug. "Deep water is deep water. It is always ready to kill you. We plan for air, we plan for pressure, and that is all we need do."

"Just don't expose yourself any more than you have to. Wakelin wants his accident, but if you can't pull that off without endangering yourself–"

"Wakelin can go screw himself," Tomaz said, with a rough laugh. "Don't go playing the old maid on me, brother."

Sebastian nodded and recited the same lines the Tarantus family told each other before taking on some dangerous task.

"*If you must lie, then speak with a tongue of pure silver. If you must cheat, then cheat death so that you may rise again. And if you must kill…*"

"*…then show the mercy that a serpent has for one who has trod on it.*" Tomaz finished. "They're just words, you know."

"They've done well for us."

"You're the poet between us," Tomaz said, as he held up his speargun. "But weapons like these…they've done far more for us than mere words. See you when I return."

The airlock door closed with a clank and a hiss. One last glimpse of green eyes and flaxen hair behind mask and porthole glass, and Tomaz was gone.

An hour later, long after Tomaz had left the sub and arrived at site 1725, the speakers on the bridge came to life again. Sebastian leapt to his feet with a curse. He knew that Tomaz would not break radio silence unless something was wrong.

The transmissions crackled and popped like gunpowder-laced paper in a wood fire. They faded in and out. But they conveyed enough.

They conveyed a nightmare of treachery as it unfolded.

"…found the submarine," came Tomaz's badly distorted

voice. "They're just…holding position. What are they doing?"

Sebastian looked to one of his crewmates. "Can we transmit back?"

A shake of the head. "Not through the thermocline down there. It's a miracle we can hear him at all."

"Leaving the sub to…" A pause, followed by a babble of voices. "What do you mean? They're out there? Where?"

A swirl of *thumps* and *bangs*.

"Where did they…they're charging us! How did they…"

Sebastian sat up, hands like marble upon the handles of the captain's seat.

The bastards at Sirenica were waiting for them, he realized, with a sick shock. If they were holding position, they were setting up an ambush!

"Get us out of here!" his brother bellowed. "Before they…"

That was followed by a skull-splitting *crack*. The horrific sounds of rending steel. A gut-wrenching burble of water.

Then silence.

The men around him had been there when bullets were flying and shells bursting like firecrackers. Yet none could meet his eyes as he got up and went to his quarters. He'd sat and smoked an entire pack of *Ljubljanas*, letting the tobacco fill the entire space with acrid wisps of smoke.

He'd let the last one burn down so that it scorched his fingertips.

Finally, there came a soft knock at the door.

"*Oprostite,*" one of the crewmen called. "It is coming time. The client will want to speak with us. Shall we raise the antenna?"

The question hung in the air. He took a deep breath as something inside him crumbled away to dust. Perhaps it was the last remaining firebreak between a Tarantus and inchoate rage.

"*The devil take Victor Wakelin!* Return to your station!"

After another minute or two, Sebastian Tarantus got up. He threw open the door and moved as smoothly as a panther on the prowl to the bridge. All eyes went to him as he arrived.

"Take us up," he ordered.

One of the men nodded. "Shall I pay out the antenna array?"

"No. Take us up to cruising depth. Come about to heading one-five six. Accelerate to full speed once we're in clear water."

"North, sir? That's directly away from Sirenica and their naval squadron."

"Yes, I know. We're going to need supplies. Special supplies."

"Has the client—"

"If anyone on this bridge mentions the client again," Sebastian said calmly, "then I shall personally tear their throat out."

The bridge went quiet.

"The crew on board the Sirenica murdered Tomaz," he continued. "Obviously, they're not in the business of making things look like accidents. Neither are we, not anymore."

Another of the men risked speaking up.

"What do you have in mind, sir?"

Sebastian's eyes burned as he answered the question.

"We're not just going to prevent Sirenica from exploring. Instead, we're going to cripple them once and for all!"

CHAPTER THIRTY-THREE

Sirenica Research Station
Deck C – Marine Bioscience Lab

For the first time in a long while, Sirenica's biology lab buzzed with activity.

Austen and Kirov transferred the sample of cephalopod flesh from the bag to a small biosafety chamber the size and shape of a desk drawer. They'd just sealed it inside when they heard a knock on the door. It swung open as Navarro entered the room.

The big man felt tired, but at least he wasn't damp anymore. A quick change into a spare outfit once they'd arrived on Sirenica solved that. The heater on board the *Lennon* had kept them from shivering, but it couldn't dry wet clothes. The trip up to the main habitat had felt like sitting in a lukewarm sauna.

He came over to the main lab table and stared down at the contents of the chamber. Once stretched out, it was clearly a single squid tentacle, along with a chunk of attached arm. A faint glow came from the gray-black surface.

The stringy, pulpy mass of flesh made a tiny twitch as he

looked it. A spatula-shaped pad tipped the very end of the tentacle. As it flexed, fishhook shaped talons extended and slipped back into recesses in the slime-covered skin.

"In case you're curious," Austen said, as she set a box of equipment down on the table next to the biosafety cabinet, "I'll be using a set of manipulator pincers instead of gloves to deal with the sample. The muscle fibers are still active, and I'm betting those claws can go right through a sheet of latex."

"Yeah, I'm not taking that bet. Not after what we've seen what they can do on reinforced wetsuits." Navarro shifted his gaze over to where Kirov was busy connecting power cables. "How many people does it take to operate the manipulators?"

"Just one. I've had more hours on this kind of equipment than Sasha, so I'll be handling it."

"That's good. As it happens, I've got something that might be more up the alley of a marine biologist."

That got Kirov's attention. She took a step towards Navarro and gave him a cautious once-over, like a cat who wasn't sure of a new person entering her territory.

"Austen says that you're someone worth listening to," she said. "What do you have?"

Navarro held up a pair of data drives in the palm of his hand. "Video of our mystery squid in action. They're from the camera mounts in our dive helmets."

Austen looked up from where she was attaching the manipulator mounts to the biosafety cabinet. "How is there any useable footage? We weren't wearing those once we entered Base Camp!"

"No, but they were set to record automatically for the entire time," Navarro pointed out, as he handed over the drives to Kirov. "We put our suits and helmets in the back seat of the *Ringo* when we headed down below the thermocline. Luckily, they were facing forward, towards our huge acrylic windshield. I'm betting that there's some useable footage here."

"Now I'm the one who won't take that bet," Kirov breathed. "*In situ* footage of a brand new deepwater species? I want to see this. I *need* to see this."

"It's all yours," Navarro said. "Leigh, I'm off to talk with Diamante. He wanted to see both of us about our impromptu expedition."

She didn't even look up from her work. "Yes, yes. Tell him I'm in the middle of something more important."

"No worries, I'll handle it. I know how scientists can get when the hunt's afoot."

Navarro went out the door, closing it behind him with a *clank*.

"That's a good man," Kirov remarked, as she went to her desk and plugged in the first drive.

Austen chuckled. "He does have his uses."

*   *   *

Count Diamante paced back and forth across the length of Topside, twisting one end of his mustache between his fingers. By now, Navarro had recognized it as a clear sign of the Conte's irritation. Sawyer and Dive Master Hanick sat at the opposite end of the long dining table. They both seemed shaken by the newest losses of personnel.

"I just want to know one thing," Diamante said, as he stopped his pacing. "How in the world did this...*calamaro* get inside the minisub?"

"There's a recessed button on the hull that allows access to the airlock chamber at the rear of the sub," Navarro said. "Once it popped that hatch, it would either swim inside, or even be sucked into the chamber."

"The airlock system isn't designed to be opened that quickly," Sawyer mused. "At least, not at that depth. I'd say there's a better than even chance that the interior cabin would've flooded as well."

"*Questo è assurdo!*" Diamante spat. "Absurd! And I suppose that this glorified mollusk simply figured out how to close the hatch after itself?"

"Cephalopods are surprisingly intelligent," Navarro pointed

out. "They've got the highest brain-to-body-mass ratio among invertebrates and are exceptional problem-solvers. What's more, they have better dexterity than a human."

Sawyer gave him an impressed look. "Didn't know you minored in Marine Biology."

A shrug. "Actually, I watch a lot of nature documentaries."

"It is good to know. *Dankeschön* for that," Hanick said. "What do you think happened down there, then?"

Navarro took a breath. "It looks like Ossberg left the sub to plant a mapping sensor. The *McCartney* would've been using their xenon lamps as usual to illuminate their work. The squid were attracted to the lights and attacked them. Wolfe was either killed while exiting to assist Ossberg, or when the airlock was breached."

The Dive Master cursed under his breath. "They should have been watching."

"I wouldn't put all the blame on them, Hanick. These animals are faster than anything I've seen, save for something like sailfish. Maybe a Mako shark. And there's a hell of a lot more of them."

"What about that other sub?" Diamante demanded. "What part did they play in this horror show?"

Navarro rubbed his chin. "Submarines aren't cheap. My guess is that our unexpected guests were hired by Orcus. However, they never got to play the part they were expecting. The squid hit them just before or after the attack on Wolfe and Ossberg. Only their minisub wasn't built as solidly. The squid managed to fracture the hull, and they imploded. But I do know one thing for sure. The men on that sub were there to take out Sirenica's dive team."

"That's a pretty damning conclusion," Sawyer observed. "The Orcus divers, if that's what they were, may have just been snooping around. How do we know—"

"You don't 'snoop around' with spearguns in hand. Very high-powered spearguns, at that. Just one hit came too damned close to shattering a foot of acrylic."

Diamante slumped in a nearby seat and ran his fingers

through his dark hair.

"I didn't think…" he said, almost to himself. "I mean, I was given two warships to warn people off! I didn't think others would be willing to kill my people over this."

Sawyer gave him a disgusted look.

"How could you be surprised? Six billion in mineral rights, twenty or thirty more billion in potential energy…people will kill for a lot less."

"I just didn't…I thought they wouldn't want to get their hands so…dirty."

She let out a short bark of a laugh. "Almost everyone down here knows how dirty your hands really are."

The nobleman sat up at that. His hands went to his shirt, just below the neck.

"This isn't constructive," Navarro finally said. "Conte, I want to bring in some help topside as well as down here."

Diamante sagged in his seat. "Fine. Figure out when they can get here, and then send Madrigal up in the *Lennon* to get them."

"I must object!" Sawyer argued. "That's an idiotic idea! We're down to one sub, Conte. One! If we lose it, then we're defenseless down here. We can't even get off Sirenica safely!"

A pause. Diamante looked up, a glint of fire returning to his eyes.

"What did you just say to me, Station Chief?"

Sawyer sensed the chill in the man's voice. She pressed on, but cautiously.

"I was merely pointing out that Navarro's request will put us all in further jeopardy."

"And yet I am ruling in favor of him. Not you. You forget yourself, *Signorina* Sawyer. Given your poor performance as of late, you should feel lucky indeed I allow you to remain aboard this station!"

Sawyer's cheeks colored with equal parts embarrassment and rage. She glared at Navarro for a second before turning on her heel and stalking out.

Michael Angel

CHAPTER THIRTY-FOUR

Sirenica Research Station
Deck C – Marine Bioscience Lab

The mechanical pincers Austen used inside the biosafety cabinet made a series of harsh *clacks* and *whirrs*. They made an almost musical counterpoint to the *clicks* and *pings* that came from where Kirov worked on her computer.

The biologist remained as riveted to her monitor as Austen was to her own work. Finally, she pushed back from the desk with an amused shake of the head.

"I can't believe it," she announced. "These are *vampire* squid, and they've single-handedly proven the Tellaro hypothesis."

Austen looked up from her work with a raised eyebrow. "I suppose I should ask what that hypothesis is, but I'm more curious about the 'vampire' bit."

"Vampire squid don't actually drink blood as a way of life," Kirov said, as she swiveled her chair to face Austen. "The name came from their unique appearance. We're seeing a supersized, highly aggressive version of a species known as *Vampyroteuthis infernalis.*"

"Any idea why it's gotten so big? And so aggressive, for that matter?"

"I've got a hunch. See, there's not much food found in the hadal zone of the ocean. That's the deepest part of the ocean, named after the Greek underworld. Species found in the hadal zone tend to be sluggish in nature. They conserve every bit of energy they can to make it between meals."

"I'd hardly call these vampire squid 'sluggish'."

"That's where the Tellaro hypothesis comes in. The food chain at the topmost, productive layers of the ocean is driven by energy from the sun. Sunlight feeds phytoplankton, the first link in the oceanic food chain. What happens if you take away the sun?"

Austen shrugged. "No sun, no energy. The chain collapses."

"Except where you find a vent field. Substitute volcanic energy for sunlight. Microorganisms that synthesize methane or hydrogen sulfide would flourish at the vents, starting a whole new ecosystem. Under the Tellaro hypothesis, we'd expect to find larger creatures, ones more willing to expend energy."

"They certainly expended it on the submarines and divers so far."

"Behavior is part of it," Kirov agreed. "And this is where the footage gets interesting. Like all cephalopods, squid communicate with their skin."

"I just told Nick that recently. They signal to each other through the color-changing cells in their skin. Certain patterns indicate friend versus foe, displays of aggression, and the like."

"And these vampire squid are doing the same thing...only they're doing it with *light*. The color changes and sequencing are all on the video."

"That's amazing!"

"It's more than amazing! It's the biggest find in marine biology in over a decade!" Kirov got up and brought her notes over to share. "Here are the patterns that communicate specific ideas. Curiosity. Fear. Challenge. Requests for help. Distress.

It's all very clear, and the entire school will respond to a single individual's flashes."

A thought occurred to Austen. "Where does the energy to make these flashes come from? There's no light-producing organ in a squid, is there?"

The biologist shook her head. "Light from squid is *bacteriogenic*. That means it's produced by a symbiotic bacteria that lives inside certain cells. Strains of *Vibrio* have been isolated from..."

Kirov's voice faded out as her eyes went wide.

"What was it that you said earlier?" Austen asked excitedly. "That *Vibrio* needs an active population of mollusks to survive?"

"I did! It's just...no one knew that a population like that would exist this far below the surface!"

"Until now," Austen pointed out. She turned back to the biosafety cabinet and began to cut out a tiny chunk of the squid flesh from next to the base of one of the pearlescent slivers. "Aside from the hooked claws, each squid's arm is lined with these two-inch-long spikes."

"The bone-deep slashes on the diver's bodies were caused by these spikes," Kirov reasoned. "The star-shaped pattern of some of the wounds must be from the squid's beak. Those are mounted in a ring of muscle that can twist and turn almost completely in a circle."

Austen nodded as she nudged the dollop of flesh onto a slide and then placed it inside a thumb-sized acrylic box. She grabbed a second manipulator to move the box from inside the cabinet to a nearby microscope. In less than a minute, she had her answer.

"It's *Vibrio*," she said triumphantly, as she stepped aside to let Kirov peer through the lenses. "The comma shape, the single whip-like flagella."

"But unlike *Vibrio vulnificus*, you can get this through a puncture wound," Kirov thought about it a minute. "Considering how lethal it is, I'd call this strain *Vibrio mortiferum*."

Austen began to pace. She couldn't take more than a handful of steps inside the cramped laboratory, but she couldn't help herself. It helped her think her way through the next problem.

"Regardless of what we call it, it's a zoonotic disease. It can jump from one species to another. You won't get it from the water, but from a vampire squid attack."

Kirov frowned. "Yet it still doesn't complete the picture, at least not from the viewpoint of a marine biologist."

"Why not?"

"Because cephalopods don't have swim bladders the way fish do. They can move up and down the entire water column with ease. Why haven't we seen these squid at Sirenica's depth? Or even at the surface?"

Austen stopped pacing. Her mind put two items together with a *click*. The first was Diamante's temperature map. The second was a line from DiCaprio's message.

"Of course," she breathed. "The squid and that symbiotic strain of *Vibrio* live in the exact same temperature zone as the human body. Blood temperature."

Kirov chewed that over a moment. "So they're kept at that lower depth because the water above is too cold for them to survive."

DiCaprio's words ran through Austen's head: *An ethereal film keeps the depth from the surface.*

"Not quite. It's the thermocline layer four hundred and two meters below the surface. The temperature inversion holding in the vent field's heat is also what's keeping those animals bottled up down there."

"You've seen that layer," Kirov said. "You saw how thin it was."

"It's no thicker than my wrist," Austen agreed. "Which leads us to the next question: *What happens if that layer gets breached?*"

CHAPTER THIRTY-FIVE

Tyrrhenian Sea
Marina Militare Task Force 512
Air Defence Destroyer Indomito

Dawn came hot and sticky, without a breath of wind.

The *Acheron* remained at the center of her tiny flotilla. The *Indomito* and her sister destroyer had temporarily ceased their slow orbit of the dive support ship. They bobbed slightly on the gentle waves.

Two silhouettes materialized out of the haze that lined the horizon.

One was small ship with a low profile and blunt bow. It came on slowly across the blue vastness of the sea. The other approached much more quickly. The silhouette resolved itself into the ungainly, bug like form of a transport helicopter.

The aircraft came in and landed on the *Indomito's* afterdeck helipad. Two men got out of the passenger compartment. Each carried a slim briefcase in hand.

The destroyer's captain sized up the pair as they were brought to the bridge. Both were dressed in charcoal-colored fatigues similar to those worn by the Italian army's sniper units.

One man was rangy, with a stern look to his face. The other was tall, with a blocky head and barrel chest that made him turn slightly sideways to get through the ship's hatchways.

"*Saluti*, gentlemen," the captain said. "Welcome aboard the *Indomito*. I am Capitano Locari. *Signore* Navarro wanted to speak with you upon your arrival here. Which of you would be Johnathan 'Red Hawk'?"

The stern-looking one spoke up.

"That would be me."

His companion elbowed him. The larger man spoke fractured English with a Russian accent.

"See? Is like I said. You are Nicholas' favorite son."

"I'm John Redhawk," the slighter man went on, ignoring the jibe. "I handle drone surveillance and communications. My friend here is October Shtormovoy. When he's not being a pain in the *tuchus*, he handles Perimeter Security."

October simply inclined his head at the mention of his name. Dark eyes peeked out from cocoa-brown brows. His toothy smile made Locari think of a bear that had somehow wandered down from the mountains and found its way onto his ship.

"*Per favore*, follow me to our executive communications suite," he said aloud. As he led the way, he added, "My apologies for interrupting your trip to the *Acheron*, but Conte Diamante has requested that we step up security since the incident with the mystery submarine below."

The captain held the door, allowing the two men access to a room off the bridge wing. To October and Redhawk's amazement, it was surprisingly well appointed. A hardwood table sat next to a trio of picture windows that overlooked the afterdeck. The opposite wall held a glass cabinet containing various pieces of antique naval equipment and a selection of alcoholic beverages.

Redhawk raised an eyebrow but didn't comment.

Different navy, different rules, he thought.

Locari tapped a few buttons on a star-shaped speakerphone that had been placed on the table. There was a buzz, followed by an exchange in Italian. The captain gestured for the two men to take seats, which they did. A couple more minutes went by before the circuit let out a triple chime, followed by a familiar voice.

"This is Navarro."

"Nick," Redhawk said, "I'm here. By the way, I found a heavy-lift helicopter for rent in Naples. So, I managed to bring October along."

"*Eto, nelepo!*" October exclaimed. "I eat just one plate of pasta. One!"

"You didn't say anything about the *size* of that plate, my friend."

"Guys," Navarro broke in, "I need you to focus. Redhawk, I want you heading over to the *Acheron* immediately. Sirenica's main sub driver, Neely Madrigal, has already been depressurized and is waiting on board for you."

"Okay, I hear you so far," Redhawk agreed. "What then?"

"I want you and your gear on her minisub. She'll take you down to Sirenica ASAP."

Redhawk pushed back from the table, his florid complexion a shade paler.

"Are you serious? You want me going *down there?*"

"I'm serious. From what I've been told, it's the safest place below the waves."

Locari cleared his throat. "We have a motor launch ready, *Signore*. It can get you over to the dive support ship in five minutes."

Redhawk let out a breath and got up. "I guess that's my cue to leave, then. See you when I get there."

"See you soon, John," Navarro agreed. "October, I still need to speak with you, so hold up a minute."

Locari opened the door and led Redhawk out. The two men left the bridge and headed down a spiral nest of a catwalk to the main deck. October leaned towards the window to watch as Redhawk boarded a motorboat. With a wasp-like buzz, the craft sped across the water towards the *Acheron*.

"He is on the way," October rumbled. "What do you want

from me, Nicholas?"

"Two things. For starters, did you and Redhawk get all the data I sent you from yesterday's dive?"

"*Da*, but we had to clean it up. Very…what is word? Bouncy."

"Couldn't be helped. That data came from helmet cameras set in the back seat of a minisub. Leigh and Doctor Kirov are fascinated by the portion where the squid show up. But I want you to look at the section around the imploded submarine."

"I did look. No markings, no serial numbers. Just so much crushed steel."

"Yeah, I know that. But we caught some footage of that diver who tried to shish-kabob me and Austen. He got close enough a couple of times for us to see the face inside the helmet. Did you manage to get hold of the INTERPOL image database I asked for?"

"Next you will be asking if I know how to hold my vodka," October scoffed, as he set his briefcase on the table. He opened it with a click, revealing a built-in laptop and keyboard. "I have it here."

"See if you can grab a couple of the best frames off the footage and run it through the database."

"I can do that. What is second thing?"

"Keep your eyes peeled for trouble topside," Navarro said. "It's great that Count Diamante has enough pull with the Italian government to get a pair of destroyers. But those ships didn't eliminate the submarine threat. If you spot any security breaches topside, see what you can do to take care of them."

"*Pechal' vo blago!* Italian military did not let me to take weapons on board their helicopter!"

"You've still got your most lethal weapon with you."

"*Da*, it is true," the big Russian agreed. "Yet I think my charms with women are not so useful on Navy ship."

"I was talking about your *brain*, but that's probably a moot point now," Navarro sighed. "Just keep your eyes peeled. I've got a really bad feeling about this."

*   *   *

Repair Vessel Nascosta

Sebastian Tarantus squinted into the bright, hot sunlight as his low-slung ship closed in on the destroyer *Indomito*. He'd had a bad moment as a helicopter had buzzed past overhead, just minutes before. If someone had talked, then that would've been an Italian Coast Guard aircraft coming in to rake his vessel with gunfire.

The *Nascosta* wouldn't have been able to fight back effectively. But she was far from the helpless civilian vessel she pretended to be. The men aboard were kitted out with concealed submachine guns. Her engines could drive her at speedboat velocities, and she could lay a dense smokescreen astern.

Yet the biggest surprise, their go-to-hell plan, was strapped to her hull below the waterline.

Sebastian brought his binoculars up again. A motor launch buzzed past and pulled up to the *Acheron*. As best he could tell, there were four crew members on board, along with a single passenger.

He scratched at his fake chinstrap beard and considered a moment. Then he went back inside the wheelhouse.

"Put it on autopilot for a moment," he told the helmsman, who nodded. "Follow me. I have a final announcement to make."

Sebastian went down to the deck below. The acrid smells of cigarette smoke and gun cleaning solvent greeted him. The men looked up from where they were performing their final weapons checks.

"Everything checks out according to the schedule," he began. "The *Indomito* has halted her patrol to allow us to board. All of you shall accompany me when we take the ship."

"Is the *Acheron* in targeting range?" one of the men asked.

"Right in the cross-hairs. So we're sticking to the plan. Once aboard, we storm the fire control center on the main deck."

"That's a big ship for us to take," another man said. "A lot of men on board."

"True, true. But we have the element of surprise. What's more, we only need to hold fire control for sixty seconds, perhaps less, before returning to the *Nascosta*." He held up the electronic key that hung from a strap on his neck. "We all have copies of the codes needed to operate the destroyer's main gun. That gun throws a five-inch explosive shell. A single shot, at most two, will cripple or sink the *Acheron*. After that, it'll be child's play to escape in the confusion."

Sebastian smiled as his mind moved on to even sunnier thoughts.

You shall be avenged, my brother. Or I shall see you again very soon. Either way, we shall win this.

*   *   *

Deepwater Cable Vessel (DCV) Acheron

John Redhawk descended the walkway leading into the cavernous sub launch platform at the bottom of the dive support vessel. He goggled at the sights. A quartet of large rectangles had been cut out of the hull. Seawater sloshed about inside each rectangle, which cast dancing bands of turquoise across the ceiling.

One of the spaces contained a bright yellow minisub that rocked with the motion of the water. He walked up to it, staring at the cyclopean acrylic dome at the front. To his eyes, it looked like a toy he'd once fished out of a box of corn flakes.

You had to fill the bottom of that sub toy with baking powder to make it dive and surface, he thought, before shaking his head to clear the memory. *Hell, I'm sure as heck getting old.*

A woman wearing a robin's egg blue jumpsuit walked up to him. She looked weary, but her face lit up with a flashbulb-bright smile as she joined him.

"You must be Mister Redhawk," she said, as she extended a

hand in greeting. "I'm Neely Madrigal. Since you're a friend of Bad John, just call me Madrigal."

"You got me nailed, I'm Redhawk." He did a double-take. "Is that what Navarro's going by these days?"

She shrugged and then stepped on a sensor plate next to the pool's lip. A ramp extended from the floor up to the entrance hatch atop the submarine.

"On Trinidad, that's what we call someone who looks like they're on the wrong side of the law," she explained. "Let's go, we need to get our propellers spinning."

Redhawk followed her up the ramp, glancing around nervously at the water on either side. She knelt and tugged the entry hatch atop the sub open with a *clank*. Madrigal climbed halfway inside before throwing him a curious look.

"Not much for the ocean?"

"Yeah, I suppose you could say that."

She quirked a grin at him. "You know how to swim, then?"

"Sure I do. Bobbing counts, right?"

Madrigal let out a musical laugh. "That's a good one! Well, I wouldn't worry about it if you can't swim."

"Why's that?" Redhawk asked, as she descended inside the sub. He followed her down as quickly as he dared move.

"It's very simple. You're not going to need to swim so long as we stay in here, and the ocean stays out there," she said, pointing to the cabin's interior, and then to the acrylic window. "Now, if the ocean ends up coming in here, trust me: You won't have time to regret anything."

Redhawk chewed that over. "Good to know."

"Close that hatch for me, if you would," Madrigal said, as she took a seat at the controls.

He set aside his briefcase and did so with a *clank*, followed by a couple turns of the hatch wheel. With a few flicked switches, the cabin controls winked on like strands of lights strung along a Christmas tree. Redhawk settled into the passenger seat.

He muttered a combination curse and Apache prayer as the engines spooled up with a high-pitched whine.

Michael Angel

202

CHAPTER THIRTY-SIX

Tyrrhenian Sea
Air Defence Destroyer Indomito

October Shtormovoy was a big man, with fingers better suited to handling meat hooks than keyboards. However, he was surprisingly adept at manipulating the delicate keys on a portable computer console. He'd once been clocked doing fifty words per minute, prompting Navarro to claim that the Russian was the fastest two-fingered typist he'd ever seen.

He'd managed to isolate a single frame of halfway decent footage from Navarro's jerky video. October made sure that it captured the green eyes, blond hair, and sharp facial features of the man who'd attacked his friend almost five-hundred meters below the surface. Then he ran it through a series of software filters and into his system's database.

The machine hummed away as the door to the communication room opened. Captain Locari entered just as October got up and stretched his back with a faint *pop*.

"*Signore* Shtormovoy, your friend Redhawk is on his way to Sirenica," he stated. "Is there anything my crew can assist you with?"

October shrugged and went to the window. "Not much, I am thinking. Database is running. Navarro said to look for security breaches, then act to close them."

"You won't find much," Locari said proudly. "We've already upgraded security measures at the Conte's request. For example, you and the monthly repair crew on the *Nascosta* would normally go directly to the dive support vessel. Now, we have everyone stop here in order to–"

October cut him off.

"Excuse me, Captain," he growled, as he leaned forward and looked down towards the afterdeck. "Who are those men down there?"

Locari joined him at the window. "Those are the *riparatori*, the repair crew I told you about. As I said, they arrive once a month to do general repairs on board the *Acheron*. Cable splicing, electronics replacement, and the like."

"Do you recognize them?"

"No, but that's not unusual. We normally just send them on their way instead of asking them on board. Why? Do you recognize any of them?"

"*Nyet*. But maybe I should."

One man after another came aboard from the repair vessel. Each shook hands and greeted the destroyer crew on the afterdeck in a friendly manner. The first man who'd come aboard sported blond hair and a neatly trimmed chinstrap beard. His eyes were a strangely familiar shade of green.

October's eyebrows descended in a frown as he felt something amiss.

He continued to watch as more men came aboard, ten in total. They still acted casual, glancing about as if curious as to the layout of the Navy ship. One coughed and stuck his hands into the pockets on his long jacket.

The big Russian blinked. His gut twisted as he realized what was going on.

"Captain, what is temperature today?"

"It is hot, I'll say that much! Thirty-five, thirty-six centigrade, I think."

"*Da.* Then why do repair men all have on heavy coats?"

Locari froze and stared only a moment longer. His face colored bright red as he slammed a fist against the table. Then he turned, grabbed the intercom, and spat a bunch of orders.

"*Questo è il capitano. Squadra di fucili sul ponte di poppa! Incontrami là!*" Once he got confirmation, he looked to October. "Remain here, *Signore* Shtormovoy. I shall handle this."

"I will help–"

"Not now, you cannot. This is *my* ship, and I say that you remain *here!*"

The Captain dashed out of the room just as a ping came from the database. October spotted the readout: *RECORDS RECOVERED. POTENTIAL MATCH 99% CERTAIN.* Rather than paying attention to the computer, he remained glued to the window as he watched things unfold.

The *tromp-tromp* of a group of booted riflemen sounded from below on the main deck. Locari appeared in October's view, leading a squad of eight men. The crewmen already on the afterdeck looked up in confusion as they approached.

"*Tutti voi! fermati là!*" Locari shouted. "*Alza le mani!*"

The blond man and his followers stared ahead calmly, motioning as if to raise their hands. With a sick sense of certainty, October knew what was to come next.

Steyr compact submachine guns and other weapons appeared from under the men's long jackets as if by magic. A pair of *BOOMS* from sawed-off shotguns opened the gunfight. The crewmen on the afterdeck fell in a wave as the shells tore them to pieces.

The air filled with the *braaap!* of the submachine guns and the answering *ka-chows!* of answering Beretta assault rifles. Locari spun as he was hit and fell to the deck. Then, one of the arrivals off the *Nascosta* fell in turn as he took a round to the chest.

That was the invading force's only setback. Locari's men began to fall one-by-one as the invading force cut them down with their snub-nosed weapons. Inexorably, they began to move forward, even as alarms began to blare across the ship.

"*Idioty vezde!*" October cursed, as his hand went to his side and came up empty. He looked around, eyes falling instantly on the alcohol in the wall case. His face lit up.

October shoved the selections of fine wine aside to snatch up the two bottles of vodka. He uncapped each and set them on the table as he ripped strips from the window curtains. Then he stuffed the dry, thin pieces of fabric down each of the bottle's necks.

Down on the main deck, the gunfight had increased in intensity. A second squad of armed servicemen had come running up from the lower decks. Though several more were gunned down, the remaining men managed to pin the attackers in place below October's position.

The big Russian paused to grab one of the table's hardwood chairs. With a grunt, he heaved the chair through the largest picture window with a *CRASH*. Instantly, the sound of gunfire doubled in volume. October smelled the stench of burning gunpowder and seared human flesh.

"*Izvinite za eto,*" he muttered, as he dug a lighter out of his pocket and ignited the first of the fabric wicks. "*Ty dyadya molotov nuzhen seychas.*"

Sorry to do this. But Uncle Molotov needs you now.

October caught a glimpse of two of the attackers crouched behind a deck stanchion as they fired at the Italian naval men. He lofted his first bottle. It hit with a *tinkle* of broken glass, followed by a *WHUMP* as the 80-proof alcohol went up in flames.

The animal cries of pain from below told him that he'd hit his mark.

Bullets greeted him as he peeked out a second time. They whined off the window frame, making him duck, but he'd already spotted what he was looking for. Directly below the window, the deck plates slanted towards the sea.

October lit the second wick and nudged the bottle over the side. It shattered, but he didn't stick around to see what happened. Instead, he made a dash for the lower decks, hoping against hope that he'd be able to pick up a weapon down below.

The explosive cocktail worked better than he could've hoped.

The flaming alcohol ran down the deck, driving two more of the Tarantus' men out from behind their cover. They went down in a blaze of rifle rounds. Sebastian, seeing half his men out of action, called a retreat.

"Go! Back to the boat!" he cried.

It was his last mistake.

More armed sailors emerged from the afterdeck as his men reached the gangplank. Another exchange of automatic weapons fire cut the air. When the shooting finally stopped, eight more of the *Indomito's* crew lay dead.

So did all of the attempted hijackers. Save for one.

Sebastian Tarantus lay crumpled on the deck, blood streaming from a quartet of holes in his gut. The pain had been sharp at first, but it rapidly dimmed. He managed to raise his head one last time.

He saw a man, one bigger and wider than the sailors, approach him cautiously. The caution was justified. Sebastian still had his left hand inside his heavy coat. He wasn't holding another gun. But it was a weapon, and it would finish the job for him.

The big man loomed over him. He spoke English of a sort, but with a Russian accent.

"It is over, *ugolovnoye*," the man said. "Who are you? Who do you work for?"

Sebastian simply smiled. He felt the last of his life slipping away, and he would still have the last laugh. He and his brother would have much to talk and laugh about, that much was sure.

"If you must kill…" he rasped, "then show the mercy a serpent has for one who has trod on it."

With his last breath, he squeezed the trigger button cradled in his hand.

The sailors aboard the destroyer stared in startled amazement as the repair ship's engines came to life with a roar. October took a step back as the craft pulled away from the destroyer without anyone at the helm. The *Nascosta* kept on accelerating, throwing up a blizzard of spray from her fantail.

Then it shifted course to port, heading straight for the *Acheron*.

A yellow light winked on below the *Nascosta's* waterline. Strapped just astern of the bow lay a huge brick of Semtex explosive. A quarter-kilogram of Semtex had been enough to bring down an airliner. Six kilograms was enough to tear apart a city street.

Sebastian Tarantus had placed fifty-eight kilograms inside his makeshift self-guided torpedo.

The bridge crew aboard the *Indomito* desperately radioed a warning to the *Acheron*. Yet the big barge-shaped vessel simply couldn't be moved on short notice. Worse, the destroyer's main battery couldn't be depressed to fire at such short range. And even if it could fire, there was a better-than-even chance they'd hit the *Acheron* instead.

So the gun crews could only watch as the craft sped on.

The *Nascosta* struck the dive support ship at the waterline on the starboard side. It vanished in a wink of hellishly bright light. October instinctively crouched down as a massive *CRUMP!* of vaporized and shattered steel echoed across the water.

A red-and black fireball rolled up into the cloudless sky. Waves rocked the two destroyers as the ocean poured into the vast hole left by the explosion.

"*Bozhe moi!*" October gasped.

With a tortured groan and the hiss of red-hot metal, the *Acheron* flipped on her side and sank beneath the waves.

CHAPTER THIRTY-SEVEN

Sirenica Research Station
Depth: 100 Meters

Far below the waves, the undersea habitat made a sudden *lurch*. Up in Topside, plates slid off counters with a clatter. Austen and Kirov grabbed onto nearby lab shelving to stay upright. Count Diamante jumped out of the way as his last bottle of *Mellone Mezzeluna* flipped over the edge of his cabin table and shattered on the floor.

Up in the Dive Monitoring center, Navarro barely managed to avoid being tossed against the chamber's window. The skin on his arms rippled with a chill as he watched the thick tempered glass vibrate in its reinforced frame. Next to him, Doctor Gimenez gripped the arms of his chair at the communications console.

The sudden bump passed. The habitat rattled through a series of gentler shakes as the lights flickered fitfully.

Then they went out, plunging Sirenica's interior into blackness.

"This *can't* be normal," Navarro murmured.

"It sure isn't," Gimenez replied, in a voice just as quiet.

A handful of seconds went by.

The lights winked back on. The hum of the station's air filtration system and its attendant electronics resumed.

It was followed by an urgent chime and flash of red lights across the communication console's monitors. Gimenez scrambled to make sense of the information and began typing in commands. Navarro heard footsteps on metal just before Sawyer entered. Otto Hanick attempted to follow in her wake, but there was only enough room for the big man to stick his head through the hatchway.

"What the hell is going on?" she demanded, jabbing a finger at the closest monitor. "That's a call from the surface, get it on speakers!"

"Trying," Gimenez gritted. "This was Jordan's job, not mine. The main circuit's fried. Going to backup."

A pair of speakers on the desktop crackled to life. A deep, Russian-accented voice came through a sea of static.

"Nicholas! *Nu zhe*, Nicholas, are you there?"

Navarro had seen October keep his cool under heavy artillery fire. To hear the note of panic creeping in now unnerved him.

"I'm here, October," he replied, raising his voice to ensure he could be heard. "What is it? What's going on?"

"The ship, the one with the...*chert voz'mi*, the one with underwater boats! Is coming!"

"Say again? You mean the ship with the submarines? Where is it coming?"

"To you!" October's voice boomed over the speaker one last time. "*SHIP IS COMING TO YOU!*"

The line cut out, leaving them back in silence.

"That blackout we just had," Gimenez stated, as he pulled up the station readouts. "It was Sirenica's air scrubbers and emergency batteries coming on line. We lost our main source of power."

"We also lost our communications," Sawyer added. "Both run through the *Acheron*. But that would mean..."

Her face went pale as the blood drained from her face.

"Oh, *God*!"

Hanick looked to Sawyer. "How long?"

"Fifteen, maybe twenty seconds."

"*Scheisse*! Kurtzmann and Ersler are down at the *verdammt* moon pool!"

"Get them out, close it off!" Hanick dashed from the room as Sawyer turned back to Gimenez. "Station-wide speakers. Now!"

A tap of the keys, and Gimenez gestured to her. "You're on."

"*All personnel, this is Station Chief Sawyer*," she stated. "*Underwater collision is imminent! Exit any room with an outside dome window and secure for impact!*"

With that, Sawyer left at a run after the Dive Master.

"Can you handle the hatch to this room?" Navarro asked Gimenez, as soon as he closed the circuit.

"I can," came the reply. "Where are you off to?"

"Biology lab. I need to get–"

Navarro's voice died in his throat. At first, the two men sensed more than heard it.

A faraway rumble, like a freight train passing in the distance on a quiet night.

The sound started to grow. A first it was just loud enough to hear inside the habitat. Then the volume built and built until it shook the very walls around them. Gimenez stood as if rooted to the spot, his eyes wide with fear.

"Out! *Out*!" Navarro ordered, his voice barely audible above the increasing roar. He yanked the man through the hatchway. Then he stepped through and took a final look back.

Now it was Navarro's turn to stare, transfixed by what he saw.

The sheer size of the half-shredded *Acheron* blotted out the upper half of the ocean as it descended. Bubbles of air and fuel oil streamed from gashes in the hull and superstructure as if the ship were boiling from within. Loose tangles of cable fell alongside the wreck, looking like something had ripped out the vessel's intestines.

The seven-thousand-ton ship hit just upslope of where Sirenica perched on the seafloor. An ear-splitting *FA-DAM!* rattled through the station. Silt and debris from the impact point rose up in a towering wave that raced towards the window.

Navarro slammed the hatch shut. He and Gimenez spun the wheel a single full revolution just as the shock wave arrived. It hit with the intensity of a locomotive crash combined with the effects of a bursting dam.

Up in Topside, the entire contents of refrigerators and storage cabinets exploded outwards as the walls flexed under the pressure surge. Lights swung violently on their fixtures, bulbs sparking and popping. Scalding-hot brown liquid spattered the wreckage as the coffeemaker's reservoir broke away and rolled freely across the room.

The foot-thick tempered glass in the Dive Monitoring center buckled under the pressure surge. It split down the middle like an iceberg calving off a glacier as the room flooded. Two more windows on B-Deck gave way with *cracks!* like gunshots, admitting the ocean in a knee-high icy torrent.

Gimenez let out a yelp as he was swept off his feet and down the corridor. Navarro grabbed for him and missed. Then he too tumbled into the rising current. The stabbing cold took his breath away just as he managed to grasp one of the protruding handrails for the stairway leading down to C-Deck.

One level down, the biology lab's heavy shelving came down like dominoes in a series of *bangs* and *crashes*. Austen grabbed Kirov around the waist. She pulled the woman along with her under the huge lab table that had featured in the video sent to Joseph Widerman.

Otto Hanick made it down to D-Deck just in time to watch the last two of his men die. The Dive Master ran down the stairs to the habitat's lowest level. He spotted Ersler and Kurtzmann as they made their way out of the moon pool room. The two men turned and began to push the extra-wide hatch closed.

But they'd run out of time.

The impact of the *Acheron* made the open moon pools erupt like watery volcanoes. The jangle of chains and the crunch of smashed machine tools was drowned out by the thunder of water as it swept away everything before it.

The heavy steel hatch was shoved back by thousands of pounds of pressure. It pulped Ersler between it and the inner wall with a skin-crawling *squelch*. The same pressure flung Kurtzmann across the hallway hard enough to leave a body-shaped dent.

The man landed in a broken heap like a marionette whose strings had been slashed. Hanick took a step towards the fallen diver just as Sawyer grabbed him by one beefy shoulder. She shook her head.

"Too late for him. Get to the internal pressure valves at the far end of the hall! Turn them up to maximum!"

Hanick stared. "If the habitat is compromised–"

"*Now*, Mister Hanick!"

The big man didn't argue any further. He plunged into the rapidly filling D-Deck and half-swam towards the controls. Sawyer made her way back up to C-Deck, where a battered looking Austen and Kirov stumbled out of the biology lab.

A rush of water came from the stairway leading up to the next level, though it quickly petered out. Navarro emerged looking bedraggled and dripping wet. He shook himself like a wet dog trying to get his bearings.

Austen ran up and grabbed hold of Navarro's elbow. She leaned him up against the wall before he could fall. He turned and spat up a bitter mouthful of seawater.

"Are you all right?" she asked. "What happened?"

"Got caught. Flooding on B-Deck." He blinked and straightened up. "What about you?"

"Just a little banged up, that's all."

"Gimenez got swept up by the water," Navarro said, as Austen released him. "But that water...I don't understand. We should be swimming by now. At least two windows gave way up there."

"It's an automatic safety protocol," Sawyer explained.

"Evidently, the leaks on B-Deck were within the station's capability to handle. In the event of a breach, sensors attempt to seal the nearest hatch within fifteen seconds."

"They *attempt* to seal the nearest hatch?"

"If the breach is wide enough, then the hatches simply can't close against the water pressure. The moon pool room's the weakest link. D-Deck was flooding, so I sent Hanick to boost our internal pressure to combat it."

"What about his two men?"

Sawyer's jaw tightened. She simply shook her head.

Kirov limped up to join them, trying to keep her weight off of one foot. "If we're increasing our internal pressure, doesn't that put us at additional risk?"

"It does," Sawyer admitted. "If Sirenica's load-bearing structure is compromised, we could simply fly apart. But that's secondary. We'll drown first if we can't hold the water back!"

Metallic creaks and shotgun-like pops began to echo through the habitat. Austen tried not to cringe, but she felt her eardrums vibrate as the pressure changed. Kirov closed her eyes, while even Navarro and Sawyer looked uncomfortable.

The noises ceased.

Sawyer shook her head and swallowed a couple of times. "Looks like we're stable again, at least for the moment. If we can just—"

"*Wait!*" Austen said. "Everyone, be quiet for a second. I thought I heard something."

The group went silent.

They heard the jumbled, tumbling sounds of the *Acheron's* remains settling, moving in a slow-motion avalanche down the slope of the seabed.

Then a soft, persistent *slithering*.

The sound of something dragging across the seabed.

CHAPTER THIRTY-EIGHT

The unnerving slithering continued from outside the habitat. If anything, it grew in both volume and intensity. It set the hairs on the back of Austen's neck quivering on end.

"Oh my God," she murmured. "What the hell *is* that?"

Finally, Sawyer spoke up. "Our power and communication cables. The ones that connected Sirenica to our dive support vessel."

"I thought we lost them," Navarro said, but his mind went to the loose tangles he'd seen spooling up alongside the descending ship.

"They've lost *functionality*. That doesn't mean they're *severed*." Her head shot up in alarm. "If the *Acheron's* sliding downslope to deeper water and we're still attached…"

The dragging sound stopped for a moment.

Silence. The creak of abused metal somewhere. The drip of water.

Suddenly, the floor was wrenched out from under them. Kirov let out a cry as she fell on her injured foot. The air filled with an irritating *rheeee* of metal on rock, followed by a series of jouncing *bangs*.

"We're being dragged!" Austen cried. "How do we cut the

cables?"

Sawyer scrambled to her feet. "Manual release! Down the hall!"

Navarro followed her. Austen trailed behind, trying her best to stay upright as the floor continued to jump and flex underfoot. Kirov tried to hobble along, but she pulled up painfully as she passed the biology lab's door.

Heart pounding, Navarro slammed into the wall as the station skidded along with another metallic crash. His shoulder twinged, but he managed to stay upright as Sawyer passed a half-dozen rooms. She turned and went through an open hatchway labeled *SWITCHING AND CABLE JUNCTURE*.

The room itself was deep and narrow. Multicolored cable trays took up the bulk of the space from floor to ceiling. Electrical and fire hazard symbols dotted the chamber. As if to emphasize the point, an extinguisher was mounted just inside the hatchway.

The cable juncture in question ran through a pair of housings as thick as a well-built man's bicep. Each housing ran from the ceiling and down to a plate of tar-black rubber set into the habitat's outer hull. Navarro stared at the two cables as they flexed with each jounce of the station.

"I've got the one on the right," Sawyer ordered. "You get the other. Grab the emergency release cutoff! Get ready to turn it when I tell you!"

Navarro had to squeeze his way up to his side of the juncture. A hand-sized valve painted in scarlet projected from the wall just below the rubber plate. Sawyer was doing the same on her side. Austen appeared in the hatchway, ready to jump in.

The *rheeee* of the station's stilts being dragged over and across rock intensified. Navarro heard the rifle crack of another window giving way somewhere on C-Deck. Sirenica hadn't been designed for this level of punishment.

"Count of three!" Sawyer shouted. "*One! Two!*"

The squeal of rending metal blotted out Sawyer's cry of 'three'! High up and to Navarro's left, a crack no bigger than a handspan in length opened up in the outer bulkhead. Water slashed overhead, rebounded off the wall, and hit Navarro like a battering ram.

He fell back from his assigned release valve even as Sawyer turned hers. With one of the two connections severed, Sirenica slewed to one side, flinging off anything that had managed to remain on a shelf until now.

The skidding helped roll Navarro away from the blast of water and back against the cable housing. Salt water stung and blurred his vision. His shoulder made a new twang of pain as he forced it to work again.

Navarro felt his way up the black rubber panel, trying blindly to find the valve. The same skidding motion that pushed Navarro one way had flung Sawyer towards the door. She ignored Austen's outstretched hand and managed to scrabble through the hatchway on her own.

"Nick!" Austen cried. "Get out of there!"

Finally, his hands wrapped around the red valve and turned it. With a final gut-churning *wrench*, the station skidded to a stop. Navarro turned, dragged his hand across his eyes and began pushing his way through the frigid waist-deep water.

To Austen's horror, the automatic safety protocol kicked in as the sensors detected the flooding. The hatch began to close. Navarro wasn't nearly close enough to dive through.

She reached inside and grabbed the fire extinguisher from the wall mount. She turned the cylinder on its side. Then she knelt and jammed it into the hatchway's path.

The closing hatchway pressed against the trigger at the top of the extinguisher, discharging propellant and powder in a weak fizz before the flow of liquid through the gap smothered it. Austen clung to the wall and reached out for Navarro even as the water level continued to rise.

"Are you crazy?" Sawyer demanded, as she got up and spotted what Austen had done. "You'll flood the rest of the station!"

Her words were ignored. Sawyer grabbed her by the arm and tried to pull her away. Austen shook her off. The water began to rush through the door even more violently, swirling into the hall and filling the corridor.

Sawyer moved to one side. Her eyes narrowed as she brought an arm up and wrapped it around Austen's neck. The epidemiologist fought her, but Sawyer was simply stronger. She wrestled her opponent away from the door.

"You're going to kill us all!" Sawyer snarled. "We've got to close that damned hatch!"

"Let me go, you *bitch*!" Austen hissed back.

She planted her feet, finding just enough purchase on the slippery floor, to shove back with all her might. Sawyer let out an *uff!* as Austen slammed her back against the opposite side of the hallway. But the Station Chief hadn't lost her grip. She began to tighten her hold on Austen's trachea.

Suddenly, she paused as she felt the sharp press of a syringe against her own neck.

"Unless you want fifty cc's of formaldehyde in your carotid artery," Kirov's voice whispered in her ear, "then you better let Austen go."

Sawyer released her grip. Austen slipped free and made her way, coughing, back to the door. She stuck her arm through the now shoulder-high gush of water.

Navarro's face appeared. He wriggled his way through, all but pushed through the gap like a cork lodged in a champagne bottle. The water surged through one more time before the empty extinguisher collapsed with a *crunch*. The hatch shut and a gurgling sound echoed through the hallway as the cable junction room filled up.

Austen and Kirov simply glared at Sawyer. For her part, the Station Chief brushed off the murderous looks. She got up and pointed to where Navarro lay shivering in the ankle-deep water.

"He'll go into hypothermic shock unless he gets into a dry outfit," she said flatly. "Come on, I know where there's some spares down here. I'm sure we could all stand a change into something less than sopping wet."

CHAPTER THIRTY-NINE

Sirenica Research Station
Depth: 106 Meters

An hour later, a less-than-sopping wet Navarro opened the door to Sirenica's Pressure Equalization Chamber with a *clank*. Neely Madrigal stepped out, one arm wrapped in a makeshift splint and shoulder sling. Her other arm was raised so that she could rub one ear.

"Welcome home," Navarro said, in a wry but relieved voice. "We weren't sure that you made it."

"By hook and by crook, we did," Madrigal replied. "But something's making my eardrums hurt."

"The pressure chamber's damaged. And believe me, that's not the only thing around here that's taken a beating."

Madrigal stretched her arm out and forced a yawn to help pop her eardrums. She gaped at the battered walls, barely-there emergency lighting, and inch-deep seawater that sloshed across the floor.

"It figures," she said. "I leave for a few hours, and...just look at this place!"

"What happened to your arm?"

"When the *Acheron* went belly-up, we got tossed around like clothes in a washer. The sub's barely in one piece. Worse, the steering column whacked me in the wrist and jimmied it up. Hurts like the devil's own, but your man helped patch me up."

With that, Redhawk stepped out next to Madrigal, briefcase in hand. He sported a blossoming shiner in one eye socket, but otherwise looked unhurt. The two Motte & Bailey men clasped hands warmly in greeting.

"Thank God you made it," Navarro said. "I wasn't looking forward to losing you."

"That makes two of us." Redhawk let out a snort as he squinted at his friend. "Safest place below the waves, my ass."

"What happened?" Madrigal asked. "Is my...I mean, is Doctor Gimenez all right?"

"He's injured, but in stable condition." Navarro gestured to them. "Come along, I'll tell you on the way up to Topside."

"Topside's still habitable? Will miracles never cease?"

Navarro led them down the curved corridor. They had to weave around heaps of smashed floor grates and duck under broken ceiling lamp fixtures as they did so. The stairways to the upper levels were in similar shape. He made sure they avoided where the stainless steel grates had been bent or washed completely away.

"We're getting intermittent communication with the surface," he continued. "As best we can piece it together, Orcus sent an infiltration team over to the *Indomito* just as you two were leaving the *Acheron*."

"What happened then?"

"October spotted the deception and the crewmen on the destroyer managed to take out the bad guys in a firefight. But their Hail Mary plan got past them – a self-guided boat loaded with explosives. Whatever they used, it opened up the *Acheron's* side from front to stern."

"Practically blew our eardrums out too," Redhawk grumbled, before doing a double-take. "That shootout on the *Indomito* – did our favorite Russian make it out all right?"

"He says he's fine. With October, anything below a sucking

chest wound is 'fine', but I'll take what I can get."

"What about down here?" Madrigal pressed. "Damage, casualties?"

Navarro's expression turned grim. "The last two members of Hanick's dive team were in the moon pool room when the *Acheron* hit the sea floor. They're gone. Doctor Kirov's ankle is in pretty bad shape. Your husband broke his leg when he was swept away by the flood on B-Deck. Everyone else has a nice collection of bumps and bruises. Oh, and I almost drowned a couple of times. I suppose I'm getting used to it by now."

Redhawk threw his friend a look, trying to figure out if he was being serious.

"Sirenica took one hell of a pounding," Navarro said. "There's damage across all levels. We've lost the biology lab, cable juncture room, multiple cabins on B and C decks, the dive monitoring center, and easy access to the moon pool room."

Madrigal let out a low whistle as they turned a corner on B-Deck. "I'm amazed the whole place didn't just fill up top to bottom."

"It might have, if Sawyer hadn't turned the internal pressure up to maximum. We risk bursting at the seams, but it's helped us force the water out."

"What about our air and power supply?"

"We're on battery power for right now, so we can charge and launch ROVs. Lights and thermostat are on line. So are most of the carbon dioxide scrubbers. Diamante was running some numbers on how long the air's going to last when I came down to get you."

"That's promising. I hope."

Navarro paused halfway up the last flight of stairs to Topside. He indicated a small alcove set off to one side. A dinged-up monitor, computer desk, and a couple cases of emergency electronic equipment sat in the little nook. The sound of people talking echoed from just above.

"John, I'll introduce you to everyone in a bit," Navarro promised. "But right now, I need your expertise to get the station's ROVs working again. If Orcus comes back right now, they could sucker-punch us while we're down."

Redhawk took the seat, put his briefcase on the desk, and opened it up. He slid out a little cache of parts and a separate laptop. He tapped a few keys on it and rummaged in one of open cases.

"You're in luck, these are similar to what I use for my drones," he said, as he hefted one of the pocket-sized controller units kept in Jordan's stash. "Give me ten minutes and I can get these working. Another ten, and I can set your ROVs to automatically orbit the place. Or automatically orbit anything approaching or leaving the station."

"You're a miracle worker," Navarro acknowledged, and he left Redhawk to begin his task.

He and Madrigal went up the last few steps into what was left of Topside. Most of Sirenica's bedraggled survivors huddled around the one remaining unbroken table. The rest of the room looked as if a bomb had hit it.

Shattered dishes, burst packaging, and spilled food turned sodden from the heavy moisture in the air covered most of the floor. Pathways had been swept or pushed through the rubble. The stench of burnt coffee overlaid the smells of hot metal and stagnant seawater.

The microwave and induction units had either been smashed or burnt out, so hot meals were out of the question. People had made do with cold tap water and anything in a still-intact foil packet. Energy bars, cookies, and snack foods were the only items in plentiful supply.

Madrigal cried out as she spotted her husband. She dashed over to where he lay sprawled on a water-damaged couch, his splinted leg held out ramrod straight.

"God, God! What happened to you, husband-man?" she asked him, as she showered his forehead with kisses, keeping her injured arm up and out of the way.

"Got caught in a flood and landed the wrong way up," Gimenez replied, as he awkwardly embraced her. "Austen brought a medical kit from sickbay, patched me up."

Kirov sat nearby, her ankle bandaged and propped up on a handy chair. She wrapped her arms around herself as if cold. Her expression was troubled.

Hanick and Diamante were busy writing on scraps of paper, discussing figures. Hanick's ever-present jacket didn't seem to be keeping the big man warm. As for Diamante, the nobleman's mustache had been turned into a drooping mess, but he looked unhurt otherwise.

Austen came up and offered him a cup of rooibos tea, which he took.

"Lukewarm is as good as it gets for now," she said, as he took a sip.

"Thanks," he replied, in a tone warmer than anything in the cup. "Where's Sawyer?"

"Down at the spare transmitter on B-Deck. She's still trying to improve the connection." Austen's face had a sour expression as she spoke about the woman. "I guess you've got to give her credit for persistence."

"Her butt's on the line as much as anyone else's," Navarro reasoned, as he tossed the rest of the cup back. "Redhawk's here, I put him to work on the ROV system. He seems happy that he got off the *Acheron* just in time."

"I'm not surprised. He's a smart man."

Diamante stepped up onto a small crate. He cleared his throat loudly. Everyone in the room quieted down and looked over to him.

"All right, I have some announcements," he finally said. "Since they relate to how long we get to breathe down here, you might want to pay attention."

Michael Angel

CHAPTER FORTY

"I've got some good news," Diamante announced. "At current *proiezioni*, we have around fifty hours of air left. If we wait patiently, we shall be rescued in good time."

"Why do we have to wait?" Gimenez asked, in a voice laced with pain. "We can take my wife's submarine to the surface. There may be enough of our escape pods still in working condition on B and C decks."

Madrigal scowled. "I'm afraid Diamante's right. Without the *Acheron*, there's no pressurization chamber. We'd be trapped in the sub or a pod at the surface until we ran out of oxygen. Or we'd experience explosive decompression when opening the hatch."

"But what about the chamber we have here, on D-Deck?"

"It's in a bad way," Navarro said. "Your wife came out with an earache."

"That serious," Austen put in. "A defect in compressing someone to high pressure is bad enough. But the reverse – decompressing from high to low pressure – is guaranteed to cause the bends. Probably even a debilitating stroke."

Navarro nodded grimly. "Even worse, the decompression process drains a *lot* of power from the batteries."

"So, we wait," Diamante said. "The *Acheron* has been lost with all hands. The *Indomito* remains above, and we are doing our best to keep the channel open to it. Sawyer is trying to find out how long it will take to bring in a new dive support ship."

"And what if we can't wait?" Gimenez said. "If one more support beam goes out on this tin can, then we're done for."

"We are not done for," Hanick insisted, with a shake of his head. "In fact, we do not have to wait. We have enough scuba gear and extra tanks for everyone. We ascend from depth, *stück für stück*. We go up in stages. By the time we reach the surface, we are fully decompressed."

"That's an extremely risky thing for inexperienced divers to attempt," Navarro warned. "At one hundred meters down, we're already at the limits of what scuba gear can–"

"Which is why my orders stand!" Diamante thundered. "You shall all *stay put* until further notice!"

A heavy silence hung over the room.

It was broken by quiet laughter.

Sasha Kirov looked up for the first time.

"Your orders? Since when do we need to keep following your orders?"

"You damn well better," Diamante snarled. "You've got a contract, same as everyone else."

"A contract binding us to work here, on Sirenica! And now, this place is trashed. You'll have to rebuild it from scratch. Unless you have a spare billion dollars in your pocket. I know that you're not all *that* rich."

"You...you had better keep quiet!"

"Or what? You'll ruin what's left of my career? That's something I care very little about compared to suffocating down here, or dying of the bends up above!"

"She's right," Madrigal chimed in. "None of us would be down here if it weren't for your threats, forcing us to stay!"

"We haven't even seen our families for more than a year," Gimenez said. "You're a crack-brained slave driver, that's what you are!"

The Count tried to speak and failed. He gathered himself

up again. "You be quiet, or I'll…"

"You'll what? Flush us out one of your airlocks again?"

"That's a truly vile lie! No one has died except for…for…"

"Except for all of my men," Hanick rumbled. "All reliable. Ones I knew for a long time. All used for their pasts by people like you, *schweinehunde*!"

"I don't have to listen to this!" Diamante declared, as he looked around the room. "Especially from the likes of you, any of you!"

He stormed off in a huff. Austen watched him leave, astounded.

"What is going on?" she demanded. "What just happened?"

Again, there was silence. And again, Kirov was the one who broke it.

"I thought you'd figured it out already," she said. "Diamante spent every penny he had, and all of his investor's money, on assets. Subs, ROVs, dive support equipment."

"Not to mention Sirenica itself," Madrigal pointed out, as she made a sweeping gesture with one arm. "All of this here."

"He had almost no money to hire staff," Kirov said. "On top of that, he wanted control. Much more control over his personnel. So he came up with a brilliant solution."

"He found *us*," Hanick said. The man turned and spat into a dark corner.

"Diamante said he didn't have to hear anything…from 'the likes of you'," Navarro said. He blinked, as if finally understanding what had been right in front of him. "You've all got checkered pasts. Criminal pasts, I'm willing to bet."

Kirov's face fell. Hanick grimaced and turned away. Austen watched, wide-eyed as both Gimenez and Madrigal nodded agreement.

Austen turned back to Navarro. "How did you know?"

"I told you, I learned that Reece Jordan was a recovering alcoholic. That didn't make sense. Not for a company that could hire the best people, and do competent background checks. My guess is that her alcoholism led to someone's death."

A snort, this time from Gimenez. "Try *six* deaths. She drank until she blacked out while monitoring a dive for some 'extreme adventure' tour. By comparison, Doctor Lici was the cleanest one down here. She plagiarized a senior researcher's notes and got taken to court, where she also committed perjury. She was only looking at some jail time and a ruined career."

"I did one better than Jordan," Kirov said. "When I was at the National University of Lisbon, I took a bribe. I falsified the cleanup data from a hazardous waste cleanup project. As a result, seven people died from a visit to the site a few months later. They absorbed toxic chemicals through their skin. No one could prove that I was guilty of anything more than incompetence, but I was hustled out the door the very next day."

"That's why Joseph Widerman lost contact with you," Austen said, finally understanding "And no one found out about your bribe…"

Kirov nodded. "Except for Diamante. As I told you: we all have secrets we keep close. Even from those we care about."

"But when you work together long enough, you talk." Gimenez put in. He raised his head defiantly as he went on. "I was part of an eco-terrorist group. We set fire to a logging company's warehouse as a protest. No one knew there were three people inside. They suffocated. I still think we were doing the right thing, even if it was the wrong way."

"My men and I were up to *nicht gut* only," Hanick said bluntly. "We came within a hair of pulling off the greatest underseas heist of all time – stealing a safe right out from the hold of a billionaire's yacht. While it was still in Copenhagen harbor!"

"That explains what Diamante was boasting about," Navarro said. "He claimed that you and your divers were trained in 'extra-special' cold water operations."

"That leaves me as the amateur of the group," Madrigal admitted. "I neglected to fill a man's emergency tank before a big freediving competition. He suffocated on the way back to the surface."

"Did you 'forget'?"

"That's one way of looking at it," Madrigal smiled mirthlessly. "That man was my former husband. I don't regret my lapse of memory one bit."

"Whenever one of us started complaining about the conditions down here," Kirov concluded, "That person would invariably be kept down here, locked away from the world. Or they'd meet with an accident. It could have been chance. But no one *dares* tarnish the reputation of Count Fiorenzo Diamante."

With that, Austen's brain clicked another piece of DiCaprio's message into place.

Diamonds make prisons harder than the strongest jail.

"Diamante is Italian for *diamond*," she whispered to Navarro, who nodded his understanding. "*Sirenica* is the prison DiCaprio was referring to."

"It would also explain the name Sirenica itself," he replied, just as quietly. "Something that lures people in and prevents their escape. Like the Sirens of old."

"This makes me wonder," Austen said to the rest of the group. "What about Dylan Sawyer? She failed the background check for Motte & Bailey. What exactly did they find in there?"

"Did I hear my name?" came Sawyer's voice. The woman entered the room with Diamante at her side. She held a couple sheets of paper in her hand. "Well, someone speak up. Who's whispering what about me now?"

Michael Angel

CHAPTER FORTY-ONE

Navarro stepped in before anyone else could speak.

"We've been swapping stories about our dark pasts," he said, with an offhand shrug. "Sort of 'Truth or Dare' style. It was my turn, so your name came up."

"Uh-huh." Sawyer eyed him carefully. "So I'm a 'dark' part of your past?"

"I'd prefer to call it a 'chocolate' part. Dark, but sweet in its own way."

She stared at him for a moment before throwing her head back in a laugh.

"Oh, that's a good one, Nick!" Sawyer leaned to one side to address Austen. "Well, I hope you enjoy being the 'next in place' part of his past."

Austen gritted her teeth at the jibe. "I'll keep it in mind."

"As it happens, I was able to get in contact with the surface again," Sawyer said to the group as a whole. "There's a new dive support vessel on the way. The *Quintana* has both a working pressurization chamber and a rescue submarine. Best of all, it will be here within the next twelve hours."

"Thank God," Madrigal breathed, as she sank back against the water-damaged couch next to her husband. "For once, a bit of good news."

"Also, I have something Navarro's been waiting for." Sawyer handed the papers in her hand over to him. "Your friend October identified both the man who shot at you with a speargun, as well as the one leading the team which blew up the *Acheron*. They were brothers."

"From the Tarantus crime family," Navarro said, as he skimmed the pages. "That would explain a lot. The whole clan is a 'terrorism for hire' group. No wonder Orcus brought them in."

Sawyer shrugged. "Perhaps they were just trying to put food on the table, like anyone else."

Navarro gave her an odd look. "A lot of people, all over the world, have that same problem. You don't see them killing others over it."

"I must agree," Diamante chimed in. "Those kinds of people are uncivilized, beyond the pale. They were the ones who've come within an ace of killing us. I'm not at all sure when we can even get the habitat repaired."

Austen cleared her throat on that point.

"Before you commit to any timeline, you need to hear what Doctor Kirov and I found out about our not-so-friendly neighbors downstairs."

"The divers and submarines have been attacked by a highly aggressive version of a species known as *Vampyroteuthis infernalis*, or 'vampire squid'," Kirov began, looking more animated again. "My working theory is that they are sustained by the unique ecology of the active undersea vents."

"This ecology is special because it's isolated," Austen added. "That's how this species developed the ability to change the color of the bioluminescence it generates. And here's the kicker: The symbiotic bacteria that help it produce the light is the same one causing the cases of necrosis."

"It's a strain of *Vibrio*," Kirov said, as the group listened raptly. "It's spread via the deep puncture wounds inflicted by the squid – which, because of its signature use of light, I'm proposing *Vampyroteuthis lucidum* as a name."

"Are you saying that we should stop all exploration?" Madrigal asked.

"Ridiculous," Hanick scoffed. "They killed my men. We should kill them, eliminate the threat. We have cases of KXT underwater explosives stored outside this habitat that could do the job."

Austen was so shocked that she asked the first question that came to mind.

"Why the hell do you people have explosives down here in the first place?"

"Seismic sampling," Gimenez said. "Only in small quantities at a time. It's perfectly safe."

"Really?" Navarro raised an eyebrow. "Is that why you have it stored *outside* of Sirenica?"

"Never mind that!" Kirov sputtered. "This is a unique species, in a unique environment! Destroying them is out of the question on ethical grounds alone. But if that doesn't work for you, then there's a concern for humanity as well."

"As if humanity has anything to fear from animals adapted to live more than a thousand feet below the surface!" Diamante scoffed. "How absurd!"

"Not as absurd as you might think," Austen said. "Unlike fish, the creatures that carry this strain of *Vibrio* are restricted by temperature, not pressure. They're kept prisoner by the thermocline layer. There's a thousand feet of cold water sitting on top of them. But if they make it through that layer, then we've got a problem."

"A problem? From a few squid? I think a few dishes of *calamari fritti* would take care of this problem."

Kirov gave the Count a contemptuous look. "For a man who invested a billion dollars in an undersea lab, you're remarkably ignorant about marine life. Each female squid can lay several thousand eggs over its lifetime. Most will be eaten, but a few always survive. And they're *mobile*. Squid can travel hundreds of miles in their lifetime."

"That's where things get really bad," Austen said. "This species has already shown that it's an aggressive predator.

They're not afraid of humans. In a large enough group, they're determined and strong enough to bend metal. Thanks to their choice of bioluminescence, getting so much as a scrape from one is enough to contaminate your bloodstream with flesh-eating bacteria."

Diamante swallowed, hard. He tried to interject. "But–"

Austen ran right over him. "And you know what's the best part? These vampire squid can thrive in water that's eighty-five degrees or warmer. If this species reaches the surface, then it'll be able to colonize any salt water in a tropical or semi-tropical zone. In months, it could overrun the Mediterranean. In a few years, it could spread world-wide. Say goodbye to a day at the beach, say goodbye to scuba diving, and God knows how introducing a new super-predator will affect the world's existing populations of sea life!"

"But they *can't get out!*" Diamante finally managed to say. "That layer keeps them trapped."

"It's an awfully thin layer," Kirov said. "It's possible that the impact of the *Acheron* has already roiled it up. But something acting on that layer more directly could create a plume of warm water that reaches all the way to the surface layers. We're just not prepared for that kind of ecological disruption."

The nobleman looked away briefly. Finally, he spoke in a humbler tone.

"Doctor Kirov, regardless of what you think of me, I do respect your opinions. Do you think our minisubs could cause enough of that kind of disruption when crossing the thermocline layer? Enough to put the world at risk?"

She bit her lip as she considered. "It might. The right disruption at the right time...I don't know. I'd be more concerned with our vehicles unwittingly transporting eggs through the barrier. Some deep water species lay them in sticky strands that could be picked up without our noticing. Those eggs could be tough enough to survive the trip through colder water."

Diamante was silent for a moment.

"All right, it seems like God himself has spoken!" he announced. "I am hereby shutting Sirenica down permanently."

Sawyer looked astonished. "Are you serious?"

"Oh, very much so." Diamante began to pace, gesturing furiously as he vented his thoughts. "I was foolish, too trusting that a show of force like the *Indomito* and her sister ship would keep others at bay. Now, people are dead because of my misjudgment. I shall have that stain on my soul until I die!"

"Conte, surely–"

"No, my mind is made up! My family will already be tarnished by this disaster, this *cataclisma*. I will not have our name forever linked to a plague unleashed upon the waters, and that is final!"

Sawyer slowly walked across the room to stand apart from the group. She came up to her boss with a strange, hard expression on her face.

"What about all the data we've collected?" she asked. "All of the work that has been done to this point?"

"And? What is it to you all of a sudden?"

"You've already found incalculable mineral and energy wealth down by the vent field. It's been mapped out, I've seen it. You just haven't stretched your hand forth to take it."

"Nor will I! The live vent field is too delicate an environment to exploit!"

"Perhaps not. But others will pay for this information. And it's all kept on a single drive. The one that you keep on a chain around your neck."

She looked to Hanick and nodded. In a flash, the big man pulled out a pair of handguns from under his jacket. He tossed one to the Station Chief and pivoted to cover the people gathered around.

"*Hör zu!*" Hanick barked. "I want to see your hands up, all of you!"

"Son of a *bitch*," Navarro cursed under his breath.

Michael Angel

CHAPTER FORTY-TWO

Navarro cursed under his breath as he and the others complied with Hanick's demand as best as they were able. Madrigal could only move the arm not bound up in the sling.

Sawyer ignored them. She moved to within a few feet of Diamante. Then she slowly and deliberately leveled her gun at his head.

"You were right, Conte. You were foolish about too many things. Especially about how firm a hold you had on the people under you." Her voice turned into pure icy grit as she continued. "You were foolish to think that criminals and murderers would remain loyal and obedient…when there were always others who could *outbid* you."

"You're insane," Diamante said defiantly. "If you or Hanick dare pull a trigger, it's the end of us all."

"He's right," Navarro said, from across the room. "A single gunshot down here will puncture the hull. We'll all die in seconds."

The edge of Sawyer's lips curled up at that. "A single gunshot? You mean one like *this*?"

She shifted her stance slightly to the side and pulled the trigger.

The sharp *blam!* echoed inside Topside like a steel drum. Madrigal let out a squeak of fear. Everyone flinched, save for Hanick and Sawyer.

"Deck A has an extra six-inch layer of aluminum to hold up the acrylic window ceiling." Sawyer said, "A nine-millimeter bullet can crack the acrylic, but it won't penetrate the metal."

The nobleman had started to sweat. "How…how did you know…"

"*It's my job to know everything*, remember? That includes every specification on this damned station of yours. Now, hand over the data drive."

Diamante jutted his chin out in a last show of bravado.

"Over my dead body, *puttana!*"

Sawyer's eyes glittered a hard, jade green. "So be it."

A second sharp *blam!* echoed inside Topside.

This time, Kirov let out a scream. Gimenez went pale. Austen recoiled a step in horror.

Count Fiorenzo Diamante swayed on his feet for a moment, a neat hole punched between his eyes. But the neat hole was in front. The back of his head was a bloody, pulpy mess. He collapsed with the wet sound of so much raw meat hitting the floor.

Sawyer bent down, found the data drive on its chain, and yanked it free with a *plink*. She stepped back and looked down at herself. From her face down to her torso, she'd been covered in a fine red spray of Diamante's blood.

She laughed as she wiped some of the iron-hot moisture from her cheek and looked at her fingers.

"Wouldn't you know it," she chuckled. "All this time, that man had me thinking that this would be colored *blue*."

"What about them?" Hanick asked, indicating the others with a toss of his head.

"All we need is a head start. Tie them up, let the rescuers from the *Quintana* release them." Sawyer turned and gestured with her gun towards Navarro. "Start with that one."

Hanick tucked his gun back into his jacket and then took out a plastic zip tie. He stepped around behind Navarro and pulled the man's wrists together.

Navarro stared back at her. "You had me fooled all this time, didn't you?"

"Not all the time. I did care for you, Nick. Probably better than the woman you brought here with you."

Austen scowled at that, but she kept quiet. Out of the corner of her eye, she'd spotted movement. Redhawk slowly crept up the stairs leading up from his alcove.

He reached down and pulled a throwing knife from a hidden leg sheath. He brought it up, ready to throw. The razor-sharp point glinted in the light.

Sawyer spotted the glint.

"Hanick! Behind you!"

Redhawk threw the knife. With a meaty *thunk*, it sank into the back of Hanick's right bicep. The man bellowed, dropping the tie just before he fastened it.

Topside exploded into motion as Sawyer made the room ring with gunfire. Kirov and Austen dove to the floor. Ignoring his splinted leg, Gimenez flung himself over his wife, trying to shield her with his body.

Redhawk cried out as he was hit. The sound of a body tumbling down the stairs added to the general din.

Navarro spun around and grabbed Hanick by the neck in one hand. His other hand went to the inside of the man's jacket and closed around the handgun's grip. His finger found the trigger and squeezed. With a *blam!* the big man's jacket billowed out in a spray of red as the bullet drilled through his torso.

Sawyer stood her ground and shifted her aim towards Navarro. She pulled the trigger twice more as the man turned and dove for cover. The bullets missed, whining off a tabletop, ricocheting dangerously close to the acrylic window above.

Then she turned and fled.

Navarro got to his feet. Instead of chasing Sawyer, he looked over to where Hanick tried to rise again. The man came close, but his strength failed him. He fell to a sitting position against wall, blood pouring from the gaping gunshot wound in his side.

Hanick looked up at Navarro, his eyes glazed with pain.

"Knew you would be trouble," he gasped. "*Geh zum teufel.*"

A rattle came from the big man's throat as he slumped to one side and went still.

Kirov looked to Navarro as she struggled to get back into her chair. "You're not going after Sawyer?"

He shook his head and held up his gun.

"She said that this top deck had a bulletproof aluminum layer. The other parts of the habitat don't. If I go after her and either of us fire our weapons, Sirenica floods."

"Then we better go help Redhawk." Austen pulled out the medical kit she'd brought up from sickbay and headed down the stairs. Navarro turned back to address the others.

"Anyone here know how to handle a handgun? Just in case Sawyer decides to double-back and try her luck again?"

"I do," Madrigal said, and Navarro handed the firearm to her. She hefted it in her one good hand. "I practiced shooting for a while. Before I had the opportunity to forget about my former husband's air tank."

"Something tells me that either way, that man wasn't long for this world," Navarro said, as he hurried downstairs after Austen.

CHAPTER FORTY-THREE

Austen and Navarro found Redhawk lying a half-dozen steps down, just outside his impromptu dive monitoring station. He groaned as Navarro helped turn him on his side for Austen to examine him. A trail of blood glistened from the man's left calf.

"Just a graze," she said, as she dug into the medical kit. "Took some meat with it. Lucky. It could have shattered your shinbone."

"Still got shot," Redhawk grumbled, even as he brought one hand to the top of his head.

Navarro stopped him. "Careful, that's a bad lump you have back there. You might've picked up a concussion when you tumbled down the stairs."

"Doubt it. We Apache are hard-headed to a fault."

"I won't argue the point, my friend."

Redhawk winced as Austen disinfected his wound. He gritted his teeth but made no sound as she bandaged it. She eyed her work skeptically.

"That's the best I can do with what I have here," she said. "You're going to need some stitches for that at a minimum. And no marathon running for a while."

"No worries there," Redhawk assured her. "Hey, help me sit up by my monitors."

Together, she and Navarro moved him as gently as possible into his chair. Redhawk tapped a couple of keys to bring up the views from outside the station. Several of the cameras were damaged, but the main array hung just outside the moon pool room functioned well enough.

The monitor showed the *Lennon* as it emerged from underneath Sirenica's bulk. They caught a glimpse of Sawyer's face as she backed the submarine out of the docking area. Once clear, she spun the minisub on its axis to turn it completely around.

"Look at that," Austen said, as she looked over Redhawk's shoulder. "A rat abandoning the sunken ship."

"Hopefully that's all she's doing," Navarro said. "She has what she wants – that data drive – and now she's on her way to whatever rendezvous she's set up."

"How do you figure that?" Redhawk asked.

"The debris field Austen and I stumbled across down by Site 1725. That was the wreck of a minisub. Miniature submarines have an extremely limited range, so it had to have come from a larger submarine loitering outside the destroyers' sonar detection range."

Austen frowned. "You think Sawyer was working with Orcus from the beginning?"

"Sawyer, the Dive Master, and his entire dive team. In fact, I'd put money on it. All the scientists here were analyzing data. Hanick and his divers were the only ones actually *collecting* it."

Navarro watched as the Sawyer did her best to guide the *Lennon* along a straight course. The submarine had been battered by the sudden sinking of the *Acheron*. Two of the propellers were either damaged or had bent blades, making the craft move in a crablike fashion.

"She's lucky the way things ended up, then." Austen observed. "She won't have to share the reward with Hanick or any of his men."

"I doubt that it was all luck. Running into the squid was

unexpected, yes. But how did the Tarantus brothers know exactly when Wolfe and Ossberg were heading out to Site 1725?"

"You're right. Someone passed on the location of Hanick's last dive team to the Tarantus brothers with the intention of killing them." Austen considered. "Unless it was Hanick himself, maybe? No honor among thieves and all that."

Navarro shook his head. "No, I'd bet it was her because—"

"Hey now," Redhawk interrupted, as he tapped a key to shift the angle of one camera. "Look at that. What's she up to now?"

The *Lennon* pulled up to the seaweed-fringed mound of piled cases that Navarro had seen during the descent to Sirenica. Sawyer brought the minisub to a stop and switched from the submarine's steering mechanism to the glove-like servo controls. She awkwardly managed to get the manipulator arms to grasp a stack of four boxes the size and shape of a dinner tray. Each box bore multiple hazard symbols and a trio of bright yellow letters: *KXT*.

"That's the explosives cache Hanick was referring to," Austen breathed. "She isn't planning to blow up Sirenica, is she?"

Sawyer shifted back to the driver's seat and started the propellers up again. The *Lennon* moved in its strange crabbing motion past the station and further down towards the deeps.

"Hell and damnation," Navarro cursed. He stepped back to call up towards Topside. "Madrigal! Sawyer's gone, she's taken the *Lennon*. I need some information, fast!"

"Sure thing," Madrigal said, after a moment. Still cradling her wounded arm, she came down the stairs as quickly as she could. "What do you need, Bad John?"

"That sub of yours, how badly damaged was it? Could we catch up to it in dive gear?"

Madrigal thought for a moment. "It's hard to keep her on the straight and narrow, but she could still make speed."

"Damn! That tears it, then."

"Maybe not. The engine's working, but the battery's low.

She'll see that very soon, if she hasn't already. That means she'll have to stop at Base Camp for at least thirty minutes to recharge."

Navarro pounded a fist on the desk in excitement. "Then that's how I can stop her. A deep dive to Base Camp takes that long to reach that habitat. The *Ringo* is still down there too, and it's still two-thirds charged."

"Hold on," Redhawk objected. "What makes you think she'll stop there to recharge?"

"Sawyer doesn't know where her pickup point will be, not exactly. She'll need power to run a search pattern while she transmits into the dark, hoping to get their attention."

"You seem very sure that she doesn't know where her people are," Madrigal said. "Why?"

"Because she took a half-dozen cases of KXT with her," Navarro said. "Sawyer heard what we said about the chaos those squid could cause if they reached the surface. She's going to trigger that chaos by de-stabilizing the thermocline layer. That should give her and her friends plenty of time to escape and cover their tracks."

"If there's a full charged sub down at this 'Base Camp'," Redhawk reasoned, "couldn't she just switch to that one instead?"

Austen gave him a look. "You didn't see the condition of the *Ringo*. There's a crack in its windshield dome that could give way in deeper water."

"That's still my best option," Navarro insisted. "Assuming that the moon pool didn't collapse in on itself like the other two, I'm willing to risk it."

"You're crazy, but that's why I like you," Madrigal said, with a shake of her head. "All right, you need to listen up about that KXT. It's the safest underwater explosive out there, so it won't go off if dropped or smashed. There's a simple settings dial on the front that controls when it will go *boom*.

"You move the dial a quarter-turn to the right and a tiny LED screen comes on. The LED screen is where you custom-set the time to detonation. You can disarm the box by turning the dial back to the left. But a *second* quarter-turn to the right means there's no going back. You're getting an explosion in sixty seconds whether you like it or not, so you best clear out."

"Right," Navarro said. "And speaking of clearing out, that's what I'm going to do."

"Hold up," Redhawk said. He grabbed one of the pocket-sized controller units and pressed it into his friend's hand. "I've managed to link this into one of the remaining ROVs. Even if you don't input any commands, it will automatically orbit within fifty yards of the controller. Take it, you might be able to use it to scout for Sawyer."

"Thank you," Navarro said simply.

Redhawk clasped his friend's free hand in his own for a moment. "Sorry I can't come. As my elders would say, 'May lightning strike where you need it.'"

"Best of luck," Madrigal added, with a smile. "You are the *baddest* of the Bad Johns."

Navarro nodded and turned to Austen. She simply crossed her arms.

"Don't say goodbye to me," she said. "I'm coming with you."

"And here I thought Sawyer was the crazy one," Navarro muttered, as he started down the stairs with Austen at his side. "Are you sure about this?"

"Only makes sense," she shot back. "You drive, I handle the sub's manipulator arms to grab or disarm the explosives. Besides, I've got two more reasons for going along when you do risky things like this."

"What's that?"

"First, it's what DiCaprio says needs to happen. *Do not breach the prison of Hades*, remember?"

"I remember DiCaprio saying it," Navarro said, as they came to the bottom of the stairs and headed towards the next flight down. "Still don't know what it means."

"Hades is the Greek underworld. It's also what Kirov called the place where those squid live – the *hadal* zone. DiCaprio's warning us that the thermocline layer had better not be disturbed."

"Okay, I'll go with it. What's the second reason for your coming along?"

She chuckled. "I'm still a slow learner."

Together, they turned the corner and headed down towards D-Deck at a jog.

CHAPTER FORTY-FOUR

Approach to Base Camp Secondary Habitat
Depth: ~280 Meters

Austen and Navarro made their way along the downward slope of the seabed. Even while wrapped in the solidity of her dive suit, Austen had to make an effort to ignore the metallic spoon taste in her mouth. She kicked her swim fins more rapidly in an effort to keep up with her companion.

"Is it my imagination," Austen began, "Or does the water look *thicker* somehow?"

"You're not imagining things," Navarro answered. "The water's more turbid. Silt's been kicked up from the bottom and it's still settling. Look up ahead and off to the left."

She turned her head to see. Her suit lights didn't penetrate the murky water all that well. However, the ROV that Redhawk had sent along with them had lamps that pierced the gloom better. Navarro had the controller for the drone stashed in a watertight pocket under his dive suit, but the drone faithfully kept to is automated program and orbited fifty yards overhead.

On its next sweep, she spotted the wreckage of the *Acheron* in the distance. The vessel had folded in on itself like a half-closed jackknife as it had slid downslope. Even now, the wreck towered over the rest of the undersea terrain, a nest of jagged metal dotted by the escaping bubbles of fuel oil.

"The Tarantus family doesn't play around," Austen observed. "Which brings me to another question, Nick. Why were you so sure that Sawyer set Hanick's dive team up to be murdered by the crew in the second minisub? It could've been Hanick himself getting rid of people who'd want a share of the payout at the end."

"I'm sure because of what October sent down to me. I'd asked him to search the INTERPOL database to identify the face of the man who attacked us with the speargun. That man was Tomaz Tarantus, and his brother Sebastian sank the *Acheron*. The two brothers have a very distinctive look. Blond hair and light green eyes for starters. Any idea who matches that description on Sirenica?"

Austen thought a moment. "Sawyer's the only one."

"That's part of what was bothering me, ever since we got back from our expedition. She's got very similar bone structure in the face, especially around the nose and jawline."

"Perhaps she's a sister to Tomaz and Sebastian."

"Maybe. She could also be a niece or cousin. Her Tarantus family connection might be the red flag that forced Motte & Bailey to pass on hiring her."

Austen's breath caught for a moment.

"I thought I just saw a flash of light."

"Let's slow down a bit, then." Navarro slackened the pace and Austen caught up to him. "I don't want us to run into Sawyer yet. If we don't have a sub of our own, we're going to be at a real disadvantage."

A second flash came from up ahead. Navarro crept up to the next set of boulders and risked a look downslope. He spotted the dimly lit, damaged Base Camp on the next rise over. The oblong silhouette of the *Lennon* came into view as Sawyer brought the sub out from under the structure.

Navarro held his breath and prayed that she wouldn't spot

the ROV whirring about in its overhead orbit. The vehicle was only as big as a large dog, but it still had its lights on. But Sawyer seemed focused on her own destination. She turned her submarine downslope and headed out as best as her bent propeller blades could take her.

"Looks like it's our turn," Navarro said, as he kicked his way forward.

Austen followed him down, though her apprehension grew as they got closer to Base Camp. The structure had been badly bent out of shape, but it still teetered on its stilt like legs. Bubbles of oxygen made effervescent little trails from the crumpled middle sections.

Still, the habitat cast two rectangles of light on the seafloor below. One rectangle was empty, recently vacated by the *Lennon*. The other was shaded by the shape of a minisub. The hull was scraped and battered all along its length. One of the four propeller housings was little more than a crushed stub thanks to the prior efforts of the vampire squid.

Still, it was a welcome sight.

"Thank God," Austen breathed. "Looks like the *Ringo* made it through okay."

The two surfaced, clambering out of the moon pool where the last of Sirenica's intact submarines bobbed in place. The head of the spear fired at them by Tomaz Tarantus still jutted from the cracked windshield dome. They quickly shucked their dive gear and carried it inside the minisub's main compartment.

Austen pulled a little sheet of notes from a jumpsuit pocket and reviewed them before moving to the passenger seat. Navarro closed the hatch with a *clank*. Slipping into the driver's side seat, he took out the pocket controller. Redhawk had placed a tiny adhesive strip on the gadget's bottom side, so he set it firmly on the console within easy reach.

The propellers spooled up with a familiar hum as Navarro submerged the minisub. The ROV, which had been circling aimlessly as they'd gone inside, happily slipped into a new orbit around the *Ringo*. It tagged along like a faithful hound as the minisub headed for deeper water.

The two submersibles continued down to four-hundred meters. The thermocline layer appeared, looking as ghostly as ever, in their reduced lamps. Austen found herself holding her breath. She berated herself silently and repeated her personal anxiety-busting mantra to herself.

God grant me the courage to handle the things I can. And to not push my luck on the things that I can't do a damned thing about.

"We're going through, aren't we?" she asked aloud.

"Don't see any way but forward. Not if DiCaprio's correct."

"In that case, I'm going to minimize our lights." Austen flipped a couple of switches on her dashboard and then pointed to the ROV circling overhead. "Might be a good idea to do the same for our companion there."

"Good idea. Don't want to attract any unwelcome attention." Navarro leaned forward to reach for the controller and found a dial on the side. In a few moments the ROV's lamp dulled to the orange glow of a bedroom night light.

The thermocline layer seemed to reach up and engulf them. They sank through the thin mist-like layer and came out into the clear water below. Almost at once, a dull warmth began to radiate into the submarine.

They descended down below four hundred and fifty meters.

Just up ahead, the steep slope turned into a sheer drop-off. The orange of the ROV's lights was overlaid by a hellish glow. Below, the sub-oceanic vent field glimmered, dim red against the shiny black of the lava surface. A sudden belch of *vapor* rippled along a chain the vents that gushed noxious off-white fumes.

The Palinuro field was restless today.

Navarro piloted them carefully along the edge of the drop-off. Austen leaned out as far as she could towards the acrylic windshield to scan the seafloor around them. She forced herself to stop looking at the spearhead embedded in the very apex of the dome. Her eyes would start playing tricks on her.

Are the cracks in the dome getting bigger? They look like...no, it can't be! Are there more cracks now? How much longer is this dome going to hold together under thousands of pounds of pressure?

"I'm not seeing anything," she finally said. "Unless she buried the KXT boxes in the ooze covering the seabed?"

"I don't think she'd take the time to do that. Plus, it would take a couple of hours for the sediment to settle out again. We'd easily be able to find where she tried to bury the explosives."

"Then I'm at a loss."

Austen sat back in her chair and let out a frustrated growl. She wiped away the sweat that had suddenly beaded at her brow. The outside water topped out at more than a hundred degrees, and the inside of the sub was turning into a sauna.

Quit it with the dead-end thinking, her brain nagged her. *If you're out of ideas, what about Nick? He's had a lot more experience blowing up stuff than you ever had!*

"Wait," she said, turned to Navarro. "Where would *you* place those charges?"

Navarro considered. "If I was in Sawyer's place, then I'd know that it's almost impossible to trigger an eruption with anything less than a nuclear bomb. Instead, I'd try to massively disrupt the thermocline layer above."

"That would maximize the chance of getting live vampire squid to the surface," Austen agreed, "or at least close enough to survive the temperature change."

"Hydrothermal vents are like hot springs. Water percolates down through the crust. It gets heated by magma and comes shooting back up. So if I wanted to create a big enough 'pop', I'd try to block the flow. The pressure from the trapped superheated water would eventually force its way past the blockage and send a plume of hot water up towards the surface."

"Then how would you block that flow?"

"There!" Navarro pointed ahead and off to the left. "That's where I would go."

He revved the sub's motors as he kept them close to the

drop-off zone. The submarine sped towards a series of impossibly steep-sided hills at the edge of Site 1725. The hills resolved into a forest of chimney-like structures. The long-dead vents from when the Palinuro field had been much younger.

Navarro brought them closer, much closer than before. Austen suppressed a shiver. The vents were narrow, fluted deposits of calcified rock the height of a five-story building. Each vent was as thick around as a suburban home at its base, but they diminished to less than a meter wide at the very tips. Chunks of rubble strewn around each vent showed just how delicate the hollow stone columns really were.

"I'd place explosives here," he said confidently. "Right where the Pinnacles meet the drop-off zone down to the Palinuro. Knock over a couple of these rock columns like dominoes, and you'd send thousands of tons of debris avalanching down into the heart of the vent field."

"You'd block the flow of the superheated water," Austen said, understanding. "Which would build up into a gigantic pressure wave. More than enough to breach the prison of Hades."

"That's what DiCaprio would say. Was that the last bit of his message?"

"Not quite. DiCaprio gave us one final line," Austen said, before sitting bolt upright in her seat. "Wait a minute! Look over there, at the base of the pinnacle to the side!"

Navarro squinted. "Yeah, I see it. Get the manipulator arms ready. I'm going to bring us into spitting range."

CHAPTER FORTY-FIVE

Survey Site 1725
Palinuro Pinnacles
Depth: ~550 Meters

Navarro gently nudged their craft into position. The very bottom of the pinnacles were masses of ropy, corpse-white rock. They reminded him of the tangled roots of an old and storm-blasted tree.

Nestled in among the stony roots lay a black box in the shape of a dinner tray. The top side sported a dial, an LED counter, and the letters KXT. Austen slipped her hands into the glove-like servo controls and the robotic arms came into view at the five and seven o'clock positions.

She reached out with the left arm and snatched up the box with the claw appendage at the end. Then she brought the package in closer to the acrylic window. The LED screen glowed faintly, allowing her to make out the numbers as they counted down to detonation.

"Ten minutes and change." Navarro read aloud. "You've got this, Leigh."

Austen brought the right arm around. She moved the

robotic pincers up to the raised part of the dial and closed them together. She blew out a breath as she did so.

"Quarter turn to the left," she said, as if to herself.

The pincers slipped off the dial just as she rotated them. She tried again, with the same result. A third time, and the pincers slipped off again.

Navarro said nothing, but she could feel his watchfulness and concern.

There wasn't anything in the job description about defusing explosives eighteen hundred feet below the surface, she thought angrily. *Sawyer was able to turn this dial, so I should be able to turn it back the same way. What's the trick?*

Then it came to her.

The pincers were slipping off as she *gripped* the slick plastic of the dial. So she brought the ends of the robotic claw as close as possible to the dial's surface, but without squeezing it. Then she spun the pincer unit as if loosening a stuck screw.

The LED screen went blessedly blank as the dial flipped a quarter turn to the left with a *CLICK* that was audible inside the submarine.

Austen sagged in her seat for a moment. "Oh, thank God."

"No rest for the weary," Navarro reminded her. "I see explosive number two at the base of the next dead vent. It's fallen into some kind of nook."

"Let's get on it, then."

She lowered the box of KXT and slipped it onto the storage rack between the skids below the hull. Navarro goosed the propellers, giving them a small burst of speed to cross the gap between the silent vents. He moved them in to hover before the second box.

Austen shook her head. "Closer. These arms can't quite reach."

"Okay. I have to be careful with that dome of ours." Navarro bent to the task, edging the submarine in towards the slope of the vent.

"Got it!" Austen reached into the narrow depression between two ropes of igneous rock and closed the pincers on it. She pulled it out, noted the LED counting down from nine minutes, and then carefully turned the dial to the left with a CLICK. "That's two."

Navarro backed off and began to circle around the bases of the nearby vent formations. He saw nothing but dark water and the bare, tumbled fields of calcified deposits. An itch of impatience began building up inside until he had to say something.

"We're down to seven minutes or less," he complained. "Assuming that we picked up the first two charges Sawyer set. We need to risk some real light if we're going to be able to locate the last two."

"I agree," Austen said, as she dialed up the xenon lamps on the *Ringo* to half power. "Let's turn the lights on the ROV so that it's brighter, though. If anything gets noticed, I'd prefer that we're not the center of attention."

Once again, Navarro leaned forward and adjusted the dial on the ROV's remote controller. The smaller vehicle went from nightlight orange to sunlamp yellow in a few seconds. From its position above the trunks of the stone forest, the ROV cast its brightness down below like a searchlight across a prison yard.

Jagged shadows swung across Austen's field of vision as the light above went through its orbit. A black glint caught her eye, then vanished. It came back on the ROV's next pass.

"The third box of KXT!" she exclaimed. "I see it!"

"Right. Direct me."

She peered ahead as if her gaze could cut through the dark water. The light dimmed, brightened, then dimmed again.

"Twenty yards ahead, at one o' clock," she said. "What's wrong with the ROV's light? Is it running out of juice?"

"Not quite," Navarro said, in a strangely breathless voice. Austen followed his gaze up through the acrylic dome. "It looks like we've got company."

A dark cloud hovered over the little submersible.

Within the shifting outlines of the cloud came the ominous glimmer of starlight. Tentacled shapes revealed themselves at the edge of the light before darting back into the gloom.

Austen jerked back from the windshield as a flight of the vampire squid cruised by within easy sight. The moved like a squadron of fighter jets as they came back and buzzed them a second time.

"I'm turning our lights down," she said hurriedly. "You might do the same thing before our friends smash the ROV to pieces."

"Don't turn things down too far," Navarro cautioned. "Won't do us any good if I run into one of these vent columns. And as for the ROV, I've got an idea."

His hand went to the little nub of a joystick. He moved the ROV far off to one side and then put it into a new, widely elliptical path. Most of the squid followed, but many remained hovering above, their eyes watching the *Ringo's* progress.

"That's amazing," Austen said, taking one final look before Navarro brought them up to the third box. "Not all of them are following your lure. It's like they're more curious as to what we're up to."

"Or they're just being wary, figuring out the best time to strike," Navarro said, while Austen stretched out the manipulator arms. "These are intelligent animals. Predators normally are."

The box of KXT slipped into one of the sub's claw like hands. The LED crossed the five-minute mark as Austen brought the second set of pincers up to the dial. Her first attempt to move the dial back slipped through her robotic fingers.

"Hold us steady," she gritted. "Getting slim on time here."

"Trying," Navarro adjusted the sub's hover, even as he kept an eye on the ROV above.

The ROV had moved off to one side, but the local cephalopods were faster. The little probe moved like a World War One biplane, while the squid shot by like shiny black stealth aircraft. Finally, an entire group latched onto the little submersible.

They swarmed the ROV, wrapping their arms about it,

trying to wrestle it down. Tentacles wrapped around one propeller housing, wrenching it off.

Navarro canceled his inputs to the controller and turned the lights to minimum. The squid let go immediately. Now free of interference, the ROV motored back towards the *Ringo* to resume its orbit.

However, the damage had been done. Its course was ragged and erratic, as if a drunk steered it. The starfield of squid eyes remained just above, though colors now flashed through the mass like technicolored lightning.

Finally, a *CLICK* echoed through the sub's interior.

"That's done!" Austen announced. "Three down, one to go. What are our mollusk friends up to?"

"If I had to guess, we've got them confused. Let's hope they stay that way a little longer."

He powered up the engines again and began searching among the thickets of volcanic columns. They circled around one house-sized vent, then another. And another. Sweat dripped from both Navarro and Austen's foreheads now as the sub's interior continued to heat up.

Chillingly, the starfield of eyes followed them, staying for the most part out of the path of the ROV or the *Ringo*. Yet a few of the school continued to harass them, shooting towards their acrylic dome before turning away at the last second.

"We're running out of time here," Navarro said, his voice tense. "This is like searching a coal mine with a pocket flashlight. If we find anything, we'll damn well have to stumble over it."

Michael Angel

.

CHAPTER FORTY-SIX

Austen continued to watch the movements of the squid outside. Now that they weren't stimulated to aggression by bright light, the meter-long animals seemed more inquisitive than murderous.

They're certainly curious about whoever wanders into their territory, she thought. *They gather around anything new.*

"Over there," she said suddenly. "At that base of the biggest vent."

Navarro headed that way. The steeply sided vent ahead was massive, easily as wide around as the trunk of a Giant Sequoia. He shook his head as he saw a cluster of midnight black bodies and golden eyes blocking their way.

"I don't see anything," he said. "Just a group of our local ten-armed friends."

"Flush them out. If they're gathered there, something new was just added to their environment."

"Worth a shot."

Navarro revved the sub's propellers and shot forward towards the cluster to startle them. The gamble worked. The squid shot off in different directions, revealing a tray-sized box they'd been investigating.

The box's LED screen blipped past three minutes even as Austen reached out with the mechanical arms. In one fluid movement, she nabbed the box with one set of claws.

"About time something went smoothly for us," she remarked, even as she lined up the pincers to grab the dial.

Navarro spotted movement out of the corner of his eye.

He turned to the left to see a mass of gray-green silt boiling up from the seafloor. A cluster of vampire squid fled before it. He made out a blur of yellow and instinctively spun the sub to protect the damaged windshield dome.

Sawyer rammed the *Lennon* full-tilt into the *Ringo's* port side with a *WHAM!* Navarro's sub flipped over twice, propeller housings flailing on their mounts. Inside, anything not tied down or belted in went flying.

Navarro's breath was driven out of him as the arm of his chair dug into his side. His remote control for the ROV ripped loose of its adhesive strip as it was flung from the dashboard. Austen let out a despairing scream as the sub's rotation was transferred to her outstretched pincer.

With a horrifying *CLICK-CLACK*, the dial on the remaining explosive charge flicked one more quarter-turn to the right. Then the box slipped out of Austen's grasp. It tumbled out of sight into the cloud of stirred-up abyssal muck.

"Shit! Shit!" Austen cried, slamming her fists against her control console in frustration. "Either we find that thing in sixty seconds, or we–"

"Little busy right now!" he shot back, as he yanked the control stick back to right the submarine. His eyes scanned the now-murky water, looking for Sawyer's next approach.

The cabin speakers crackled to life as Sawyer's voice echoed in their ears with crystalline clarity.

"Couldn't leave well enough alone, could you?" she asked coldly. "Of course not. Always have to be the star player, Nick."

Navarro spotted the tell-tale churn of approaching propellers to one side. He threw his own sub into reverse. The *Ringo* took a glancing blow on her starboard side. This time, the

WHAM! of the impact came with the *squeal* of rending metal from the outside.

"She took out another of our propeller housings!" Navarro warned.

"But—"

"No choice! We have to get out of here while we can!"

He spun the sub around and cranked the engines to full power. The clear midnight blue of the ocean reappeared as they escaped the cloud of kicked-up muck. Austen craned her neck, doing her best to look behind out the side of the dome.

The yellow shape of the *Lennon* emerged from the cloud not twenty yards astern. It roiled up a vortex of dark water and silt in its wake. Sawyer's voice rang in their ears as she pursued them.

"Thought you could leave me behind, didn't you? You can't run from me, Nick!"

He grimaced. "Sure as hell can *try.*"

Navarro took the minisub deep into the forest-like tangle of undersea vents. He wove among the columns at full speed, barely avoiding the walls of stone. Sawyer followed, pushing her craft to its limits with reckless disregard.

Austen held on for dear life, hands white knuckled as Sawyer bore in again. She struck another glancing blow to their rear deck. The *Ringo* shuddered and threatened to corkscrew. The three collected boxes of KXT were flung off their place on the sub's skids and went sailing off into the darkness among the tangled vent remains.

She's going to batter us to death, Austen thought despairingly. *And that's only if the coming explosion doesn't kill us first!*

She looked up through the topside viewing dome. The starfield of eyes remained overhead, impassively watching the spectacle below. Glints of color coursed through the school of squid. Her mind flashed on the last of DiCaprio's words.

A flicker of starlight may yet save you.

She shook her head in frustration. *How was* that *going to help us now?*

Navarro's face was a sheet of sweat now. He knew that

Sawyer wasn't trying to crack their hull. She was going for their propeller housings. Once those were gone, he and Austen would drift helplessly to the seafloor. If they didn't implode, they're run out of air in a few hours.

As it was, the *Ringo* was down to her last two propellers, making them slower than the *Lennon*.

Maybe I can use the ROV as a distraction, he thought desperately. His hand searched the console and came up with nothing. The earlier impact had knocked the pocket-sized controller into some dark corner of the sub.

Sawyer bore in yet again. Navarro chose to dive this time. The *Ringo* jounced violently downward with a *SKRIIIKK!* as the belly of the *Lennon* turned their topside viewing dome into a smear of scrapes.

"Time left?" Navarro asked, as he fought to keep the sub from plowing into the seafloor.

Austen checked her monitor. She looked to Navarro and shook her head.

"Damn it!" He yanked the controls around to follow the curve of the closest vent. "Going to try and put as much cover between us and the KXT."

A flicker of red danced alongside the edge of the column. The light and the dull wave of heat building inside their cabin spoke eloquently to him. He realized they were getting closer to where the slope dropped off into the active part of the Palinuro.

He pulled up short.

Just ahead, Sawyer's sub appeared from around the curve. She'd gone around the opposite side of the vent in order to cut them off.

"Too slow to get away," Sawyer said, gloating. With one hand, she brought the *Lennon's* manipulator arms up, ready to grab onto the *Ringo* once in range. "You've got to accept the inevitable!"

"You first," Austen shot back.

Sawyer drew close enough for Austen to make out the woman's confused look as she heard those two words. Then her face went pale as she both heard and felt it: a deep, chest-thumping *BOOM* that shook the depths.

The two subs collided just as the KXT's initial blast wave rolled by. Austen and Navarro lurched in their seats with the impact. There was a *crinkle* as Sawyer latched her sub's claw appendage onto one of the *Ringo's* mechanical arms.

The explosion was followed by the massive *CRACK* of an iceberg splitting off from a glacier. The sequoia-sized vent column toppled over in slow motion. Dozens of smaller chimneys were flattened as it came to rest.

"Hang on!" Navarro shouted, as he saw a roiling wall of sediment and debris rolling forward to engulf them.

The impact flipped the two subs end over end. A grotesque sucking, howling sound buffeted Austen's ears. The rush of water, the howl of abused motors, and a single *plink!* as one of the bolts holding her seatbelt gave way.

Navarro let out a pained grunt as part of his console erupted in sparks. The arm of his jumpsuit blackened and smoked. He slapped at it, cursing.

Finally, the turbulence passed. The two subs emerged from the passing wave, one still clinging to the other. The *Ringo* and the *Lennon* circled each other, though Sawyer's sub was able to bulldog the other to one side.

"She going to smack us into the–" Austen began.

"I see it!" Navarro said, as he fought as best he could. The whine of the overloaded engines grew shrill. The hot, iron smell of metal rubbing on metal began to seep into the cabin.

The *Ringo's* side crunched into the steep slope of the nearest vent. Rocks from the destabilized column crumbled and fell around both submarines, bouncing off the hull with loud *clangs*.

Sawyer glared at them through her viewing dome. Slipping into the passenger seat, she grabbed the controls. Leaving one pincer clamped onto the *Ringo's* arm, she brought the other forward to grab the spearhead still embedded in the windshield between Austen and Navarro. With a grinding *crick*, she began to turn it.

Austen brought the sub's free arm up and tried to pull

Sawyer's pincers away. A tingling, grinding noise came from the acrylic as Sawyer began to rotate the sharp piece of metal. Another crack went crazing along the dome's surface.

Navarro reversed the engine again, dragging the *Lennon* along with them. Suddenly, his gaze locked on what he saw through the battle-scarred topside dome. Something out the darkest reaches of a nightmare materialized out of the depths.

"Holy Mother of God," he whispered.

CHAPTER FORTY-SEVEN

An entire galaxy of flame-red and star-yellow eyes came pouring out of the fallen vent column's stump.

Like an angry swarm of hornets whose hive had been destroyed by a firecracker, the vampire squid seethed into a swirling mass. That black-bodied mass blotted out the miniscule form of the ROV and the subs below. Flickers of multicolored light ran through the school in such quantity that they pulled Austen's attention from her struggle with Sawyer.

Finally, something clicked into place in her mind.

She finally understood DiCaprio's final words.

A flicker of starlight may yet save you.

Austen let go of the servo controls. As she did so, Sawyer's grip on the spearhead slipped. With a cry of frustration, the woman pulled her mechanical arm back and then swung it like a barroom brawler. She pounded on the *Ringo's* dome with a series of ear-rattling *thumps.*

"Leigh!" Navarro shouted, as he tore his eyes away from the swarm. "What are you doing?"

"Using a flicker of starlight," she replied, as she ran her hand along her console in one sweeping motion.

The cabin lights, outside emergency lights, and the sub's

high-powered xenon lamps jumped to maximum brightness. Sawyer paused in mid-swing and drew back as she shielded her eyes. That small break was all that Austen needed.

She flicked the switches for the lamp's special lens colors. The xenon lamps flickered from blue, to red, and then to green. Navarro stared at her, uncomprehending.

"Kirov figured out these squid use their bioluminescence for communication," Austen explained, as she continued the pattern. "I took notes on what each color sequence meant. And right now, I'm *signaling for help*."

The mass of squid moved as if they were one organism. Already riled up by the explosion, they darted down towards the submarines like a giant alien hand with multiple sets of fingers. The ROV was buffeted by their passing, but the mollusks ignored the small vessel and swarmed over Sawyer's sub.

The woman let out a panicked yelp as the squid all but blotted out her vessel. The two subs were tossed around even more violently as the *Lennon's* pincers refused to let the *Ringo* loose.

Austen's seatbelt gave way with a second *plink*. She tumbled out of her seat just as she turned off the *Ringo's* lights. She struck her head on the side of her console and didn't get up. Navarro called to her, but he dared not release his grip on the submarine controls.

Nails-on-a-chalkboard screeching blotted out all other sound as the squid indulged in an orgy of destruction against Sawyer's sub alone. Metal joints and muscular plastic fibers on the mechanical arms were nearly bitten through by dozens of parrotlike beaks. With a pop, the *Lennon's* free arm came off at the base.

The sub's propellers became clogged with masses of gelatinous flesh. The rotating blades killed the cephalopods that had been sucked in. But once jammed, they allowed still more to latch on and wrench the housings off at the base.

Thousands of tiny claws stripped every ounce of paint from the hull. In their wrath, the squid even ripped the xenon lights out of the armored sockets. In no time, they turned Sawyer's vehicle into a battered hulk.

Finally, the swarm's fury turned the two submarines loose. They skidded across the seabed, still locked in a death grip by a single set of pincers.

The *Ringo* came to rest upright. The *Lennon* slipped downslope to the very the edge of the drop-off, dragging the attached sub along for the ride. Navarro pulled back on the controls with all his might.

The straining propellers managed to bring the two submersibles to a halt.

"Leigh!" Navarro called. "Leigh, can you hear me?"

Austen let out a pained groan, but she didn't sit up. Navarro looked around. He didn't see a First Aid kit anywhere. Outside, the little ROV continued to circle, though its damaged propellers made it waver from its course in strange elliptical patterns.

On the other submarine, a pair of quivering hands appeared and grasped hold of the console. Navarro frowned as Sawyer sat up groggily. Blood streamed down the side of her face from a cut above one eyebrow. Her nose was swollen and jutted off to one side as if broken.

Their eyes met. When Sawyer spoke, her voice was fragile.

"I underestimated your...pets," she said. "Just like I underestimated you."

"That tends to happen when you try to kill someone," Navarro shot back. "What's your connection with the Tarantus clan, Dylan? What's Orcus paying you?"

"A hell of a lot," she admitted. "I'm one of that clan, Nick. Sawyer was the surname I took as my cover."

"Explains why you dated and then dropped me. You just wanted to infiltrate Motte & Bailey."

"That wasn't all I wanted," she insisted. "But my family...don't you see that this isn't my fault?"

Navarro gave her a skeptical look. Outside, the ROV whirred its way past their two domes, closer than before.

"No," he finally said, "I don't see it that way."

"I didn't know any better! It was how I was raised!"

"My parents were no bargain either. I didn't go down your path."

"Then maybe something's wrong with me," Sawyer admitted. Her eyes brimmed with moisture as she pleaded with him. "Something in my brain, something in my temper that makes me snap at everything. Look, I'm...I'm at your mercy now. I'll tell you everything you want to know."

Still he hesitated. The ROV buzzed past, even closer this time.

"Please," Sawyer's voice dropped to just above a whisper. "Nick, if you ever cared for me at all, help me. I don't want to die!"

Navarro fought the churn of emotions inside. Looking around the cabin, he reached out and grabbed the diving suit.

"All right," he finally said. "I don't know if this will work, but I'll use the airlock to get over to your—"

The ROV swung around in its latest orbit. It struck the juncture of the two minisubs, snapping the mechanical arm still clasped in the *Lennon's* pincers. Released from its anchoring weight, the *Ringo* slewed backwards and upslope.

Sawyer screamed as she felt the sub go into free-fall. Her vehicle's control fins flapped uselessly without any source of propulsion. Navarro watched, horrified, as the woman was backlit by the hellish fire of the vent field.

The speakers inside his sub relayed the wrenching, creaking sounds of the *Lennon's* hull coming apart as the pressure mounted. Finally, there was a *crack*, followed by the *hiss* of boiling-hot water flooding into Sawyer's cabin.

She screamed once more, a mortal cry of fear and agony.

Then, with a final CRUNCH, the sub's structure collapsed in on itself. A gout of air bubbled past the *Ringo* on its way to the surface.

Navarro moved his vessel into a stable hover. He locked the controls and then went to kneel by Austen. She groaned as he checked her over for injuries.

"Come on Leigh," he said quietly. "Don't scare me like

this."

She opened an eye.

"My head hurts. Help me up, would you?" He eased her to a sitting position. She winced as she touched the side of her skull and came away with a smear of blood. "What happened? Is it over?"

"It's over," he said, before casting a glance outside the windshield dome. The mass of lidless eyes still glowered outside. "So long as you know the magic squid word for *friend*."

Michael Angel

CHAPTER FORTY-EIGHT

Orcus Teleconference
Harstaad Island
Dårlig Mann Fjord

Victor Lawrence Wakelin was back to hearing voices in his head again.

This time, it bothered him.

He strode up and down his home's hallways, clad in an ermine-white bathrobe over a pair of bathing shorts. The same miniaturized speaker had been plugged into his ear canal. Once again, he played the Moderator to today's batch of miscreant billionaires. For the umpteenth time, he wondered why he even bothered.

To make matters worse, for the umpteenth-and-one time, his feet were cold.

Wakelin wasn't particularly fond of slippers. Unfortunately, the marble and glass cubist fantasy that made up his home wasn't particularly good at keeping the chill out of the floor slabs. So he listened to the byplay as his toes grew numb.

A Russian woman's voice took center stage at the moment. "*Kakaya katastrofa!* None of us knew that the Tarantus brothers would go…what do Americans say? Flying off hook."

"They also lost Diamante's data," a second voice added. "A major opportunity to add to our assets has been lost forever."

A *sniff*. "Well, those of us who already have interests in the energy markets are safe."

"*Mne fse ravno*," the Russian woman said. "The way it was done…it exposes us to much danger now."

"Don't be absurd!" came another voice, a gruff one. "International law enforcement can't follow a trail of ants back to their nest. I won't lose sleep over it."

Wakelin gently cleared his throat.

"I'm glad that our esteemed colleague from the transportation sector can sleep so soundly," he said. "As your Moderator, I cannot be as sanguine. The involvement of the Tarantus brothers has left a trail of destruction a mile wide. Investigations will be inevitable. Sacrifices on the part of some of our members will be required."

The line went silent as each attendee digested that tidbit of news.

"I'm glad that I finally have your undivided attention," Wakelin said, in a wry tone. "As to the 'sacrifices' needed, I shall be contacting you individually. To put it bluntly, you have all made your beds. Now you must lie in them!"

Wakelin switched off his earpiece. He pulled it out and tossed it onto his desk as he passed by his office. He then pushed through a mist-covered glass door and entered his solarium.

Right now, the room had been made up to look like a Mediterranean retreat with saplings of cypress, bay laurel and Oriental sweetgum. His guest had taken one of a pair of beach chairs set by the main window. The panoramic view from there down the mouth of the fjord was at once relaxing and breathtaking.

His guest wasn't bad looking, either.

The woman reclined in a beach chair, clad in a dress the exact color of lemon chiffon cake. A trail of smoke wafted up from the cigarette she'd just stubbed out in a nearby ashtray.

An empty margarita glass decorated with a wedge of lime sat on a low table next to her.

She sat up and looked at him inquisitively. High-wattage green eyes, gull-winged eyebrows, and hair the color of India ink gave her an intense, feline look.

"*Bonne après-midi*, Victor," she said mildly. "I assume your call went well?"

He let out a snort.

"Helen Lelache, you are the next thing to a mind reader. I think you know very well how it went. The people I play Moderator for have the attention span of a house cat. If you aren't giving them food or scratching them at just the right spot behind the ears, they can't be bothered to learn a damned thing."

Wakelin shrugged off his robe and stretched out in the chair next to her. She said nothing, but merely watched him in silence. Finally, he spoke again.

"All right," he finally said. "How did you know? How did you figure out that our Sirenica project was going to fail from the start?"

"Not from the start," Lelache corrected him. "Only when Leigh Austen and her friends from Motte & Bailey arrived."

"The woman is of no consequence," Wakelin scoffed. "She happened to know the right people to come to her aid, that is all."

Lelache shook her head. "You are wrong on all counts. Did you not find Motte & Bailey's involvement at all interesting?"

"It was a little unusual for Niles Bailey to get involved. Why allow Austen to hire this Navarro character?"

"That is only the start. It was *more* than a little unusual for two of Navarro's best men to be immediately on call. They were on standby if anything went wrong aboard Sirenica."

"Perhaps Mister Bailey had a personal interest in Diamante's work?"

Lelache waved one hand as if to brush the question aside.

"That is a trivial matter. You are wrong to dismiss Leigh Austen's involvement. She seems to have some sort of...*insight*

273

into these situations which others do not."

"And she's one of these so-called 'Angels' that everyone at the CDC talks about?"

"*Tête de noeud*, there are only Seven Angels, and they have been marked by the Centers for Disease Control as special people. She is one. I am another."

Wakelin considered a moment as feeling began to return to his toes. He liked that.

"Then tell me...would you handle things differently from here on?"

She made a Gallic shrug. "I might have some ideas."

"Explain, please!"

Lelache smiled. Her teeth were pearl white and more than a little pointed around the canines. She nudged her empty glass towards him.

"Refill my drink, *mon ami*. Then I shall tell you."

EPILOGUE

Aeolian Islands
Isle di Lipari
Castello dei Crociati

The Italian Navy had put all but one of Sirenica's survivors up in a Crusader-built castle.

Austen stood on the renovated stone battlements and looked out to sea. She inhaled gratefully, relishing the freshness of the air. Down on Sirenica, all she'd ever smelled was salt, bleach, mold, and metal. Up here, she could take in the intoxicating scent of the island's vast lemon groves.

The normally sleepy town port below was a hive of activity.

Most of the harbor was taken up by the bulk of the *Quintana.* Her football-shaped rescue submarine perched serenely on her afterdeck like a modern art sculpture. In contrast, the dive support vessel's foredeck helipad had been pressed into almost constant use.

Government officials, insurance investigators, salvage operators, environmental groups, and marine biologists of every stripe had demanded access to Sirenica. Some to assess ecological damage, others to research what they could about the new species of deepwater cephalopod.

A few came to set up monitoring stations in case a few squid had made it through the thermocline layer. More came just to preen for the press. And many came simply to pluck the remaining meat from Sirenica's billon-dollar carcass.

Austen had also been on that foredeck, shortly after everyone had been rescued and safely depressurized. The ship's surgeon aboard the _Quintana_ had assured everyone that the hospital on Lipari would be able to handle bruises, bumps, and the odd broken bone. But he insisted on sending Redhawk via helicopter for additional surgery in Naples.

"It's only a thirty-minute flight," Austen said reassuringly, as she stood over her friend's gurney. She had to raise her voice over the sound of the helicopter's motors as they warmed up. "No need to worry. You're going to be fine."

"Oh, I'm fine as it is," Redhawk chuckled. "They've got me pumped so full of the good stuff, I'm _already_ flying."

"_Ne bespokoysya,_" October added, as he stood opposite her. "I shall be coming along for ride. To watch over friend."

Redhawk rolled his eyes. "Okay, _now_ I'm worried."

The Italian airmen called over to them.

"_Tempo di salire a bordo!_"

A pair of orderlies wheeled Redhawk over to the helicopter. October followed along, his big frame bent almost double to avoid the whirring blades. The aircraft took off with a roar, swinging around to the north. She'd watched the helicopter until it disappeared over the horizon.

But that had been yesterday. This morning, she'd finally been able to escape the poking and prodding of the local doctors. Now, she had a new mission.

Austen made her way down the stone steps of the battlements and around to one of the structure's side gates. A gravel-strewn path led through sculpted hedges of fragrant rosemary bushes. The path became a rough trail that zig-zagged its way down a steep slope to the waterside.

The trail ended at a shingle beach armored with a skein of pink and white pebbles. The sea gently murmured and hissed among the stones. She looked around. There were no boats docked directly offshore here, nor were there any houses with a direct line of sight.

She did, however, hear the heavy tread of someone's footsteps.

Navarro emerged from the trail, looking relieved to have spotted her.

"I saw you heading this way," he said, joining her. "If you want to be alone, I'll just move on."

"I meant to be alone for a bit," she admitted. "But if there's anyone's company I don't mind, it's yours."

Navarro's face broke out in his trademark gap-toothed grin. "Well, that's easily the best compliment I've gotten all day."

"Any news about our friends? Good or otherwise?"

"Only good. The governor here helped put Madrigal and Gimenez back in contact with their families, so they're very pleased about that. Sasha Kirov looks happy and relaxed for a change as well. Her wife and daughter are flying in tonight."

"What about Doctor Lici?"

"She's in stable condition and improving. The drugs prescribed for a *Vibrio* infection are working. As a matter of fact, Redhawk's sharing the same hospital wing."

"I hope he's doing well. He's had a rough bit of luck lately."

"Redhawk's an Apache through and through," Navarro said. "That means he's as tough as saddle leather. Surgery went fine. His only complaint is that October keeps beating him at poker."

She raised an eyebrow. "What about you? How are you handling…well, all that happened on Sirenica?"

"I'm fine. Remember, I didn't bash my head against anything down there. Unlike certain people I could name."

Austen reached up and touched the small round bandage they'd placed just above her temple. The throbbing had stopped, but like most scalp wounds it needed to remain covered. She'd almost forgotten about it already.

"Maybe I'm part Apache," she said. "Hard headed to a fault. But I didn't lose anyone down there who I cared about,

Nick."

Navarro looked out over the water for a while. He had to clear his throat before speaking again. The happy grin from earlier had been replaced with a thoughtful look.

"It's sad, what happened. I can't deny it. Dylan...she was once a fine person. Maybe it was all an act, maybe not. I'd like to give her the benefit of the doubt. Like she said at the end, maybe there was something wrong with her. Something that got inside and drove her to do the things she did."

"Maybe," Austen agreed.

"At the end, I decided that I was going to rescue her. I don't know if I'd have survived that. The water pressure down there would've been a hell of a lot for a deep dive suit to handle."

"Don't forget the water temperature," Austen pointed out. "It was a hundred and thirty degrees at the drop-off point. You'd be looking at a second-degree burn all over your body in less than a minute."

He took a deep breath. "I'd have still tried. But the universe just didn't cut me enough slack. It was bad luck that the squid damaged the ROV. Bad luck that it crashed into the *Lennon* when it did."

"Depends how you look at it, Nick. From my perspective, it was good luck that you didn't end up throwing your life away after Sawyer's."

Navarro gave her an appraising look. She returned his gaze with a cool one of her own.

"I guess you're right," he finally said. He stepped close, taking her hands in his own. "Perhaps later tonight...we could talk some more? Not about Sawyer. I've had just about enough of my past. It would be nice to talk with you about the future."

"The future." Austen stood on tiptoe and planted a kiss on Navarro's warm and stubbly cheek. "I like the idea. I'll be along in just a little bit, okay?"

"I'm looking forward to it."

Navarro turned and headed up the trail. The big man quickly disappeared into the island's thick underbrush. She waited until she couldn't hear his footsteps anymore.

Austen turned back to face the sea. Digging into her pocket, she pulled out the ROV's miniature control module. It had fallen into her hand when the *Ringo* had been tumbled end-over-end by the KXT's detonation.

She'd had a devil of a time working the nub of a joystick. It had taken three tries to get the ROV on target. Her head had been swimming with pain after hitting the edge of the sub's console. But Austen had come to her senses just as Sawyer made her final play to manipulate Navarro into coming to her rescue.

Nick, you'd never have survived that rescue attempt, she thought firmly. *And yet you'd have gone anyway. Courage and sacrifice aren't just words to you. They're promises still to be kept. But I have my own promises to live up to as well.*

Austen's mind went back to when Nick had served her dinner. When she'd convinced him to come with her to Sirenica. When she'd told him about her veterinary experience with the rabid coyote.

I may be a slow learner, but I made my mind up right then. I made up my mind to do what needs to be done. Especially when it's the right *thing.*

She took a step back and firmly planted her feet. Then she wound up and threw the control unit as far as she could out into the harbor. It made a tiny splash as it disappeared.

Austen realized with a shock that something Sasha Kirov had told her was very true.

We all have secrets we keep close. Even from those we care about.

With the merest wisp of a smile, she turned and walked up the slope to rejoin Navarro.

The End

Michael Angel

AFTERWORD

Thank you for reading *The Blood Zone*! I hope you found it as enjoyable to read as it was for me to write.

There are some research notes involving *The Blood Zone* that I'd like to share. Effort was taken to ensure basic accuracy in many areas of this book. However, most of the story is equal parts speculation and imagination.

The organism *Coclia Salemovirus* and the related disease Salem Valley Fever are both fictional. However, in some ways they are similar to tularemia, a rare infectious disease caused by the bacterium *Francisella tularensis*. This disease is also colloquially known as rabbit or deer fly fever.

Vibrio mortiferum may be fictional, but *Vibrio vulnificus* is unfortunately all too real. It is the second-best known pathogenic bacteria from the genus *Vibrio*. The award for the most notorious killer from this genus must go to *Vibrio cholerae*, the causative agent of cholera.

V. vulnificus is present in marine environments such as estuaries, brackish ponds, or coastal areas. It has also been found in the guts of oysters and fish inhabiting oyster reefs in the Gulf of Mexico. Reports persist of this bacteria causing necrotizing fasciitis, or 'flesh eating disease' after the 2005 flooding caused by Hurricane Katrina.

As of this writing, there are several underwater habitats currently in operation for both research and entertainment purposes. For example, Florida International University operates Aquatica, a research center which sits in 60 feet of water off Key Largo. The larger La Chalupa habitat operated as a research base off Puerto Rico in the 1970's. It has since become the Jules Verne Underseas Lodge and has hosted over 10,000 guests in the past three decades.

By comparison, the fictional Sirenica cost a great deal more to build, is placed in much deeper water, and is a great deal plusher that many real life aquatic habitats. Yet many aspects of life on Sirenica are depicted properly, such as the chill, damp conditions and the squeezed-flat foodstuffs. For this I am indebted to papers published by the National Oceanic and Atmospheric Administration as well as James Nestor's book *Deep: Freediving, Renegade Science, and What the Ocean Tells Us About Ourselves.*

The exotic breathing gases mentioned in this book such as trimix and hydreliox are both real. They reduce the effect of high pressure on the human body, though each comes with their own set of side-effects. Hydreliox alleviates the symptoms of high pressure nervous syndrome over trimix, but hydrogen narcosis then becomes a factor at depths over five hundred meters.

Several other aspects of deep sea exploration were greatly simplified or fictionalized for the purposes of this book. Pressurization and de-pressurization times are vastly shorter and easier on the human body. Make no mistake, deep water diving is a much more hazardous and uncomfortable exercise in real life.

The process by which undersea hydrothermal vents form is real, as is the Palinuro vent field itself. Mineral extraction from dead or dormant vent fields are being explored in real life. The first major mining expedition was carried out in 2017 within the back-arc basin known as the Okinawa Trough. Multiple international agencies are working on legislation to ensure that live vent ecosystems are not exploited.

Finally, while the Tellaro hypothesis and the species *Vampyroteuthis lucidum* aren't real, the vampire squid *Vampyroteuthis infernalis* does in fact exist. It's much smaller than its fictional counterpart at a barely a foot in length. While this cephalopod is covered in light-producing organs, perhaps the best aspect of this creature is that it's not known for attacking humans, let alone steel-hulled submarines!

Again, thank you for spending time with me, Leigh Austen, Nicholas Navarro, October Shtormovoy, John Redhawk, Count Fiorenzo Diamante, Neely Madrigal, Reece Jordan, Miguel Gimenez, Alexandra Kirov, Victor Wakelin, Otto Hanick, the Tarantus brothers, and Dylan Sawyer.

Michael Angel

Michael Angel

ALSO AVAILABLE ON AMAZON

THE DEVIL'S NOOSE: A PLAGUE WALKER PANDEMIC MEDICAL THILLER

**The thing that wiped out the dinosaurs
is about to make its comeback.
It's a trillion times smaller than a killer asteroid.
And it's fallen into the hands of a madman.**

After surviving a horrific outbreak of the Black Nile virus, epidemiologist Leigh Austen's done her best to bury memories along with the bodies.

But when a call for help from the World Health Organization (WHO) arrives at her lab, she's got to face her nightmares all over again. Something's wiping entire villages clean of humans and wildlife in a war-torn former Soviet Republic.

Leigh's skills are desperately needed to identify and stop the pathogen's spread before it explodes into a global pandemic.

Austen's team of scientists and armed security set off into the epicenter of the hot zone: over a mile straight down the throat of the Karakul, the deepest open-pit mine in Asia.

From there, they'll contend with treacherous military officers, caverns filled with scalding-hot poisonous gas, and an organism so deadly it annihilated the dinosaurs sixty-five million years ago.

What Leigh and her people discover will shake them to their very core.

If they survive.

Michael Angel

CHAPTER ONE

Former Soviet Republic of Kazakhstan
Breakaway Region of Ozrabek
Central Asia

Seven-year old Aliya Nizova darted through the trees, her little horsehair-trimmed boots slipping on the carpet of wet pine needles.

Her breath rasped in her throat as she ran, desperately seeking someplace to hide. She came to a stop at the edge of a clearing and looked around. To the right, a granite boulder jutted from the earth, a rime of dirty snow clinging to its base. To the left, the ground sloped down to a cluster of tangled berry bushes.

A not-so-distant shout filtered through the dark forest. She made her decision and moved to the left. Cold mud squelched under her boots as she knelt behind one of the bushes.

She waited, ears keen to pick up any sign of her pursuer.

Aliya heard a *thump.*

Unlike the shouts, the strange noise had come from nearby.

It had sounded a little like a heavy pinecone hitting the ground, she thought. She craned her neck to look around at the nearby trees. But none of them had cones dangling from their branches.

A second *thump*.

The sound was followed by a strange *scuffling* noise.

Then silence.

Jumping to her feet, she stepped out from the bushes and back into the clearing. At first, she saw nothing but tea-colored earth and gray-green sedge grass. The breeze picked up, cutting and cold.

Aliya skipped back a step as more *thumps* sounded next to her, *one-two-three,* like rifle bullets burying themselves in the earth. The clouds parted, allowing a thin shaft of sunlight to bathe the clearing in golden light.

They were all around her: small, broken black shapes.

The ground was littered with the bodies of carrion crows. Their heavy beaks and ebony plumage glistened as they lay sprawled on the ground, necks broken and wings shattered They'd fallen from the sky as if expiring in mid-flight.

Even at seven years old, Aliya knew enough about the world to think: *Something's wrong here.*

She'd never frightened easily. But a chill skittered down her spine.

One of the dark shapes moved. The bird's wings fluttered, beating against the ground with a scuffling sound before going still. She knelt next to it, grabbing a twig in one hand. She gave it a poke in its side.

No reaction. She poked it again.

The crow's head whipped around as it struck with a convulsive *snap*.

Its beak, made razor sharp to dig into rotting flesh, closed about the twig less than an inch from her index finger. The wood splintered in Aliya's hand, causing her to hop back in surprise.

The bird let out a guttural *caw*. Then it arched its neck back, further and further as if pulled by a powerful, unseen force. Wings thrashed, legs pistoned, and four-toed feet flexed, clawing at the air. Caws like shrieks erupted from its beak as it yawned unnaturally wide.

Finally, its death agonies over, the bird fell silent. One eye stared dully up into the sky, as still and inert as a damp black pebble.

A crashing sound came from the bushes at the edge of the clearing. Aliya's twelve-year-old brother Serik emerged to join her. His breath puffed steam into the air.

"Mama's called us back," he announced. "But I still found you, I win."

"I wasn't hiding anymore," Aliya said. "Look over here. Dead crows."

Serik's eyebrows rose as he took in the sight. "A whole flock of crows! What happened to them?"

"This one here just died. I thought I saw something in its mouth."

Aliya grabbed a sliver of her shattered twig and leaned in close again. She poked at the lower portion of the bird's beak. She steadied her feet as she bent the neck back towards her, until she spotted what she'd glimpsed before.

A smear of color pooled in the bird's mouth. The substance shimmered and ran like sludgy oil. An oil that shifted from a pale, sickly blue to slime green.

Her brother let out a gasp of surprise and alarm.

"That's what Taras coughed up, right before he died!"

Taras had been their neighbor. Like many of the men from the village, he got up at dawn and then vanished in a haze of bus fumes every morning to commute to work at the mine.

She didn't know who'd been the first to cough himself to death. But now more and more of her friend's fathers were falling ill. Her mother had taken to smudging the house with smoke from bundles of mountain sage.

A runnel of the liquid edged towards the pink flesh of her finger. Aliya blinked, not understanding. She held her makeshift twig in such a way that it couldn't drip down on her.

Had the stuff run *up* the wood, climbing it like a snake?

"Come on, leave it!" Serik said, knocking the sliver from her hand and pulling her to her feet. "Mama's worried, she says that she saw a bunch of people driving this way up the old mountain road."

She fell into step beside him as they started back, the clearing with the dead crows vanishing behind them. The last hint of autumn sun faded away.

"Soldiers?"

"Looks like. They're in the green trucks."

They felt a rumble through the soles of their boots. Then the grumble of diesel engines began to filter through the trees. Picking up their pace, they soon emerged from the forest next to their family's home.

The Ozrabek village was a simple cluster of rough, timber-framed homes. The village's roundabout and the road leading down the mountain were choked with military trucks. The children watched as armed soldiers jumped down off the vehicles and began forming up into squads.

Aliya's parents, who wore their traditional upturned Kazakh headgear and fox-trimmed coats with solemn dignity, were being berated by one of the officers. She couldn't make out any of the words at this distance, but the exchange of words quickly grew more heated.

The officer let out a curse as he grabbed a rifle from one of his subordinates. Her mother screamed as the man raised the rifle's butt and brought it down upon her husband's forehead.

Serik cried out something unintelligible and ran towards them. Aliya hesitated for a moment, then watched in horror as something completely alien stepped out of the back of the nearest truck.

It looked like a man, but with a bulbous, baggy silver outline. It had soulless black disks for eyes and a flared pair of nostrils on either side of its snout. It wheezed like a demon as it moved.

Aliya ran for the house, making it through the door just as the *pok! pok!* of pistol shots filled the air. Screams, followed by the rattle of automatic weapons firing. Blood drained from her face as what little courage she had left drained away. Whimpering, she ran for her favorite hiding place.

She'd been smaller when she had first hidden under her parent's bed. Now she had to push with her feet in order to make it into the comforting darkness.

She jammed her knuckle into her mouth, biting down to keep from whimpering, and waited.

The noises outside went on for a what felt like forever. Dim cries of pain, barely-there shouted orders, the rumble of trucks. She closed her eyes, praying for this nightmare to pass.

A single footfall inside the house sounded like a thundercrack in her ears.

She heard the raspy wheeze of the silvery demon's breath. The steps drew closer. She saw a pair of tinfoil-colored boots at the door. Her prayers that the thing would go on down the hall went unanswered. Instead, the boots moved around the bed and behind her, out of sight.

Her heart leapt into her throat as the bed frame above her sagged with a sudden *creak*. The springs flexed as the demon sat above her. Flecks of rust dribbled across her cheek. She desperately covered her nose to hold back an explosive sneeze.

More steps. More wheezing sounds. A second pair of silver boots entered the room. At least these stopped where Aliya could see them.

To her amazement, she heard a woman's voice! It had a strange accent, and it sounded muffled, as if wrapped in layers of cloth. Still, she could make out the words.

"The village has been secured, Commander."

A second voice, a man's this time. Aliya frowned, suddenly understanding. The two silver-skinned demons were people, then.

"What about Captain Baurzhan?"

"He's not exactly happy about being pistol-whipped."

A snort of contempt. "He shouldn't have struck the village elder with his soldier's rifle. This place would have given up without a fight."

"What does it matter? These people are dead anyway."

Aliya bit into her knuckle so hard that blood flowed, so hot that it surely steamed.

"They're still my people. It's not their fault that they needed to be sacrificed."

The woman sounded surprised. "You, sentimental? I wouldn't have thought that possible."

The man ignored her comment.

"We are in the elder's house. The richest family in the village. It's why he has a Western-style box spring bed. And why each of the two rooms in the back have a single, smaller bed. The children didn't have to share."

"I don't see why—"

"Husband, wife, and son make three. Yet there are four in this family." A pause, followed by another *creak* as the man shifted his weight. "I grew up in a place like this. Learned to hunt in the forest. You learn to see the signs. You learn to track even the smallest of animals."

"Good luck picking up tracks on a bare wooden floor."

"It's not the floor I'm concerned with. Look at the wall over here."

Aliya's head pounded with fright. She froze, not even daring to breathe.

"Scrapings of mud?"

"Oh, yes," the man's voice said. "Mud off someone's boots. Small boots. A child's, I would bet."

Suddenly, a heavy hand clamped around Aliya's ankle. She kicked out, but it was useless. In this confined space, she had no leverage.

She let out a last despairing shriek as she was pulled out into the light.

CHAPTER TWO

―――――――――⎯⎯⎯◇⎯⎯⎯―――――――――

Whitespire Laboratories
Reston, Virginia
Biosafety Level 3 Lab Area

On an otherwise unremarkable Tuesday morning, Leigh Austen was forced to decide how she was going to amputate her boss' left hand.

Ironically, that wouldn't be the most surprising thing to happen to her that day.

An hour earlier, she stood barefoot in the chill confines of a locker room the size of a walk-in closet. Her pale pink skin pricked up in goose pimples, but that wasn't what concerned her. She held up one hand. Freshly scrubbed fingernails gleamed in the light.

A barely-visible shiver ran down her wrist, making her fingers twitch. She closed her eyes and the antiseptic smells of the room vanished. Her nose filled with the wet rot of the rain forest, the sickly-sweet odor of diseased flesh.

Austen felt her heartbeat picking up, like a runaway freight train.

She slowed that train with a sequence of deep breaths and

her personal anxiety-busting mantra.

God grant me the courage to change the things I can. And to not push my luck on the things that I can't do crap about.

The shivers vanished, as they always did. Donning a spearmint-green surgical scrub suit she then focused on getting her hair under the cloth surgical cap. If pressed, Austen would admit that her hair was one of the few luxuries she allowed herself in her choice of career. At home or in the office, she let her auburn locks hang loose below the shoulder. In the lab, she kept them tightly braided into submission.

One set of footwear later, she went through a set of self-closing doors which operated like the airlocks on a spaceship. The shower area in between bathed her in a cool blue UV light that served to obliterate stray viral particles.

As the doors closed, she felt the gentle tug of air at the shoulders of her gown. Biosafety laboratories were constantly kept at a slight negative pressure. This ensured that the air currents always flowed into the lab, trapping anything airborne inside. Usually.

Finally, after a dash of baby powder and the snap of nitrile surgical gloves, she donned a two-part PAPR, or powered air-purifying respirator. A chunky piece of headgear with a clear face mask made up the first part. This was connected via an air hose that ran from behind the head down to a gold brick that hung from a clipped waist belt. The brick contained a battery, filter unit, and fan motor to deliver pathogen-free air to the user's face and mouth.

Austen continued through a second pair of self-closing doors and walked past the chemical decontamination showers. Her movements were smooth and languid, in part from a year-and-a-half spent practicing *tai chi*. Graceful, purposeful movements were a good thing in a biosafety lab.

Clumsiness in a Level 3 environment could mean a horrific death.

She entered the lab, where another green-gowned figure took note of her arrival with a mock checking of a non-existent watch. Joseph Widerman's amused expression was easy to make out, even behind a face mask and a pair of tortoiseshell glasses.

"And...right on the dot once again," he said, with a gleam in his eye. "I can set my watch by you, Leigh."

She looked at him, not quite understanding his comment. "How do you mean?"

He jerked a gloved thumb towards the observation windows along one wall. She'd only been working at Whitespire Labs for a couple of weeks, and she'd already forgotten about the things. They allowed potential investors to sit outside and watch the lab in operation, a feature that Widerman had smartly exploited to the fullest.

"You can just make out the door leading to the gowning area," he explained. "When I see you walk through, I start a slow count from two hundred on down. So far, you've never failed to enter the lab right as I get to zero. That's consistency."

Austen let out a rueful chuckle. True, she took a certain pride in her gowning discipline. Widerman didn't know that every time she entered Level Three, she had to beat back a case of rattletrap nerves. And as the new hire, she wasn't about to let her boss in on the secret.

"That's what I get for following procedure to a 'T'," she said. "So, let's look at those samples of Crucero, if they're ready."

"After an overnight incubation, they better be. You want Station Two again?"

Austen raised an eyebrow. "Do I have a choice? Or am I going to have to fight you for the spot by the centrifuge?"

"I'm closer to the dissection tools, you wouldn't stand a chance." Widerman shrugged. "Besides, if I'm the one paying a quarter-million dollars for a piece of equipment, I want to be the one who gets to use it for a while."

Together, they took their places at the connected biosafety cabinets. Each cabinet was its own self-contained, gas-tight compartment under negative pressure. Austen and Widerman could only work with the contents through pairs of gloves attached to arm-length rubber sleeves. The sleeves in turn were secured to openings cut into the cabinet's clear acrylic sides.

Austen tapped a sequence of buttons on her keypad, and a set of reddish vials slid in front of her. The vials had been filled with samples of equine blood and exposed to Crucero, a newly emergent member of the *poxviridae* family. A member that would fry nerve tissue and leave victims to die writhing in agony.

She slipped her hands into the secured sleeves and lifted one of the vials. She frowned as she realized that overnight, the bright scarlet of the blood had gone a sickly, rusty color. The color change indicated massive amplification of the virus.

The vial wasn't warm to the touch. But to an epidemiologist, it was 'hot'. Hot as the surface of the sun. She easily had enough virus in her hand right now to infect a third of the people living on the Eastern Seaboard.

Austen drew samples from the vials with a pipette and added them to a set of slides for later examination. Meanwhile, Widerman called up his own set of Crucero vials and began adding them to the centrifuge's arm holders. The state-of-the-art device he'd had installed inside his biosafety cabinet could spin out the wrecked cellular matter from the liquid remains in under a minute.

The work got routine in a hurry, so the day filled with small talk. This was one reason Austen preferred working in a Level 3 lab as opposed to a Level 4. In the lower level laboratory, they could speak easily enough over the PAPR's hum. Level 4 meant that you worked inside a cross between a deep-sea diving suit and an isolation chamber.

Widerman's latest family issues took center stage today.

"...so we finally found a Chabad in Lewiston that offers pre-Bat Mitzvah classes," he said absently. "But of course, it's going to be a drive, and God forbid that my wife has to get behind the wheel. She just won't do it."

"That might be a blessing in disguise." Austen pointed out. Elaine Widerman was a truly sweet woman, but she had a habit of putting dents in her SUV's bumper whenever attempting to parallel park.

A *chime* from the laboratory's paging system cut into their conversation. Widerman nudged the speakerphone button next to his station with his elbow and kept on working. The admin's voice sounded loud and clear in the laboratory.

"Doctor Widerman, I have two guests to speak with you."

"I'm gowned up and in L3," he replied, not bothering to look up from his work. "Tell them to leave a number and I'll get back to them."

"Actually, they're here in person. They're from the WHO, under authorization by the CDC."

Austen filled the last pipette and removed her hands from the biosafety cabinet's sleeves. The World Health Organization only worked hand in glove with the Centers for Disease Control and Prevention when an international emergency cropped up. That made this visit serious.

Widerman slipped the final vial into place and switched on the centrifuge. The machine hummed and he watched it carefully as he began to slip his hands out. Austen looked up and saw two men at the window. She didn't recognize the first one, but a frown blossomed across her face as she made out the second man.

Ian Blaine. I wondered when I'd see that son of a bitch again.

The rattle of metal on metal broke her thoughts. A *bang!* like the report of a rifle echoed through the room. The centrifuge blew apart, tossing a deadly ring of shrapnel in all directions.

The biosafety container's acrylic sides held, but the vials of Crucero shattered, spraying liquid throughout the cabinet's interior. Chunks of metal slashed through the sleeve compartments, shredding the gloves.

Joseph Widerman cried out and shoved himself backwards. His eyes goggled at the deep slash across the back of his left hand. Scarlet dripped through the torn nitrile glove, mixing with the viral-infected blood.

"*Vey is mir!*" he gasped. Alarms sounded shrilly in the air and the nearby monitor flashed red and green, making the spilled blood look black as tar.

Austen didn't hesitate. She threw open the emergency cabinet and grabbed a medical kit. She'd taken no more than two steps towards her boss when she realized that he wasn't in danger from bleeding to death. He had a far worse problem in his veins.

"Leigh, you've got to help me!" Widerman gulped. Sweat beaded on his brow, and his skin had gone ash white. "Get the fire axe! Take my hand off at the wrist!"

She stared at him. "Don't be ridiculous, I can't do—"

"Quick! Before the virus can circulate in my bloodstream!" He staggered back another step, chest heaving, and yanked open the dissection drawer. His right hand came up with a scalpel clenched in its fist. "God help me, I'll do it myself!"

Austen moved in, hands out in supplication. "Joe, stop it! You'll never get past the bone, and you'll just sever an artery!"

Panicked, animal sounds came from Widerman's throat. He slashed at Austen as she stepped forward, missing her suit by inches. Beyond reason, he put the blade to his left wrist and started to dig in.

Austen glanced at the windows. The two men outside were pressed to the glass, watching helplessly. She made her decision in that moment.

"Damn it, all right!" she shouted, and she reached back into the emergency cabinet to grab the long-handled fire axe. "Table! Arm across the table!"

Widerman scrambled desperately to comply.

"My elbow!" he hissed, as he stretched out his arm. "Too late for the wrist, aim for the elbow joint!"

Austen swallowed, hard. She raised the tool in both hands. Then she took one long, sure step as she swung. The axe's razor-sharp blade hissed in the air as she brought it down.

CHAPTER THREE

Austen turned the blade as she brought it down. Instead of aiming for Widerman's left elbow, she brought the flat of the blade down on his right hand. He cried out as the blow made him drop the scalpel. The surgical knife landed on the floor with a *ting*.

"Come on!" she said, even as she set the axe aside and moved towards him.

Austen managed to prop up Widerman before he collapsed. She slung his right arm over her shoulder and steered him out of the laboratory. The man had a slight build, but it was hard to hold onto him in the suit. Her facemask was fogged by body heat and sweat by the time she got him into the decon showers.

"Hold out your left hand," she instructed him, even as she pulled the lever labeled EMERGENCY DECON. "Turn it palm side down."

The chemical showers kicked on with a *hiss*. Purple spray turned into sparkling white foam that cascaded down the sides of their masks and surgical scrubs. Widerman winced as the disinfectant flowed over his open cut.

"I think you broke the middle finger on my right hand," he

groaned. "Dammit, I'm sure of it."

"Sorry about that," she said. "Tell you what, when you get it splinted, you can shoot me the bird all you want."

"Leigh, you should have cut my arm off. That was a catastrophic exposure. You know what that means for me, don't you?"

"It means you get a vacation in Stoney Lonesome, yeah."

'Stoney Lonesome' was the name that everyone at Whitespire jokingly called the medical isolation ward. Anyone exposed to a hot-zone environment won instant admission and 24x7 care from nurses and doctors wearing Class 4 safety suits. Those who died earned a thorough hazardous biowaste disposal of their body, HEPA-filtered incineration, and a page in the company's 'Lessons Learned' manual.

"Let Elaine know where she can see me, okay? Don't sugarcoat it. Three days incubation, and then I get a first-class ticket straight to hell. All I've got is a 50-50 shot at walking out."

"You'll be walking out," Austen assured him. "And you'll have *both* of your hands. Remember what you promised me after the bat mitzvah."

"I remember..." he said faintly.

With a bustle of noise, a quartet of medical technicians entered the decon area. They carried a biocontainment stretcher between them. The first pair slapped a temporary bandage on Widerman's wound, sealed him in the stretcher, and then carried him out.

The second pair performed an integrity check of Austen's suit. Once that had been confirmed, they brought in a set of pressurized tanks on rollers, filled to the brim with the nastiest of chemical cocktails. They snapped nozzles and brushes to sets of flexible tubing, hooked the base of the tubes to the tanks, and went into Biosafety Level 3 to obliterate all trace of the Crucero testing.

Leigh made her way out, relying on her innate knowledge of the de-gowning process to get her back to the locker room in Level 0. She made it as far as the halfway point, where she stripped down and entered the water shower.

The numbness that had enveloped her in the decon area dissolved like so much grime as the hot water jets thrummed against her skin. She let out a single sob and nearly collapsed upon the shower stall's molded seat.

Is this really what it's all about? She shook her head as she contemplated the idea. *Working every day with things that will reward even a tiny slip-up with excruciating pain and death?*

Then there were the smells that plagued her every time she gowned up. The beating of the African sun on her back. The sickly-sweet smells of the jungle, mixed with the piles of bodies that—

Austen shook her head. That was past, this was present. And she was learning to move on.

I held it together today, she reassured herself. *I held it together for Joe. Maybe there's hope for me yet. Maybe.*

She stood and turned off the shower.

It took another quarter-hour for her to complete the exit from the laboratories, get re-dressed, and confirm Widerman's admission to the isolation ward. The report said that his hand had been successfully stitched up, and that he was in 'stable condition'.

For now.

With these pleasant thoughts circulating in her head, Leigh straightened her sleek silver cardigan so that it slipped over her granite-colored ankle length slacks. She normally chose what to wear based on what was practical versus stylish. But Elaine Widerman assured her that supple gray-on-gray clothes set off her coppery locks and softened her lean, severe frame.

Finally, she took a breath and stiffened her resolve. She pushed through the doors into the observation room to meet Widerman's two visitors. The first man was tall and well built, with wide shoulders jutting out from an off-the-rack sports coat.

His coffee-colored hair had been buzzed short enough to reveal the outline of his skull. Watchful eyes were set deep in a lantern-jawed face. That face might have landed in the outer suburbs of handsome, save for a jagged scar that wended down the left side from hairline to below the cheekbone.

The second man had no such imperfections. Ian Blaine was a virologist and geneticist, but he looked as if he could have stepped off the cover of a catalog for an upscale men's store. He certainly dressed the part. An immaculate center part threw back twin waves of golden hair. That in turn highlighted symmetrical cheekbones and a white, toothy grin that made women sit up and take notice.

He certainly had Austen's attention.

"Of all the people to arrive on a day like today," she said, as she strode up to him, her heels clicking and echoing on the marble floor. "It would be you, Ian. As usual, you have perfect timing."

The man seemed to be expecting her greeting.

"It's good to see you too, Doctor Austen," he replied smoothly. "I realize that we didn't part on good terms, but I was hoping for professional courtesy, at the very least."

"Then you can keep hoping," came the blunt reply. "What are you doing here, and how can I move you along? Whitespire doesn't handle government contracts, so I doubt the WHO or the CDC will have any interest in our work."

Blaine paused a moment before flashing his trademark winning smile.

"As much as I'd like to catch up, I didn't come to see you. In fact, I'm here to request the services of your top field epidemiologist. Someone experienced in handling emergent diseases outside a laboratory."

"That could be a problem," Austen said, "since I just threw him into the medical isolation ward. As you saw, Doctor Widerman's been exposed to Crucero. It's a Bolivian virus that's jumped species from horses into humans. The locals call it 'Crucero' because it inflames the nerve endings. Survivors report that it feels like one is being crucified."

Blaine, cool as ever, didn't blink an eye.

"About half the victims die within fourteen days," she continued. "Doctor Widerman's chances are slightly better.

But either way, it's the most lethal pathogen we deal with. So, my advice to you is to check back with me in a fortnight. I'll let you know whether to make reservations for a flight. Or a wake."

The two men traded glances as they absorbed the information. For the first time, Blaine's companion spoke up. His voice was deep, and it held the barest hint of western twang.

"If Widerman's out, then who's the next best?"

The question made her quirk a grin.

"The next best? Well, that would be *me*."

Michael Angel

THE PLAGUE WALKER PANDEMIC MEDICAL THRILLER NOVELS

The Devil's Noose
The Reaper's Scythe
The Blood Zone

The Plague Walker:
(A Leigh Austen Short Medical Thriller)

FANTASY & FORENSICS BY MICHAEL ANGEL

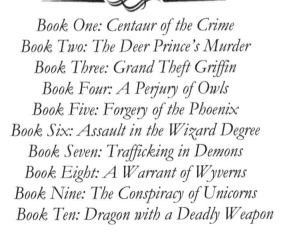

Book One: Centaur of the Crime
Book Two: The Deer Prince's Murder
Book Three: Grand Theft Griffin
Book Four: A Perjury of Owls
Book Five: Forgery of the Phoenix
Book Six: Assault in the Wizard Degree
Book Seven: Trafficking in Demons
Book Eight: A Warrant of Wyverns
Book Nine: The Conspiracy of Unicorns
Book Ten: Dragon with a Deadly Weapon

Forensics and Dragon Fire
(Fantasy & Forensics Novella)

ABOUT THE AUTHOR

Michael Angel's worlds of fantasy and science fiction range from the unicorn-ruled realm of the Morning Land to the gritty 'Fringe Space' of the western Galactic Frontier. He's the author of the bestselling *Centaur of the Crime*, where C.S. Lewis meets CSI. His many books populate shelves in languages from Russian to Portuguese.

He currently resides in Southern California. Alas, despite keeping a keen eye out for griffins, unicorns, or galactic marshals, none have yet put in an appearance on Hollywood Boulevard.

Find out more about his latest works at:
www.MichaelAngelWriter.com

Editing/Proofing services provided
by Leiah Cooper from
SoIReadThisBookToday.com.

Cover art by
DerangedDoctorDesign.com.